USS Lightning Rod

Battlefleet Series: Book 1

Theo Mann

Invisible Publishing Company

Contents

Chapter 1

E llis "Sailor" English threw his weight against the heavy blast doors and shoved with all his might to close them. They swung on their hinges, but before they could lock into place, a massive fireball smashed against the doors from outside.

The explosion boomed out from the Acheron Space Colony on Ganymede and curling flames billowed across the dusty terraformed landscape. The fire enveloped the colony and the *USS Lightning Rod* shuddered under the impact.

English ducked behind the blast door and shut his eyes. He strained every muscle to force the doors closed, but the shockwave overpowered his efforts. The flames pushed the doors back against him and his feet slipped on the diamond-plate floor.

Flames curled around the doors and licked his face. He turned his head aside, but he didn't stop pushing even when the doors swung a little bit farther inside the *Lightning Rod's* cargo hold.

English braced himself harder, and at that moment, two more people hurtled out of nowhere to collide with the doors at his side. All three worked to their utmost to push back against the flames, but a second later, another catastrophic boom thumped across the colony.

The blow hurled the blast doors wide open. English and his unknown companions flew backward and English slammed into the hold's back wall.

He picked himself up with difficulty. Two other men rolled on the floor next to him. English grabbed the nearest one and helped him up while the third got painfully to his feet.

All three men stared at the fire raging all over the colony. English couldn't even see the towering industrial complex that should have risen high into the atmosphere.

"Holy shit!" the man at English's side murmured. "The whole Extension Mill has gone down!"

English started to reply when he noticed something moving inside the flames. "Come on!" He sprinted for the open blast doors, sprang down into the stinging dust and smoke, and charged toward the colony.

A line of people snaked out of the chaos to meet him. Their black protective suits covered their heads and bodies completely. They didn't look human.

English squinted to protect his eyes and dove into the searing heat. He grabbed the first person and bellowed at the top of his lungs. "This way! Follow me! I'll guide you to safety! Follow me!"

The other colonists staggered and then veered in the direction of his voice. English held his breath as a great rush of scorching air whooshed back toward the colony. "This way!" he roared. "Hurry! The backdraft is......."

He shoved the first colonists toward the *Lightning Rod*, dove behind the group, and herded them into a run. They stumbled, but he finally got them moving as a deafening blast ripped out of the colony.

Another shockwave slammed English in the back. He toppled into the colonists in front of him and knocked them the rest of the way to the *Lightning Rod's* cargo ramp. Rough hands seized English by his uniform and dragged him the rest of the way inside.

The doors pounded shut and English collapsed on the floor wheezing for every tortured breath. Someone came over to him and grabbed his arm. "Are you okay?" It was one of the men who helped him try to shut the doors.

English wobbled on unsteady legs, but he eventually got to his feet and nodded. He turned to face the person next to him....and came face to face with a carbon copy of himself.

The guy wasn't as tall—maybe three or four inches shorter than English. This man was stockier in the shoulders and his legs were thicker, but he had an identical buzzed haircut with salt-and-pepper flecks around his temples and the back of his neck.

The guy eyed English with a flinty, searching look that English knew only too well. The nametag on the guy's uniform read, *Frasier*.

Frasier's eyes dipped to English's neck. "You got some bad burns there. You should go up to Sick Bay and...."

Retching coughs interrupted him. Frasier and English both turned to the colonists. Twenty men wriggled on the floor as they started to peel their suits off.

The first few crawled to the nearest wall and propped themselves against it while they gasped and coughed for breath.

English squatted down next to the first man and touched his shoulder. "What happened? What caused the explosion?"

"Sab.... sabotage!" the guy croaked. "Sabotaged....us......"

"The Tecrium reactor...." another blurted out. "......overloaded......"

English stared at one man and then at the next. Then he looked up at Frasier. Frasier scowled, but at that moment, the medics from Sick

Bay charged in. They mobbed the colonists and shoved English out of the way.

He backed off to give them space, but the colonists' claim that someone sabotaged the Acheron Colony's Tecrium reactor unsettled English too much to ignore. What should he do about this? He should report it, but to whom?

Someone bumped his elbow and he found Frasier at his side again. "That was goddamn incredible, man! I've never seen anything like it. You deserve a medal for that." Frasier stuck out his hand. "Gunnery Sergeant Charlie Frasier. It's an honor to know you."

English shook Frasier's hand and muttered, "Ellis English. Good to meet you," but his mind drifted back to the colonists.

He wanted to question them more about the explosion, but the medics were already guiding them away to the elevators.

"No damn way!" Frasier blurted out. "Not *Sailor* English! Not *the* Sailor English!"

"Huh?" English turned around. "Oh, yeah."

Frasier gaped at him in slack-jawed shock. "*You're* Sailor English—*Captain* Sailor English? What the hell are you doing here?"

"I'm not a captain. I'm a gunnery sergeant the same as you. I just showed up and then this happened."

Frasier looked around the rapidly emptying cargo hold. "I mean......what the hell are you doing *here*? Shouldn't you be at the United Space Force Command Center or something? Aren't you something like the most highly decorated officer in USF history? This...."

Frasier waved at the blast doors. The impact of what they just witnessed was starting to sink in.

English shrugged Frasier's comments away. "I'm not any of that anymore. I'm just a rank-and-file grunt like you. Anyway, I just showed up for active duty, so maybe you can tell me where to go."

Frasier gawked at English like he had three heads. "You're.... a gunny.... but why? You could have any post in the whole Force. What are you doing slumming it out here with us?"

"I don't want any post in the whole Force. Now, if you aren't going to help me out, I guess I'll just have to go search the ship on my own."

Frasier shut his mouth and scowled again. English settled himself in for the long haul. His first days and weeks and months and years on this ship were going to include a lot of this.

Everyone and their mother would want to know why the famous, decorated superhero Sailor English had been busted down to gunnery sergeant on a low-level destroyer like the *Lightning Rod*.

Frasier pursed his lips. "All right, man. I get the picture. I won't ask any more questions."

"Thanks. I appreciate it."

Frasier jerked his thumb over his shoulder toward the elevator. "Come on. I'll show you where you can change into a new uniform. That one is ruined."

English snapped out of his trance. The whole back of his uniform jacket had been scorched out. He'd been so busy saving the colonists that he didn't notice until now.

The burned uniform left his back exposed with numerous burns bubbling up in puss-filled blisters on his back and neck. His back started to hurt now that the adrenaline was wearing off.

Frasier turned to lead English to the elevator when the doors opened from the other side. Four people came out and English froze when a woman in captain's bars strolled toward him.

English and Frasier snapped to attention and English trained his eyes straight in front of him to avoid meeting her gaze, but not before he got a good look at her.

She wasn't any taller than Frasier and she wore her long, chestnut hair down past her shoulders. It wasn't regulation, but she could get away with it since she was the captain of the *Lightning Rod*.

Her sharp black eyes flicked from English to Frasier and finally to the third man who had helped Frasier and English try to shut the doors. The guy hustled up next to Frasier, snapped to attention in line, and faced the captain with the other two.

A young man even taller than English hung close to the captain's elbow. Two other members of the bridge staff followed them into the cargo hold.

English knew who they were from the ship's records. He studied as much of the crew as he could before being posted to the *Lightning Rod*, but he paid special attention to the command staff.

Captain Georgia Ogden had been in command of this ship for five years. That made her a fixture and not likely to welcome anyone challenging her authority.

Her records said she was fair, but she kept her distance from her crew. She didn't make friends easily, not even among her peers.

Her XO, Commander Matthew Radcliffe, was an up-and-comer destined to captain his own ship one of these days. He was likable and he had already made friends with several people on the USF Command Staff. The guy knew how to network and keep his connections alive.

The other two were Lieutenant Julio Avila and Master Chief Santiago Terranova, both of whom had decent service records but nothing outstanding.

English noticed all three of the bridge staff trying to catch his eye, but he didn't waver. He fixed his gaze on a spot behind them and kept it there.

Captain Ogden halted in front of English. "You're out of uniform, Gunny."

"Yes, Ma'am," English said.

"Explain yourself, Mister."

"The Acheron Colony, Ma'am," Frasier interrupted. "I came downstairs and the whole colony was on fire. English was trying to close the blast doors alone, and when Lloyd and I tried to help him, another explosion went off and knocked us all flat.... Ma'am."

Captain Ogden took her eyes off English to glance at Frasier. "How did you get the colonists inside?"

"English did that," Frasier explained. "He saw the colonists first and he ran out into the fire to guide them in. That's how he got burned, Ma'am. He would have gotten scorched in the backdraft, but he was near enough to the ramp that Lloyd and I were able to haul him in.... Ma'am."

"Is that true, English?" Captain Ogden asked in a low, silky voice. "Did you go out into the fire without permission?"

English stiffened. He knew it would be like this, but he still didn't look at her. He only replied, "Yes, Ma'am."

She waited for a second, but he kept his mouth shut and didn't say anything else. "Well, English?" she prompted. "Don't you have anything to say for yourself?"

"No, Ma'am."

English felt everyone present watching and holding their breath to see what Captain Ogden would say. English even felt Frasier and Lloyd listening even though they stayed at attention and didn't look at him.

English held his ground. He resolved never to give Captain Ogden or any other officer on the *Lightning Rod* any reason to complain about his conduct. He was already in a delicate enough position as it was.

Captain Ogden finally sniffed. "Go get yourself into uniform, Gunny. You're scheduled to review your fighter wing in an hour and then the whole squadron has a joint training run in two hours."

"Yes, Ma'am."

"You can get back to work, too, Frasier. You're all dismissed."

English headed for the elevator. Commander Radcliffe and the other two bridge officers darted out of his path to let him through.

He picked up the duffel bag he'd been carrying when he first walked into the *Lightning Rod's* cargo hold. He had just stepped inside the ship for the first time when the explosion went off. This was not how he envisioned his first minutes on board.

The elevator doors closed and he let his shoulders slump. He drew in a shaky breath. His back and neck were really starting to smart, but he didn't have time to go to Sick Bay now to get them treated. He had one hour before he had to get back down to ./ the flight deck ready to do his job.

He exited the elevator on Deck 14 and made his way to the enlisted barracks. He didn't have any quarters or even a locker yet. He didn't have time to take a shower, either.

He went into the locker room, dropped his duffel on the bench, and winced when he peeled off his ruined jacket and shirt. He only had one other uniform so he would have to replace this one as soon as possible.

He unzipped his duffel and took out his other uniform and a clean t-shirt. He was just wondering if he should put something on his burns when the door burst open. Frasier gasped when he saw English with his shirt off. "Jesus Christ, man!"

"Keep your shorts on, son," English muttered. "I'm not dead yet."

"Holy crap!" Frasier muttered again and went over to the first aid kit mounted on the locker room wall. He pulled out a tube of something. "You can't go back on duty like this. You better report to the bridge that...."

"Like hell!" English snarled. "I'm not reporting anything to anybody."

"Jesus!" Frasier whispered again. He walked around behind English and started dabbing the ointment on the blisters without asking English first.

English shut his eyes and didn't complain. He gritted his teeth against the sting and let Frasier fuss over him.

Frasier kept swearing through the whole process, but English said nothing. This might be the last and only time he got any kind of special treatment on this ship. He was grateful to think he might have made a friend so quickly.

Frasier finally screwed the cap on the tube and swiveled around in front of English. "There. It isn't much, but it's better than nothing. You really need to go to Sick Bay and get that tended to. I don't know what the captain is doing by putting you back on duty when you...."

English snorted. "I think we both know what the captain is doing by putting me back on duty, pal."

Frasier blanched and lowered his eyes. "I don't know about that."

English stuck his arms into his t-shirt and gritted his teeth to pull it down over his chest. "Thanks for speaking up for me down there. I owe you one."

"Forget that. What you did out there was...." Frasier grimaced. "I won't say it was heroic, but.... I guess I understand now why everyone makes such a big deal about you."

"Well, don't, okay? Don't make a big deal about me. I'm nothing. I'm a gunny like you. That's all I am and that's all I want to be."

"What happened to you?" Frasier asked. "Do you have any idea what people in the service think of you?"

"Yeah, I know." English picked up his jacket. "Believe me, I know."

"What are you doing here?" Frasier asked again. "You're goddamn royalty, man. You don't have to be here."

"Yes. I do." English shrugged into his jacket and buttoned it up. "I gotta go. I gotta review my crew before the training run. I guess I'll see you down there."

"Yeah." Frasier watched him finish adjusting his uniform. "See ya."

Chapter 2

E nglish stepped onto the flight deck and stopped. His practiced eye roved over the fighter craft parked in orderly rows on their launch pads. Mechanics and pilots buzzed all over the place. Welding torches spat fountains of sparks and tools clanged against metal.

The air smelled of smoke and chemicals and grease. The noise made a happy symphony of teamwork, comradery, and bawdy jokes. It was a world English knew well and liked. He could get comfortable here.

He approached the Squadron Command desk. A harassed lieutenant sat on a high stool slaving over ten different computers. The guy reminded English of his son when he was graduating from high school.

The young man's nametag read, *Eismann*. English saluted. "Sir! Gunnery Sergeant Ellis English reporting for Fighter Wing 17, Sir!"

The lieutenant looked up and his eyes widened. "Sailor English? *The* Sailor English?"

English stiffened and let his eyes drift to a spot behind Eismann's head. "Yes, Sir."

"Jesus!" Eismann hopped off his stool and held out his hand to English. "It's such an honor! I didn't think it was the same person on the roster. What are you doing here? I mean, are you here to review the squadron?"

"No, Sir," English growled. "I'm here to take command of Wing 17. I'm the new gunny on deck, Sir."

Eismann frowned. "Are you sure? This is highly out of order."

"Yes, Sir."

Eismann went back to his desk and rummaged and tapped on his computers. He kept muttering to himself. "I don't believe it! It can't be."

"It is, Sir. If you could just tell me where to go, Sir, I need to review my crew before the joint training run. I don't want to let Captain Ogden down."

Eismann's head shot up and he gaped at English in disbelief. "Are you sure? I mean...."

"I'm sure, Sir. I'd appreciate it if you could tell me where to go. You can work out the details later if you need to.... Sir."

Eismann gulped. "Um....okay.... Gunny. Wing 17 is over there. Your crew is all waiting for you."

"Thank you, Sir." English saluted again and walked off in the direction Eismann indicated. English sighed once he got out of earshot. This was only the second time and it was already getting old.

He spotted Fighter Wing 17, and when he made his way around the fighter craft launch pads, he saw his crew. They looked like the saddest excuses for USF pilots that English had ever seen.

They slouched and reclined and leaned and sat on equipment, stores, and tool chests near one of the fighters. None of the pilots even bothered to stand.

His one comfort was that they were all extremely young. Hopefully they would be too young to know who he was, but even that might be asking too much.

He slowed his approach to give them all plenty of time to notice him. Four young men hopped to their feet and snapped to attention. The rest stayed where they were.

English strolled over to them and paced up and down between them and the fighter. He took his time measuring each one with meticulous precision.

The four that stood up formed a line in front of him. A flabby, sloppy thing in a grubby uniform occupied the farthest end. His nametag read, *Janacek*, and English knew from the boy's service record that the kid's first name was Henry.

English didn't see how this kid managed to pass the physical fitness test, but at least Janacek knew enough to stand to attention before his commanding officer.

The next boy kept his eyes straight in front of him. Every detail of his uniform was perfect. His nametag read, *Duran*, and English stopped in front of the kid.

The name Duran was almost as famous in the United Space Force as English's. English knew three other Durans from his own time in the Force. They were all crackerjack pilots with more decorations than anyone could count.

This kid couldn't be more than seventeen and his record said his first name was Ezra. He was just starting out, so English didn't say anything to him. He would let Duran prove himself first.

The next boy was named Babbitt—Harlow Babbitt. He'd come up from nothing and worked as a janitor in the barracks while he went through basic training. He'd been making his mark ever since, so English didn't worry too much about him. He'd be too anxious to keep the spot he worked so hard to earn.

The last pilot standing at attention was Emory Thorpe. He didn't cut as crisp a picture as Babbitt and Duran, but English didn't find anything to complain about in Thorpe's presentation.

"Sir!" Thorpe barked. "Fighter Wing 17 reporting for duty, Sir!"

"At ease, Airman," English told him. "Why don't you introduce me to your slack-ass crewmates here?"

Thorpe made a disgusted face. "Excuse me, Sir, but they should all be bumped out of the service right now if you ask me, Sir. None of them respects the uniform....and I don't think they even know how to fly."

"You watch your mouth, Thorpe," a black-haired girl snarled from the back of the group. Her nametag read, *Franz*—Natalie Franz—and her service record told English far more than he wanted to know about her.

She had spiked her hair with what looked like axel grease so it stuck straight up from her scalp. Thick, black makeup lined her eyes and she wore purple-black lipstick that made her pale skin look skeletal.

"What's the problem, Franz?" English asked. "Do you want me to believe a derelict like you knows how to fly? You better pack a lunch if you want to convince me of that."

She flashed him a hateful glare. "Oh, I can fly, scarecrow, and don't you dare call me 'Franz'."

"Don't mind her, Sir," Thorpe interrupted. "Our last CO was.... well, he was drunk a lot and there hasn't been another one to run our wing.... until now."

"I see." English turned back to Franz. "Well, Franz? What's your story?"

She bared her teeth at him and Thorpe cut in again. "She's been bumped from every other flight crew, and if she bumps from this one, she's going straight back to the Lunar Detention Center—the adult section this time....and we all call her Racer, Sir."

"Racer!" English widened his eyes. "Does that mean she can fly after all?"

"She's damn good, Sir. She isn't the best, but she's pretty good."

Thorpe's eyes darted toward Duran when he said Racer wasn't the best. So it was true. Duran must be the best pilot in this wing. That figured. Did any of these kids know his pedigree? They didn't act like it.

English tore his eyes away from Racer. Thorpe didn't tell English anything he didn't already know from her record. English would be the one to pack a lunch to deal with her titanic attitude.

He could bump her down to the Lunar Detention Center right now for mouthing off to him and showing up out of uniform, but if she was that good in flight, why waste her?

He turned his attention back to the others. "Which of these shit-heads do you say doesn't know how to fly?"

"That would be me." A tall boy with white-blonde hair and brilliant blue eyes raised his hand from English's left. The kid cracked a wicked grin and his eyes twinkled.

So this was the notorious Ben Ritchie. He'd already racked up ten disciplinary actions for insubordination and conduct unbecoming, mostly due to his incessant wisecracks.

"I can't fly, Sir," he volunteered. "Are you going to bump *me* down to the Lunar Detention Center?"

Racer laughed loudly. A miniature girl with babyish blonde curls standing next to Racer giggled once and immediately stopped when English caught her eye.

"Don't listen to him, Sir," Thorpe interrupted. "Ritchie's not too shabby when he tries.... which he never does.... Sir."

"Aw, Thorpe, I didn't know you cared!" Ritchie jeered. "All this time, we could have been best friends."

"Why are you here if you don't try, Ritchie?" English asked. "Tell me you don't want to wind up back on the streets of Chiang Mai where you came from."

Dead silence fell over the wing crew and Ritchie looked away. That shut his mouth like nothing else. English struck the first blow and they all felt it. He knew enough to cut each of them to shreds. They better start learning who was in charge here.

English strolled over to the tiny girl standing next to Racer. "Why are *you* here, Manheim?"

Her frightened eyes skipped to Racer. Ada Manheim opened her mouth more than once and finally squeaked out, "…. Sir…." before she looked at Racer again.

Racer pretended to ignore her, but there was obviously something going on there. Manheim didn't even blink without checking with Racer first.

No one said a word. Manheim must be who Thorpe meant when he said someone didn't know how to fly. English didn't see how this tiny girl could even reach a fighter craft's controls, much less summon the backbone to shoot anything.

He walked back over to the fighter and faced them all. One more pilot remained leaning against a stack of crates to one side. The kid kept studying his fingernails in between watching and listening to every word English said.

The kid didn't move or volunteer anything. English knew his name was August Stoval and he didn't have anything distinguishing on his record yet. He also didn't have any black marks against him which was saying something on this crew.

"All right, people," English began. "All of you line up over here."

He waited while Stoval and Ritchie joined the other four in line. Racer finally gasped and rolled her eyes before dragging her feet over to join the others. Manheim waited until Racer came forward before Manheim did the same thing.

"My name is Gunnery Sergeant Ellis English," English announced.

No one reacted except Duran. His head snapped around so fast he almost dislocated his neck. He stared at English and Duran's jaw dropped, but he was the only one who noticed.

Duran gulped, but he didn't say anything. He had to work hard to make himself face front again and come to attention. Duran's relatives must have told him all about English, but apparently this Duran decided to wait for English to prove himself first, too.

"Janacek, you go change into a clean uniform," English began. "You don't want Captain Ogden seeing you like that, and the next time you show up out of uniform, you won't be flying. If any of you shows up out of uniform or breaks protocol ever again, you won't be flying, either. Is that clear?"

They all chorused, "Yes, Sir," some more enthusiastically than the others, but at least they all got the message.

"We have a joint training run in a little over an hour," English told them. "I can see that you people have all been sorely neglected, but this is our chance to show everyone we aren't totally useless. Go on, Janacek, and get back here as soon as you can. The rest of you load up and we'll get started."

No one moved. "But, Sir...." Thorpe began. "What about.... don't you mean.... aren't we going out for the joint run?"

"That's right, but I wouldn't send you out against the other wings without doing a few practice runs first. Load up. We're going out now to stretch our legs. By the time the training run starts, we should be ready to give the other wings a run for their money. Go on. Get moving."

Thorpe, Duran, and Babbitt gaped at English like he was speaking Chinese. Racer eyed English with suspicion, but when Janacek broke out of line and walked away, the rest snapped out of their trance and scattered.

Chapter 3

E nglish went back to Lieutenant Eismann's desk. "I'm taking my crew out for a run around the block. We'll be back in time for the captain's review."

Eismann blinked at him and stuttered, "Uh.... okay.... Gunny. Whatever you say."

English bit back the urge to laugh at him and returned to his fighter wing. All his young pilots were already loaded up except for Janacek, who came waddling back looking better, but not as good as he could.

Janacek wedged himself into the last fighter in line and then English loaded up in the larger wing leader craft. The controls switched on and the engines powered up when English's weight sank into the seat.

He slipped into his safety harness and clipped it while he read the controls. Each of his pilots showed up on his dashboard where he could read their vital signs and the mechanical readouts transmitting from their fighters.

They were all adjusting and fine-tuning their controls exactly the way they should. None of them missed a beat which meant Thorpe may have been downplaying their abilities. They were all perfectly capable, so what did he mean about them not being able to fly?

Even Ritchie dialed in his plasma cannons down to the micron. He might not have tried with his former drunken CO, but he was sure trying now.

The communications system switched on inside English's cockpit. "Squadron Command to Wing Leader 17," Eismann chirped in English's ear. "You are clear to launch, Wing Leader 17."

"Thank you, Lieutenant. Keep the home fires burning for us."

Eismann laughed. He was softening up.

"Wing 17—launch," English ordered and the pilots punched their throttles one after another.

Thorpe went first with Babbitt and Duran right behind him. Racer blasted off the flight deck on their tails.

A second later, Janacek, Stoval, and Ritchie hit it, too. Manheim took the longest and she didn't fly as fast as the others.

She dropped off the flight deck and English launched right behind her. He sprinted past her. "Keep up, Airman. Don't let these gasheads leave you behind."

She giggled and sped up a little, but not enough. English dropped his throttle down and turned a somersaulting loop around her.

"See that, Airman?" he told her. "You don't want these chumps going back to the ship telling everyone that a fossil like me flew rings around you. Punch it, girl! Get up there with your crew."

She didn't laugh again. She nailed the throttle and plowed straight through the fighter wing until she overtook even Duran.

"Whoo!" Ritchie hooted. "Did you see that? I didn't know you had it in you, Manheim!"

English crawled up on them from behind. "Keep it frosty, boys. The drones are deploying. Go on, Racer! Show us how it's done."

"Yes, Sir!" she called and plunged nose first into the gas clouds over the USF training arena on Cyllene.

The clouds parted and Racer swooped parallel to the moon's surface. She rocketed into the arena as dozens of drones launched from underground. They opened fire at the same time with many launching higher to attack the fighters advancing from behind.

Racer, Duran, Babbitt, and Thorpe unleashed their cannon fire to destroy the drones.

Thorpe hadn't been lying about Racer's abilities. She dodged the drones and pelted them with fast, sure shots. She never missed once. Her fellow pilots also made short work of the drones and the four of them vaulted out of the arena on the other side.

"Look at her go!" English cheered. "I take it all back, Racer. You can show up in black lipstick anytime you want if you keep shooting like that."

Racer actually laughed. "I'm gonna hold you to that, Sir."

"What about me, Gunny?" Ritchie asked. "Can I show up in black lipstick, too?"

"Show me what you got and I might consider it. Stoval—Janacek—do your thing!"

Stoval, Ritchie, and Janacek dropped in right behind their crewmates and another flock of drones launched to attack them. English sprinted in formation with the pilots and his spirits lifted. He targeted the drones and ground gun positions that opened fire simultaneously.

Stoval and Janacek flew more slowly and missed more often. Ritchie must really have been trying because he only missed a few times. He could dodge and weave almost as well as the first four, so maybe he just needed someone to inspire him to try.

"Excellent shooting, boys!" English called. "I'm impressed. You can definitely wear black lipstick, Ritchie."

The others exploded in laughter. "I can't wait to see this!" Racer exclaimed.

English wheeled back to their starting point. "Your turn, Manheim. Let's go!"

He motored up next to her and glanced over. She sat in her cockpit as white as chalk. She stared down at the arena hardly blinking her huge eyes.

"I told you so," Thorpe grumbled. "It's always like this."

"Shut it," English snapped. "You can do it, Manheim. Shadow me. We'll do it together."

She glanced over at him and looked right through him.

"Ada!" he called. "Look at me!"

She blinked and her features cleared, but she didn't look any less terrified.

"Shadow me, Ada," English ordered. "You fly where I fly and shoot where I shoot. Understand?"

She nodded, too petrified to speak.

English tapped something into his controls. "None of the drones will shoot at you, Ada. I'm signaling Lieutenant Eismann to disable all the weaponry in the arena. None of the drones or ground positions will shoot at you. You fly with me. Understand? You're perfectly safe. Okay?"

She nodded again and English dropped into the arena. She followed, but she flew more and more slowly as she approached. No wonder her crewmates said she was useless. She was scared out of her wits. She would have bumped out of the service ages ago if she had a decent CO.

English slowed to fly at her side. "You ready? Shoot that drone right in front of us."

English fired, but Manheim didn't. "Pathetic!" Ritchie muttered in the background.

"The next one of you that opens his mouth is out!" English snapped. "You'll be flying back to the *Lightning Rod* to pack your bags. You hear me?"

No one said anything.

"Let's go, Manheim. The next one is all yours. I'm right with you. Ready? Fire!"

She fired at the next drone. It hung right in front of her and exploded in flames. Her fighter flew through the fireball and out the other side.

"Come on, Manheim!" English urged. "You and me together—on the next one! Fire!"

They both fired at the same time and hit their target together.

"Good girl!" he yelled. "Come on! Pick up the pace. Put your throttle down. You can do this."

She started to speed up. She fired faster hitting one target after another. By the time they got to the end of the arena, she was flying at full speed.

"I don't believe it!" Ritchie murmured. "She's doing it!"

English ignored this, but the words electrified Manheim. She slammed down her throttle, zoomed high overhead, and beat it back to the starting point.

English kept pace with her. "One more time, Manheim! You and me! The rest of you drop in behind us, but don't overtake."

Manheim streaked through the arena hitting targets right and left. She squealed when she got to the other side. "I did it! I can't believe it! I did it!"

"You're damn right you did it," English told her. "One more time—live fire, this time!" She froze in her cockpit, but he didn't give her a chance to pull out. "Go!"

"Go, Manheim!" Racer hollered. "Show us how it's done!"

Manheim faltered again when the time came to drop into the arena, but English rocketed past her. "You better beat me, girl, or I'm gonna hit all your targets for you."

Her features hardened behind her cockpit cover and she blasted to full speed. She overtook him and started shooting as never before. She dodged one drone and almost got hit by the next, but she adjusted her course and didn't take any damage.

She hurtled out of the run and whizzed around to the starting point again. "Keep it going!" English ordered. "Every man for himself!"

"Whoo-hooo!" Babbitt cheered and shot past English gunning for the drones.

The fighter wing scattered, and in a second, English lost sight of who was doing what. He revolved through the target range hitting everything in sight. He only took his eyes off his targets to make sure Manheim still held her own.

She did. She whizzed between her crewmates and even stole several targets from Racer. The pilots' voices drifted out of the noise of explosions.

"Look at her go!" Thorpe screamed. "You're scaring me, Manheim!"

"Right behind you, shithead!" Babbitt called. "Quit watching her and mind your ass!"

"Holy shit, look at Duran!"

English vaulted high over the arena and looked down at his controls. The rest of the wing occupied themselves with the drones and sprinted over the ground targets pelting them with plasma.

Duran was in a class by himself. He descended so low to the ground that a danger signal came from his fighter's signal feed.

He skimmed the moon's surface spitting shots three times faster than the others. He hit the drones from below and took out ground targets faster than the arena's apparatus could re-launch them.

He made it as far as the arena's edge, but instead of rising upward to join the rest of his crew, he slammed the engines into reverse, skidded in a sharp circle, and rocketed back the way he came.

The others ran several passes and cycled back to the starting point where English waited for them.

"Outstanding, boys!" English told them. "That's what I'm talking about! Great work, Manheim! You're as good as Babbitt now."

"Hey!" Babbitt shouted. "That was a low blow, Sir."

"Hardly," Janacek corrected. "Did you see the way she was flying? That was a damn compliment, boy."

"Head back to the ship," English ordered. "We have a joint run coming up, and after that session, you folks should be able to school the other wings big time."

"Hell, yeah!" Ritchie crowed. "This is gonna be a first for Wing 17."

"Let's go, Duran," English called. "We'll be back out here in a few minutes."

Chapter 4

W ing 17 landed on the flight deck. All the pilots unloaded and mobbed Manheim in a crowd.

They buried her in hugs and cheers. Thorpe rumpled her hair. Janacek picked her up, squashed her against his giant belly, and jumped up and down with her.

They kept yelling and recapping her success in the arena—all except Stoval. He stood back and watched their antics with a mild smile.

English laughed at them and he even saw Manheim blinking back tears of laughter. Her crewmates kept slapping her on the back, knocking her tiny frame back and forth, and grabbing their own heads in amazement.

English turned to go check in with Lieutenant Eismann....and froze. Gunnery Sergeants Frasier and Lloyd stared at English and his pilots in shock. Dozens of other pilots stood around gaping at Wing 17, too.

No one noticed the elevator open. Captain Ogden, Commander Radcliffe, and the rest of the bridge staff stepped out onto the flight deck.

English stiffened as the captain's eyes settled on the party going on in Wing 17. The rest of the flight deck fell dangerously silent as the captain advanced.

One by one, English's pilots realized that all the usual flight deck noise had gone quiet. Stoval bumped Duran's elbow and the party stopped. The eight pilots turned around and someone cleared their throat.

The pilots of Wing 17 lined up on either side of English. They faced the captain and all the other fighter wings came to attention, too, but it was too late.

Captain Ogden halted in front of English as usual. She cocked her head and pierced the young pilots with a critical eye. She finally said, "You have a joint training run scheduled, Gunny."

He stared at the wall behind Lieutenant Eismann so English wouldn't see her staring at him. "Yes, Ma'am."

"Is this the way you execute your duties, Gunny?"

The tension spiked off the charts, but English didn't flinch. "Yes, Ma'am."

"I'm surprised at you, English. I thought you would be more concerned with protocol."

"Yes, Ma'am."

She sniffed again, but he didn't check her facial expression. Commander Radcliffe shifted his weight from one foot to the other behind Captain Ogden's back.

"This wing has been the worst on the deck, Sergeant. They've consistently failed to meet minimum standards in every training run to date."

"Yes, Ma'am," English replied.

"I thought this would be a perfect place for you, English. You seem to fit in well with this wing."

Someone gasped, but it didn't come from his wing. English didn't rise to the bait. "Yes, Ma'am."

"Are you agreeing with me, English? Are you telling me you're a failure who belongs at the bottom of the heap with these washouts?"

"Yes, Ma'am," English growled.

She chuckled to herself and now Commander Radcliffe wasn't the only person fidgeting in discomfort. Shocked whispers went around the flight deck, but English was gratified to hear that none of them came from his crew.

Captain Ogden finally gave up needling English and wandered off to review Frasier's wing. English stayed at attention and his crew did the same. No one moved until Captain Ogden and her staff went over to Lieutenant Eismann's desk.

"Load up, squadron," she ordered. "Show me what you can do."

The flight deck exploded in noise. All the pilots turned to their fighter craft and the mechanics rushed in to finalize adjustments.

English turned around to see his crew gathering in a cluster. They grabbed each other and dragged each other toward their fighters. Duran, Babbitt, and a few others tried to break away and walk back over to where Captain Ogden stood, but the others stopped them.

"Who the hell does she think she is?" Duran snarled. "I'll tear her goddamn head off!"

"She's got some balls calling us washouts!" Babbitt hissed. "The four of us have hit minimum standards on every run and she knows it!"

"Did you hear what she said to Gunny?" Janacek whispered. "She's pure evil!"

"Break it up," English ordered. "Get loaded up and show 'em what you can do."

"But, Sir......!" Ritchie protested. "We can't let her talk about you like that—about all of us!"

"Quiet!" he breathed. "You want to prove her wrong? Now's your chance. Put some numbers on the board and let me see you hand Wings 10 and 12 their asses. Come on! You, too, Manheim! We don't have the numbers because one of our crew wasn't scoring. Go! Load up—now!"

They kept shooting death glares at Captain Ogden, but they finally relented and loaded up. English climbed into his fighter and their voices swamped his ears the minute he sat down.

"You hear that, Manheim?" Racer asked. "We're all counting on you."

"Gunny English will be right with us, Manheim," Janacek told her. "You're gonna kick ass."

"We all are," Thorpe added. "That means you, too, Ritchie. Don't let us down."

"You don't worry about me, boy. I'm gonna stuff those words right down her rotten little throat."

"Keep it clean, people," English ordered. "She can hear every word you're saying."

"I hope she can. Come on, boys," Racer fired back. "This one is all ours."

Everyone agreed, and a second later, the order came down from Lieutenant Eismann. "Squadron Command to Wing Leader 17. You are clear to launch, Wing Leader 17."

"Punch it, boys!" English ordered, and this time, they all launched fast and hot.

English dropped out into black space and had to gun it to catch up with his crew. Wings 10 and 12 dropped out at the same time and all three fighter wings raced each other to the arena.

English flew in formation with his wing, but once they got down on the target course, things went to pieces real fast. Every fighter flew at top speed with all the pilots trying to hit as many targets as possible.

The arena got so chaotic that many pilots hit each other. They gained points every time they hit an allowed target and lost points if they hit a friendly fighter.

Plasma deflected off English's fighter craft. His eye flicked back and forth between other ships, drones, and ground targets.

Duran plunged all the way down to the ground. He flew so fast that no one could hit him. The numbers on the scoreboard kept mounting next to his name. Even Manheim was scoring.

English lost track of the score. He rotated and somersaulted between three drones and hit them all. He blasted out the other side and almost collided with Frasier. Frasier had been trying to hit the same drones but got there a fraction of a second too late.

The two gunnery sergeants rocketed toward each other on a collision course, but Frasier didn't pull out in time. His plasma cannons pelted English's fighter in the nose as English pulled into another roll. He skimmed Frasier's craft and wheeled off somewhere else.

"You cocksucker!" Frasier cursed as his numbers dropped by three points. "I'm gonna kick your ass for that!"

English laughed. He was already too far away for Frasier to get near him.

"Don't worry, Sir!" Ritchie banked and dove straight for Frasier. "I'll handle him for you."

"You little shit!" Frasier snarled. "I'll show you......."

Ritchie hit another drone that Frasier had been targeting.

"Call off these dogs!" Frasier yelled. "English! You bastard!"

More rowdy laughter rang in English's ear as Wing 17 ganged up to steal every shot from Wing 10. The numbers kept mounting until a deafening siren echoed through all their cockpits.

"Hell, yeah!" Racer bellowed. "Eat plasma, slackers! Take a good, long look, Wing 10! Wing 17 all the way!"

English laughed in delight when he saw the score. Wing 17 had beaten Wing 10 by seven points and Wing 12 by ten points. That was the first time since the *Lightning Rod* started running three squadrons.

"All fighter wings—return to the flight deck," Lieutenant Eismann ordered.

Thorpe sighed. "It had to end. Oh, well."

"Next time," Frasier growled. "This isn't over, Wing 17."

"Oh, it's over," Ritchie countered. "It's so over. You'll never beat us again, Wing 10."

"Keep it respectful, Airman," English interrupted.

"Let 'em enjoy their victory while it lasts," Frasier told him. "It will never be repeated."

Hoots and challenges broke out from the other pilots. Even Wing 12 joined in the playful ribbing on their way back to the ship.

The Wing 17 pilots lost their composure once they unloaded from their fighters. The celebration got even wilder and more unruly than before, but English didn't try to stop it. His pilots earned this.

Wings 10 and 12 landed on their pads and all the pilots came over to congratulate the winners. English's crew blushed with pleasure when the other pilots shook their hands and told them how well they did.

Frasier stuck out his hand to English and English shook it gratefully. Frasier wouldn't stop grinning. "You really are a miracle worker if you licked that crew into shape. Everyone said it was impossible."

"Naw," English countered. "They're good kids."

"They have a good commander. You'll be getting promoted soon."

English colored, but he made sure not to look over at Eismann's desk. He didn't want to see Captain Ogden watching him. He only said, "I doubt that."

Lloyd joined them and the three sergeants talked together until the noise died down.

Eventually, everybody noticed Captain Ogden watching from one side. The pilots settled down and formed up in a mixed jumble. No one stuck to their wings as they lined up and came to attention.

Captain Ogden strolled over and stopped in front of English again. "Well done, Gunny."

English looked at the wall behind her head. "Thank you, Ma'am."

"Maybe putting you down here with these pilots was the right thing after all."

"Yes, Ma'am."

He waited for her to say something insulting, but she only turned away. "We'll see if you can do it again next week."

He said, "Yes, Ma'am," but she was already walking away. She went back to the elevator. Commander Radcliffe shot English a glance over his shoulder. Then the bridge staff all entered the elevator and the doors closed.

As soon as she left, the flight deck exploded in even more noise. Lieutenant Eismann left his desk to congratulate English and a few people brought out drinks and food to share.

The pilots got all mixed up with each other talking loud and fast about their runs. English observed his crew enjoying the festivities and he knew by the delighted glows on their cheeks that this had never happened before. They'd been outcasts until today.

Chapter 5

T he elevator doors slid closed with Captain Ogden, Commander Radcliffe, Lieutenant Julio Avila, and Master Chief Santiago Terranova inside it.

"That was absolutely, drop-dead incredible!" Master Chief Terranova murmured. "I never would have believed it if I didn't see it with my own eyes."

"Did you see the way English dodged Frasier?" Avila replied. "That man can fly! Jesus Christ, no wonder he's so famous!"

Commander Radcliffe glanced sideways at the captain, but she didn't move or speak. She stared straight ahead at the elevator doors.

"I didn't think he'd be able to stomach such a big reduction in rank, but he sure did," Terranova went on. "He handled it perfectly. That on its own is an achievement. The guy could have been an admiral by now if he'd only stayed in the service."

"So what's he doing here?" Avila asked. "He vanished off the face of the Earth seven years ago and no one has heard from him since. I can't believe the Force would waste a guy like that out *here.*"

No one spoke for a minute and the two officers glanced at the captain. It wasn't like her to let an event like Wing 17's victory go without comment.

Then again, after the way she went out of her way to humiliate English in front of everyone, she probably had egg on her face about now. Good. It served her right.

The elevator doors opened again and she led the three senior officers across the bridge to her ready room. The tension dissolved as soon as she got inside. She sat down behind her desk and brought up the *Lightning Rod's* duty roster.

"Assign quarters to the Acheron colonists, Matt," Captain Ogden told Radcliffe. "As soon as they're out of Sick Bay, schedule interviews and take reports on the explosion."

"Yes, Ma'am," Radcliffe replied. "No problem. We'll need to put in at the Mars repair shop and get the blast doors resurfaced."

She perked up and cocked her head. "What's wrong with the blast doors? Did they get damaged?"

"Only the exterior protective shielding. The fire softened it, so it needs to be resurfaced. That fire was astronomically hot. There must have been Tecrium in the combustion mixture."

She settled down in her chair frowning. Did she honestly think she could bust English for damaging the blast doors while he was trying to shut them?

Radcliffe drew her attention back to the roster. "What do we have up next? Your schedule says, *Personnel Meeting*."

"We do." The doorbell rang at that moment. "Come in!"

The door opened and Radcliffe stood rooted to the spot when Sailor English strode into the ready room. He stood at attention in front of the captain's desk, but he didn't look at her. He locked his eyes on a spot above her head. "You asked to see me, Ma'am."

"That's right." She stood up. "I took a big risk accepting you on my ship, English."

"Yes, Ma'am." He spoke in the same clipped, mechanical tone he used on the flight deck. He barely even blinked.

"I don't know what you were trying to pull by bringing in those colonists. You just can't stop yourself from playing the big hero, can you?"

"Yes, Ma'am," he clipped.

She sniffed at him and strode around her desk to stand right next to him. He didn't flinch. He showed no sign of even noticing she was there.

"I don't know what you thought you were trying to accomplish by getting yourself sent out here as a lowly gunnery sergeant, but you won't get away with it, Mister. I'm here to tell you that you won't get any special treatment on this ship. I don't give a shit who you are or who you were back in the day. As long as you're on my ship, you'll conduct yourself the same way the other gunnery sergeants do. You'll do your duty, and if you screw up even once, you'll be out on your ass. Do you understand, English?"

"Yes, Ma'am."

Radcliffe watched the words bounce right off English. English didn't react at all. He acted like he expected this. Maybe he had prepared himself for this very conversation.

She strode back to her chair, but she didn't sit down. "Well?" she demanded. "What are you doing here? Who did you piss off to get stripped of your rank?"

Radcliffe couldn't listen to this anymore. "Excuse me, Ma'am, but Gunny English hasn't faced any disciplinary action since he was a raw recruit. There's nothing on his record to indicate he was ever stripped of his rank."

The captain turned around and gave Radcliffe such a look of scorn that he instantly shut his mouth, but he didn't quite resolve himself not to intervene again.

What was wrong with her? Radcliffe had never seen her attack anyone like this, not even that drunk Gunny Brooks who sent Wing 17 so far down into the gutter.

Now she was doing it to a decorated, respected, almost godlike icon of the United Space Force. She kept talking about what English was trying to accomplish with this. What could *she* possibly hope to accomplish by tearing him apart like this?

Radcliffe always respected Georgia Ogden. He had always been glad to serve under her—until today. Could she really feel this threatened by a man who only wanted to do his duty and be a part of the service? Could she really be that fragile?

"Well?" she snapped. "What do you have to say for yourself, English? Are you going to answer my questions or are you just going to stand there saying, 'Yes, Ma'am' to everything I say?"

"No, Ma'am," English returned.

She smacked her lips in exasperation. "Get out of here—and remember what I said. If you mess up once, I'll bump you back to Earth where you belong."

"Yes, Ma'am."

English walked out of the ready room. Avila, Terranova, and Radcliffe stared at each other in horror and Terranova's eyes kept darting over to the captain. None of them could believe what they just witnessed.

She gave orders to the other two and they left, too. That left Radcliffe alone with her. Captain Ogden sighed and turned to him. "I want you to keep an eye on English, Matt. He's up to something."

"What are you talking about, Ma'am? English is straight up. You don't have to worry about him."

She snorted. "I don't believe that for a minute. There's no reason at all why the Command Staff would send him out here unless they were trying to spy on us—on me. If they wanted to do an inspection, they would have sent a uniformed officer, not some undercover spy."

Radcliffe gasped and his jaw hit the floor. "You can't be serious! He isn't even posted to the Command Staff. He was a civilian up until three weeks ago. His request to be posted to active duty on a destroyer is right there in his record."

"That's bullshit, Matt! You aren't telling me the late, great Sailor English just up and requested to be posted to active duty. That's nonsense."

"How do you explain him being off the USF roster for more than seven years? He was captain of the USF flagship *Siskiyou,* and the very next week, he quit without a word of explanation. He's been rotting in civilian life ever since. I'm telling you he was NOT on the Command Staff before now."

She made a face. "Not that we know of, anyway. He's here for some underhanded reason. I know he is."

"Why did you accept him on board, then? You could have turned down the posting."

She shrugged that away. "Maybe I was curious. Maybe I wanted to know why the Command Staff would go to such lengths to plant someone of higher rank on my ship."

"He isn't of higher rank. He was never more than a captain."

She huffed under her breath again. "No way did he just come out of retirement and wind up here. He could have been reinstated at his former rank at the USF Command Center. He could have been a diplomat or a senator. He could have had the whole world on a plate.

He didn't request to come out here to deal with those pieces of space trash on Wing 17."

Radcliffe winced. His respect for Captain Ogden was rapidly flying out the window with every hateful word she said about English.

Now Radcliffe understood why she found English so threatening. She thought he was here to undermine her or trip her up by finding something questionable about her command.

"I'm putting you in charge of finding out what he's up to, Matt. You served under him in the past. You know him better than anyone. You can get into his confidence and find out what he's doing here."

Radcliffe gulped down bile stinging his throat. This conversation made him sick.

He spent his early years in the Force worshiping the ground Sailor English walked on. Everyone did. English was a god amongst ship captains. Everyone worshiped him, but Radcliffe worshiped him more than most.

Radcliffe did a lot more than serve under English. There was no one in Radcliffe's life, not even his own father, who Radcliffe wanted more to be like than Sailor English.

Radcliffe modeled his whole career and ambition on English. Radcliffe wanted to be just like English and he still cherished that dream now.

Radcliffe couldn't look at Captain Ogden. She made him question everything he ever held sacred about the United Space Force.

Had his career really come to this—spying on his own crewmates? Was this a job worthy of the XO of a USF destroyer?

"Sailor English is going to be a thorn in this crew's side," she went on. "He's a troublemaker—a lightning rod for trouble. He'll attract every troublemaker on the crew and they'll rally around him to bring this ship to the brink of ruin."

She said a few more things about English and then started talking about Radcliffe interviewing the colonists. He lurched through the conversation without hearing much of what she said. He had to get out of this room fast.

When she finally dismissed him, he stumbled to the elevator and headed down to the Sick Bay.

He meant to check in with Dr. Cassidy about the colonists, but when he got into the corridor leading to the Sick Bay, someone came out of it in front of him.

Gunny Frasier halted in the corridor and narrowed his eyes at Radcliffe. "Sir."

"What's up, Charlie? Did you just visit the colonists? How are they?"

Frasier compressed his lips, scowled even more ferociously, and lowered his voice to a rumble. "I've got something to say to you, Commander. I'm sorry if it's out of line, but it has to be said."

Radcliffe jolted backward. "Really? What is it, Charlie?"

Frasier straightened up and squared his shoulders. "I'd prefer if we talk in private, Sir."

Radcliffe stared at him. This must be the first time in months that Charlie Frasier had called Radcliffe, 'Sir'. Whatever he had to say must be serious.

Radcliffe looked around and waved behind him. "Come this way."

Radcliffe led the way into Dr. Cassidy's office and shut the door. "All right, Charlie. Fire away. I'm listening."

Frasier straightened up a second time and took a deep breath. "It's about Gunny English, Sir."

Radcliffe wilted. "Oh. That."

"He's been on duty for the last ten hours, Sir, and he's injured. He got badly burned on the Acheron Colony. Captain Ogden ordered him to carry out that training run and he's been on duty ever since. We all heard her dress him down in front of everyone on the flight deck. It ain't right, Sir. It's downright unbecoming if you ask me."

"I realize that, Charlie. I was just about to go talk to him."

"She's the one you should be talking to. There isn't a man on this crew that doesn't respect Sailor English except maybe those punks on Wing 17 and now they all worship him, too. We all saw the way they were acting at the training run. He lit a fire under those kids. No one else could have done that."

Radcliffe had to grin. "Yeah. I know."

Frasier lowered his voice to a hushed rasp. "There's something else. The colonists…. after English brought them in, they said the explosion was sabotage. They said someone sabotaged the Tecrium reactor and that's what caused the fire."

Radcliffe froze staring at the man in front of him. Did he just hear that right?

Someone sabotaged the Tecrium reactor. Of course. Radcliffe's own reports from the engineering crew indicated there had been Tecrium vapors in the fire. The fire couldn't have weakened the *Lightning Rod's* heat shielding otherwise.

Radcliffe's mind reeled taking all this in. None of the colonists would have made it to the *Lightning Rod* alive if English hadn't been there to save them.

Was that the saboteur's plan—to eliminate every witness? If English hadn't guided the colonists to safety, no one would ever have known the reactor was sabotaged at all. The saboteur would have gotten away scot-free.

"I don't know what the hell she thinks she's trying to do by discrediting him, but it won't work," Frasier whispered. "If she keeps badmouthing him in front of everyone, we won't turn against *him*.

It will only turn us against *her* and we'll all start hating her instead. Someone should tell her, Sir, and you're the closest to her. She trusts you. She'll listen to you."

Radcliffe winced. "She won't listen to me, Charlie. Believe me."

"Well, someone has to. If she won't listen to reason, she'll ruin her own career and he'll be more popular than ever. Do you think for an instant that everyone on the flight deck isn't wondering when she's gonna light into us next? Does she seriously think she can treat a well-respected, decorated captain like this and get away with it?"

Radcliffe sighed and shook the tension out of his shoulders. "English is lucky to have a friend like you, Charlie. Thank you for telling me."

"What are you gonna do? Are you gonna talk to her?"

"About English? I doubt it. She won't listen to reason when it comes to him."

"What about the sabotage? Are you gonna tell her about that?"

Radcliffe drifted off for a second thinking so many things he couldn't make sense of them right now. "I'm not sure. I need to think about this."

"English was standing right there when they said it. He heard the colonists say it was sabotage. He'll tell you....and Lloyd was there, too."

"Okay, Charlie. I understand. I'm going to be interviewing the colonists about it anyway, so if they confirm this, I'll have no choice but to include it in our report."

Frasier relaxed. "Okay. Thank you, Sir."

Radcliffe tried to smile at him. "Can we go back to being on a first-name basis now?"

"I'm not sure, Sir. As long as the *Lightning Rod* is putting on this whole bridge-versus-English bullshit, I'm not sure I can do that."

"I'm not against English, Charlie. English is my goddamn hero. He always has been."

Now it was Frasier's turn to wince. "I'm sorry, Matt. I shouldn't have said that."

"It's okay. I'm as disgusted with the captain's behavior as you are."

Frasier raised his eyebrow. "You are?"

"Of course! I served under English, for Christ's sake! I would take a bullet for Sailor English."

"Okay. I'm sorry. I didn't know that."

Radcliffe squeezed his shoulder. "I'm going down to talk to him right now. After I see him, I'll order him to Sick Bay to see his burns tended to. Don't worry about it. Leave it with me."

"Thank you, Matt. That means a lot to me."

Radcliffe nodded toward the door and Frasier walked out. Radcliffe didn't tell Frasier how much this meant to *him*.

The worst part of this was that Radcliffe now found himself in a position of being English's superior officer. Radcliffe wasn't sure he could really go through with this.

At least English had people like Charlie Frasier sticking up for him. Radcliffe would give anything to be that person in English's life right now, but Radcliffe couldn't do that. He had to stand at Captain Ogden's side and listen to her spout all that venom at him.

Radcliffe had to stand by and listen to English say, "Yes, Ma'am" and "No, Ma'am" to the worst insults Radcliffe had ever heard uttered in this Force. Radcliffe hated himself for that.

He shook himself and went outside. He discarded his idea of visiting the colonists and went down to the flight deck instead.

Chapter 6

Commander Radcliffe found Sailor English tinkering with one of Wing 17's fighter craft. English wore a mechanic's jumpsuit with the sleeves rolled up his burly forearms. Tattoos snaked down to his wrists. His uniform usually covered them up.

Grease smeared English's arms, blackened his hands, and a few streaks of it marred his face and hair.

"Tell me you aren't shortening the controls for Manheim," Radcliffe teased when he walked up.

"This is Duran's bird," English replied. "I'm adjusting the plasma feed so he can fly faster."

"Faster! If he flies any faster, he'll disintegrate."

English grinned. "How ya doing, Matt? It's good to see you."

Radcliffe winced. "I wish I could say the same thing about you. What brings you out this far?"

"I just got bored without any fighters to work on, so this seemed like the right place to come." English cocked one eyebrow at him. "What's on your mind?"

"I was never any good at keeping secrets from you, Sir."

English fixed him with a hard glare. "Don't call me that. I'm not the man you used to know."

"Of course you are. How the hell am I supposed to act like your superior officer? I can't help it."

"Well, you have to. I'm not a captain anymore."

"What the hell is wrong with you?" Radcliffe exclaimed. "What the hell are you doing down here working on fighter craft? You should be upstairs running this ship."

"Well, I'm not. I'm down here and I'll stay down here. This ship already has a captain—a good one, too, if her record tells me anything."

"This is nuts, Sir." Radcliffe pulled his head in. "Sorry...." He had to stop himself from saying it a third time. He didn't seem to be able to stop himself. He couldn't think of English as anything but a captain.

"You have your own duty, Matt. You can't keep doing this. Just stick to the chain of command and let me do my job."

Radcliffe didn't say anything for a second. "Is it true the colonists claimed the Acheron fire was sabotage?"

"Who told you that?"

"Charlie Frasier."

English tossed his wrench back into the tool chest. "Yeah, it's true. They said someone blew up the Tecrium reactor."

Radcliffe let out a shuddering breath. His job just kept getting more excruciating by the second.

"That was something incredible that you did with Wing 17," he remarked. "You haven't lost your touch."

English chuckled. "They're good kids. They'll shape up, now that they have someone pulling for them."

"You......" Radcliffe stopped himself from telling English again what a gem he was. English obviously didn't want to hear that.

English halted next to the tool chest and gripped Radcliffe's shoulder. The old warmth and affection flooded Radcliffe's being. "I'm proud of you, Matt. I'm happy to see you doing well and rising in the chain of command. Don't give Captain Ogden any reason to doubt your loyalty."

"Loyalty! You call that loyalty? How the hell am I supposed to stand by and watch *that*?"

"You just have to. She'll come around, but only if I hold the line and keep my head down."

Radcliffe shook his head. He hated this. He didn't want to tolerate it. He hated the resigned submission in English's tone. "What the hell happened to you? How did you fall to...to *this*? Couldn't you get anything else?"

"Ogden was the only captain who would take me on. The Command Staff sent my request to eight other captains and they all turned me down."

"I know that, but couldn't you have stayed at the Command Center or something? You could have gotten any post you wanted."

"I didn't want to stay at the Command Center. I wanted to get back on a ship, so here I am."

Radcliffe lowered his voice to a murmur. "They're saying you made someone mad and got stripped of your rank. Is that true?"

English laughed, but Radcliffe detected a healthy dose of sadness underneath the surface. "I didn't make anyone mad. I'm right where I want to be. I got exactly what I asked for."

"Oh, bullshit, Sir!" Radcliffe blurted out and immediately regretted it. "I'm sorry."

"I was lucky to get this post. Ogden didn't have to take me, and as long as I'm here, I won't give her any reason to regret it. She needed a gunny, not a headache. I'm giving her the best gunny I have. That's all there is to it."

Radcliffe grimaced. This conversation was making him as sick as the last two he had. His day just got worse by the second.

He swallowed hard. He couldn't think of anything else to say to English. What did Radcliffe really think would happen when he came down here?

Did he think he would convince English to pull rank on Captain Ogden, take her command, and become the officer Radcliffe knew seven years ago? That would never happen. That wasn't English's way.

Radcliffe would give anything to turn back the clock. He would give anything to serve under English again and put him in Ogden's place, but Radcliffe couldn't do that, either.

English came to a stop in front of Radcliffe and jutted his chin at him. "Get out of here, Matt. You coming down here will only make it harder for both of us."

Radcliffe hauled his eyes up to match English's. "I hear you got injured earlier, Gunny."

English burst into a huge grin. He tried to bite it back and failed. "Yes, Sir. That's right."

Radcliffe dipped his gaze to English's neck. The burns still showed above his jumpsuit collar, but English showed no sign that he was in pain. Of course he didn't. He was on duty.

"You get yourself to Sick Bay, then, Gunny. Don't come back down here until Dr. Cassidy clears you for duty."

English burst out laughing. It was the same deep-throated, chesty laugh Radcliffe remembered. He could never forget that laugh. "Yes, Sir. Thank you, Sir."

Radcliffe winced again. He hated English calling him that, so Radcliffe let the laugh trick him into thinking they were playing a game.

In a few hours, the world would right itself on its axis. Then English would be the captain and Radcliffe would be the younger officer looking up to him like some kind of god.

English grinned at him with genuine affection. Nothing made him happier than Radcliffe finally pulling rank on him. That grin completely shattered the illusion.

English finished wiping his hands on a rag and clapped Radcliffe on the shoulder again before he started rolling down his sleeves. "It's really good to see you. I'm really glad you're on this ship. It's nice to see a familiar face."

"You don't need me," Radcliffe grumbled. "Your crew and the other gunnies are all pulling for you."

English beamed. "I guess they are."

Radcliffe nodded toward the elevator. "Go on and get up to Sick Bay. Don't make me have to give you the first disciplinary notice of your career."

English laughed again. "Yes, Sir. I'm going."

He headed for the elevator stripping off his jumpsuit. He wore a regulation t-shirt under it and the whole back was saturated with puss from his burns.

Chapter 7

R acer hit the bell outside Captain Ogden's ready room. Racer shuddered when the captain's voice came from inside. "Come in!"

She walked in and found Captain Ogden alone at her desk. She smiled up at Racer and Racer cringed.

She crossed her arms over her chest and glared at the captain, but facing the captain made Racer shiver again and she wound up rubbing her arms. Captain Ogden's ready room was the last place in the galaxy Racer wanted to be, now or ever.

"Come in, Airman," the captain lilted. "Thank you for coming to see me."

"What do you want?"

The captain only smiled which made Racer squirm even more. "I wanted to see you, Natalie. You're becoming quite the pilot under Gunny English's command."

Racer bit her tongue. She would never have tolerated anyone calling her by her real name, but she couldn't exactly tell the captain to suck it, could she?

"I wasn't sure you really wanted to be a pilot, but after Wing 17's second joint run victory yesterday, I can see you have the makings of a fine officer. I'm even thinking of recommending you to the USF Flight School. Congratulations."

Racer narrowed her eyes at the captain. Now Racer knew this was a trap. "What do you want from me?"

"Nothing, Natalie. I called you here to congratulate you on your success. I can do that, can't I?"

"Don't give me that bullshit. If you recommend anyone to the Flight School, it will be Duran, not me. What the hell do you want? Stop blowing sunshine up my ass and tell me the truth."

Captain Ogden just kept smiling that infuriating smile of hers. "All right, Natalie. If you insist. Your fighter wing is taking part in the colony dry run three days from now. I want you to throw the run and let the other fighter wings show up Wing 17."

Racer snorted and looked away. "Now I know you're screwing with me. I'm outta here."

She headed for the door, but Captain Ogden's voice cut her off. "I'm serious, Natalie. You're good enough to miss your shots and you're also good enough to make a few mistakes by hitting your own wingmates."

"If I do that, Gunny English will bump me off the squadron. This is my last chance and he's the only sergeant who has ever believed in me. I wouldn't let him down like that—no way."

Racer stopped herself from repeating some of the things English had said to her after their first practice run and since. Racer would take those comments to her grave.

She would never let anyone know how much his encouragement meant to her. They were some of the nicest things anyone had ever said about her. In fact, they *were* the nicest things anyone ever said to her.

English had never looked back after that first practice run on Cyllene. He never once suggested that she take her makeup off and he always included her as a full member of their crew. He never treated her like she was an outsider or like she wasn't good enough to be one of them.

The thought of leaving Wing 17 was starting to haunt Racer's nightmares. What would her life be without this sense of belonging—without English's encouragement and approval? She'd never felt this way about anyone in her life, not even her own father.

Captain Ogden slowly got to her feet. Her eyes gleamed with an unnatural light. She spoke in a soft, comforting tone. She kept smiling like she was Racer's best friend, but the words coming out of the captain's mouth hurt worse than any pain Racer ever endured.

"I determine who serves on this ship, Natalie. If I decide *you* will stay on this ship, you will stay. If I decide you will go, you will go. Gunny English has nothing to say about it, and if I decide that *he* will not stay on this ship, he has nothing to say about that, either."

Racer gulped. Captain Ogden didn't have to spell it out for her. If Racer didn't do what she said, Captain Ogden would bump her off the ship. How could Racer face English knowing she deliberately undercut her own crew?

"You will throw the dry run and let the other fighter wings take the credit," the captain went on. "I can't believe I actually have to say this, but since Wing 17's second training win, I have no choice but to take drastic measures. If Wing 17 wins the dry run, I'll know you disobeyed my orders and I will be gravely disappointed, Natalie. Do we understand each other?"

Racer nodded and rubbed her arms again. Now she felt really cold. She couldn't bring herself to speak. This was the greatest disaster of her life.

She never minded the idea of getting sent to the Lunar Detention Center—not until English got posted to the *Lightning Rod*. Now the thought of letting him down made her want to die. Anything would be better than that.

"I'm glad we understand each other. You can go, Natalie."

Racer stumbled out of the ready room, across the bridge, into the elevator, and headed down to the enlisted decks. Now what was she supposed to do?

She leaned against the wall trying to clear her head. She couldn't throw the dry run. Her crewmates would never let her live it down. What would Duran think.... or Thorpe? Then she thought of Manheim and almost fell over.

Thorpe actually told English on their very first day that Racer was one of their best pilots—maybe not as good as Duran, but damn good. Thorpe actually said that. How could she go back on that? How could she open herself up to Ritchie's derision?

The elevator doors opened on the flight deck. She had completely missed the enlisted deck. Babbitt, Stoval, Manheim, and Duran all stood talking next to English's fighter, but she didn't see English anywhere. Should she be happy about that or not?

She stumbled onto the floor. Lieutenant Eismann didn't notice her. She crossed the deck in a daze. Her body went through the motions automatically.

"The dry run is our chance to really put the screws on Frasier and Lloyd," Babbitt was saying.

"We don't have to put the screws on them," Duran replied. "We already beat them in the last two training runs. We have them on the ropes."

"What do you think, Racer?" Manheim asked. "Ritchie wants us to cooperate with the other fighter wings. He says it's better if we get a good result for the whole squadron instead of trying to outdo the other crews."

"So now you're taking advice from Ritchie?" Babbitt fired back. "He doesn't know shit. We have four years of score points to catch up on. Wing 17 is still at the bottom of the barrel. We have to prove we're as good as the rest of them or they'll start trying to push us down again."

Racer glanced over at the launch pads. Her brain didn't seem to be working.

"Racer?" Babbitt asked. "You okay?"

Just then, Thorpe, Ritchie, and Janacek showed up from somewhere. "What's going on here?" Thorpe asked.

"We're trying to decide what we should do in the dry run," Babbitt replied.

"There's nothing to decide," Thorpe replied. "We're gonna kick some ass. That's all we're gonna do."

"He means will we work with the other fighter wings or try to make them look bad," Duran explained. "He wants to make the dry run like another training competition instead of trying to get a good result for the whole squadron."

"It's obvious, isn't it?" Babbitt replied. "We have to make them look bad. If they look bad, we look good."

"What do you think, Racer?" Manheim asked again.

Just then, the elevator whisked open and English crossed the deck toward them.

He carried a large box and set it on the tool chest next to Thorpe's bird. "You folks deserve a reward, so I thought we'd have a little pilot picnic on the pad."

Ritchie burst out laughing. "Say that fifty times as fast as you can. Pilot picnic on the pad. Pilot picnic on the pad. Pilot picnic on the...."

"That's enough," English cut in. "Sit down. We got some serious relaxing to do."

English sat down on a stack of crates and dug into his box. He pulled out two packages of cookies, a tube of hard-rock candy, and an enormous submarine sandwich.

He started tearing into all the packaging and passing the food around along with bottles of juice and a few pieces of fruit.

Ritchie, Duran, and Thorpe sauntered over, hesitated, and then found seats for themselves. English took an enormous bite out of an apple and cocked an eyebrow at Duran, who was still frowning at the nearby fighter craft. "Did I interrupt something here, folks?"

"It's nothing." Thorpe took the candy out of English's hands, opened the tube, and took out a piece. "We were just talking about the dry run."

"I said we should use the dry run to whoop the other fighter wings again," Babbitt blurted out. "These patsies want to cooperate and make the other wings our best friends now when we all know the other wings will all be gunning to make us look bad. We have to beat them to it first or we'll be in the doghouse again."

English cut off a piece of the sandwich, took a bite, and started carving off hunks to pass to the others. They all settled around him in various attitudes of relaxation—all except Racer.

She stood apart and kept looking at the fighter craft parked near her. Was she really going to do this? Was she really going to throw her own crew?

She actually started to feel like a part of this crew, but that was obviously a mistake. She was an outsider. She would always be an outsider. Nothing could change that. She was rotten—rotten to the core. Even Captain Ogden knew it.

"What are we supposed to do during the run, Gunny?" Manheim asked. "What do we do if the other wings try to dump on us? Are we supposed to fight back?"

English chewed his sandwich studying them all for a second. "Well, the dry run isn't a competition like the training runs are. The dry run is a simulation of an alien attack on an Earth colony. It's our chance to prepare ourselves for a real invasion, and in that case, we would all be working together. If aliens invaded our system, no one would be thinking about competing with anyone. Only hitting enemy targets would matter."

"What about Frasier and Lloyd?" Thorpe asked. "You know they'll be telling their wings to dump on us. What are we supposed to do then?"

"I doubt Frasier and Lloyd will be telling their wings to do that. If they do, their pilots could earn demerits from hitting a friendly fighter craft the same way you would earn demerits if you hit one of them."

Babbitt looked away. No one answered.

Racer shivered again. She should leave right now. She didn't want to hear about how many demerits she would earn by sabotaging the run and making her crew look bad.

She couldn't leave, though, not without making the others suspicious. Even standing aside while they enjoyed their picnic must have set off English's alarm bells. He was too smart not to notice something like that.

Could he see right through her? Did he suspect even now what she was planning to do—what she had to do? Did he hate her for it? Did he hate her as much as she hated herself?

"You do the best you can in the dry run," he was telling them. "Do your best flying and do your best shooting. Make sure you aim for the enemy instead of your fellow pilots the same way you would in a real alien invasion. That's the best way you can earn your crewmates' respect. That's what you want, isn't it?" English turned to Stoval, who slouched against a welding block nearby. "What's your poison, Auggie? Are you a health nut or a junk food junkie?"

Stoval cocked his head to study English. This was the very first time English had ever addressed Stoval except to give him orders in the arena. Even Racer turned around to see Stoval's reaction.

Stoval rarely spoke. In fact, Racer couldn't remember Stoval saying anything to anyone since he came on board. He always listened, though. Nothing escaped his notice.

English pulled a few cookies out of the package and handed them to Stoval along with an apple and a piece of the sandwich. He smiled at Stoval and a hint of fire flashed in Stoval's eyes.

Without warning, Stoval blurted out, "You were in the Battle of Kolla Station when the Sozai attacked, weren't you, Sir?"

English stiffened and then looked down at the stuff in his box. "Yeah. I was."

"What was it like?" Stoval asked. "What was it like to fight in a real war against real alien invaders?"

English rustled something inside his box and then put the box on the floor.

"It's the most terrifying thing there is," he finally replied. "It's the worst feeling in the world knowing you and your fellow pilots are the only thing standing between Earth and a horde of bloodthirsty aliens. You want to run away and save yourself, but you know that if you do, the aliens will overrun Earth. If you run away, everything and everyone you care about will be destroyed and you won't have a home to run to. You know you have to hold the line no matter what, even if it means you dying."

Dead silence fell over the group. No one spoke as his words sank in.

"There's no competition then," English murmured. "Your fellow pilots are the only thing keeping you alive. If you screw up and hit the wrong target, you'll be making the Force weaker and the aliens stronger. That's why it's so important that you go into the dry run with the right attitude. This is just a trial for a real invasion. You need to get your heads screwed on straight. There will be plenty more training runs where you can school the other fighter wings. You don't need to do it in the dry run."

"But we won the Battle of Kolla Station," Thorpe prompted. "We drove the aliens off."

"We won, but at a huge cost. We lost a lot of really good people in that war and it took the Force years to rebuild to our full strength. I lost my own brother in the Battle of Kolla Station. You gotta look around you at your crewmates and realize that, if anything like that ever happened again, not all of you will make it back alive. It's the same with Wings 10 and 12. These people are not your enemies. Any one of them might be the person who gives their life so you can make it back alive.... or you might be the person who dies so they can make it home alive. You have to be okay with that because someone is going to make it back home alive and Earth will continue. That's the most important thing. One person doesn't matter. Who lives doesn't matter as long as someone does."

Another long silence answered him. Racer clamped her eyes shut tight and swallowed hard. She didn't belong on this crew. She didn't belong in the same Force with people like English, Duran, and Babbitt. They believed in the Force. They could do it right.

What was she? She was trash. She was a liability to her crew, to English, and to everyone, including herself.

Some of the food wrappers rustled and Racer opened her eyes to see Janacek reaching for what was left of the sub sandwich.

English spotted him in time, picked up the sandwich by its wrapper, and snatched it out of Janacek's reach. "Oh, no you don't, boy! You are not getting any of this."

The whole crew erupted in laughter that only got louder when English pulled a carrot out of his box and held it out to Janacek. "You eat this instead."

Duran thumped Janacek on the back. "Nice try, son! You're on hard tack now."

Racer caught herself starting to laugh, too, and stopped herself. She cringed when English saw her and the smile faded from his face. A question mark hung over his head when he pierced her with that deep, knowing look. He had to know. How could he not?

She couldn't stand him looking at her like that. She turned away and walked off the flight deck, but she only ended up taking her problems with her.

Chapter 8

E nglish stood over Lieutenant Eismann's desk and pointed out landscape features on a chart while the Wing 17 pilots listened.

"See this mountain here?" he told them. "This can give the enemy cover, so you'll need to be careful they don't ambush you from there. This group of buildings also provides cover, so if the enemy has already established a position on the moon, they'll probably come from there."

"How do we know if they've established a position on the moon?" Duran asked. "How do we find out before they start shooting at us?"

"You don't. That's the problem," English replied. "That's why you have to stay frosty and watch every possible angle. You can see these open areas when you're flying on approach to the region. You'll be able to see that the enemy doesn't have any positions or ships there. It's the covered positions you have to worry about."

"Which direction will the enemy be coming from?" Thorpe asked.

"You won't know that, either. They're going to try to surprise you, so keep your eyes and ears open."

Babbitt frowned at the chart on Lieutenant Eismann's computer. "This doesn't help us at all."

"Remember what I said and imagine you're in a real battle scenario. You wouldn't know anything about the enemies' plans ahead of time. You're lucky you know the sizes and capabilities of the enemy ships coming in because you wouldn't know that if this was real. You wouldn't know what weapons they were going to use against you or how fast they were or how many they were bringing."

"Why are you showing us this, then?" Duran asked. "Isn't this cheating?"

"It isn't cheating because this moon is in our system. We know the terrain already, so if this was real, we would be looking at the chart and evaluating our strengths and weaknesses before landing on the moon anyway. This kind of planning is all part of fighting a war. Checking out the scene beforehand isn't cheating. It's just good strategy."

"So how does this work?" Racer asked. "What's the plan for how to get down on the surface?"

English pointed to three other destroyers in orbit over Saturn's moon of Fenrir. "The *Lightning Rod* will be moving in formation with the *Hermes*, the *Solar Flare*, and the *Nostradamus*. All four destroyers will descend on the colony together. The destroyers will cover the colony until we get near the surface and then the enemy will attack. The four captains won't deploy their squadrons until after the aliens attack."

"You ARE cheating!" Ritchie countered. "You couldn't know that."

"Of course he could, jackass," Racer growled. "None of the captains would need to deploy their squadrons if the aliens weren't there. Use your brain."

English laughed. "You need to take some lessons from Racer, Ritchie. The four destroyers are on a mission to lift off the colonists and get them to safety. The squadrons would all stay home twiddling their thumbs so long as the moon was secure, but it won't be secure. That's where we come in."

The pilots studied the chart, but no one asked any more questions or raised any more objections. They all took in the details he pointed out. They were learning fast and he got prouder of their maturity by the day.

Lieutenant Eismann stood off to one side and watched English brief his crew. English kept looking around the flight deck, but Frasier and Lloyd didn't show up. Were they briefing their people at all? English couldn't understand why they wouldn't. How did they expect their pilots to handle the dry run without all the relevant information?

English checked his watch. "You folks still have an hour left before we start. You can relax. Don't hang around the flight deck. Just go about your business the way you would if this was real."

"How are we supposed to relax when we know what's coming?" Duran asked.

"I know it's hard. Just do your best. I'm sure you'll all do great down there."

They wandered off one after the other, but none of them left the flight deck. They were all jumpy and nervous about the dry run. English didn't blame them.

Racer stayed behind. She glared at English across Lieutenant Eismann's desk, but she didn't say anything. She had massively toned down her makeup and she didn't take so much trouble to spike up her hair anymore, but she'd been getting surlier and more snappish ever since the crew's second training run victory.

What was wrong with her? She kept glaring at him like she hated him, but he couldn't remember doing anything to set her off. He tried to encourage and praise her, but that only seemed to make her more hostile.

"Do you have something you want to say to me, Airman?" he asked.

She narrowed her eyes slightly and her nostrils flared, but a second later, she wheeled away and stalked off without saying a word.

English sighed and turned away to find Lieutenant Eismann grinning at him. "You're as popular as ever."

English snorted. "Apparently the Lunar Detention Center is looking a lot more appealing than hanging out taking orders from me."

"You'll win her over. You always do."

English went back to looking at the chart. "I hope you're right 'cuz she's a damn good pilot."

"You're really something else, you know that?" Eismann ventured.

"Huh? What do you mean? I'm just doing my job."

"This." Eismann waved at the computer. "That briefing you just did. It's amazing. You have them eating out of your hand."

"I don't get you. All I did was explain the situation to them. I'm their CO. That's what I'm supposed to do."

"I was a pilot in the service for four years before I got promoted to this post. None of my COs ever did anything like this for me."

English's jaw dropped. "Are you serious?"

"Of course not. Dry runs are supposed to be a total surprise."

"Yeah, but......"

"Frasier and Lloyd never do anything like this."

"Are you saying this is considered cheating or something? How can it be when the pilots would be given this information before a real battle?"

Eismann cocked his head. "Are you sure about that?"

"Of course! We were all briefed before every battle during the war. Our COs would never leave us in the dark about any information that might help us handle the situation. Are you crazy?"

Eismann shrugged. "Okay. I believe you."

English studied him for a second. "Are you telling me none of the other gunnies ever brief their crews—seriously?"

"Of course not. I told you I've been doing this for years and this is the first time I've ever seen this—ever."

English's mouth fell open. He could hardly believe this. Was he really that unusual to want his people to succeed?

Eismann moved over to the desk and went back to tinkering with his many computers. "I think you better go check on your people. Janacek is doing something to his bird that I don't think you'll like."

English shot the computer a look and walked away. He went over to Janacek's bird. The kid had his head inside the repair hatch and was loosening the fuel pump attachment bolt. "You don't want to do that, son," English began. "Leave that for the mechanics."

"I was just trying to...."

A deafening alarm went off above Lieutenant Eismann's desk and the whole crew jumped, including English.

The loudspeaker started blaring, "Alien invasion imminent! All fighter wings—prepare to launch. Alien invasion imminent! All fighter wings—prepare to launch!"

"You said we had an hour!" Babbitt yelled.

"We're starting early! That's the Command Staff's way of surprising you. Load up on the double!"

English whirled away searching for the rest of his pilots. Racer, Manheim, and Ritchie all came running. The launch bay doors boomed open and Duran, Thorpe, and Janacek all blasted into space.

The *Lightning Rod* was still well out of orbit and the other three destroyers hadn't even moved into formation yet. Fighter wings streaked out of their holds and plunged for the colony.

English took a few steps back toward the elevator to look for Babbitt and Stoval when they came running over from across the deck.

They scrambled into their fighters and English launched right behind them.

Fighters plummeted into the atmosphere from all over. English burst through the cloud cover and roared in surprise when a fountain of lasers pelted him in the face. They scattered across his cockpit cover and he dodged hard to starboard to avoid them.

He took a split second to see twelve spherical enemy ships positioned over the colony. Three massive vessels covered the settlement with more stationed near the mountain. Knowing they were unmanned drones didn't make them any less terrifying.

Lasers flew thick and fast. English throttled to his top speed and wove as never before to avoid the shots. He heard his pilots yelling in the background, but he couldn't make out anything they said.

More lasers spouted from the ground positions. Damn it. The aliens must have planted gunners there, too.

He wheeled through the battle and out the other side. The squadrons had to clear a path for the destroyers to get to the colony.

Someone screamed in English's ear and he snapped wide awake. Manheim was in trouble. She had descended between two enormous alien battle cruisers and they pinned her between their guns and the ground positions not far off.

Duran, Stoval, and Ritchie whizzed around her trying to break her out, but it was no good. The three of them together couldn't stop the alien ships from slamming her from both sides.

English gunned his engines and rocketed into the battle. He hammered the alien ship, but one fighter couldn't do anything.

He checked his instruments one more time. "Racer! Janacek! With me! Flank this asshole and draw the enemy's fire away from Manheim. Duran, coordinate your boys and strike in unison. Target the top and bottom of the sphere."

"On it, Sir!" Duran replied. "Come on, boys! Bring it around to port."

English revolved away and met up with Racer and Janacek. English turned back to make his first assault just as Babbitt and Thorpe appeared out of the mayhem, too.

"Fire in unison on my mark." English punched his throttle and his formation rushed the enemy ship. Manheim's screams echoed in his ears. "Fire!"

The five fighters opened fire at the same instant. They dumped plasma on the sphere's very top point—all except Racer. Her shots zinged past the sphere and hit Manheim's bird.

Duran and the others hit the sphere's bottom edge. The sphere twirled and all its lasers followed English's formation in a spiral corkscrew around the enemy ship. English hauled his craft into a steep climb while he dumped plasma on the enemy.

Lasers stuttered his hull, bounced off, and as he pulled out of the climb, the strikes hit Janacek who flew right behind English.

The rest of English's formation rotated their guns backward to keep the assault going—all except Racer who missed her aim again. Her plasma zinged past the sphere to hit Duran instead.

"Hey!" he yelled. "What the hell!"

There was no time to question. Racer jerked her cannon back into position, and as soon as her plasma joined the streams coming from the other pilots, the sphere detonated.

A blistering shockwave hurled Wing 17 away into the path of more lasers coming from all over the field.

Racer vaulted into the air, plunged for the next sphere in line, and flew straight into a fresh laser barrage. The shots smashed her craft and an alarm went off on English's controls. *Franz: Kill Hit.*

"Head back to the ship, Racer!" he ordered. "Thorpe, bring Manheim and Stoval over to the settlement. We have to clear these aliens to land our destroyers."

English's wing reassembled around the next sphere in line. He was in the middle of giving orders to repeat the same maneuver when Charlie Frasier's voice interrupted him. "You need some help here, pal?"

"Always. You bring your crew in from the east and we'll take the north side. We need to draw the enemy fire away from the settlement."

"Hey, leave some for me!" Lloyd called.

English laughed. "There's plenty for everyone. Lloyd, take your crew in from the south. Hold your fire until I give the word."

The next coordinated attack by all three wings destroyed the second sphere much more quickly. This left a sizeable hole in the enemy ranks and the *Lightning Rod* started to descend.

English found himself giving orders not only to his own pilots but to Frasier, Lloyd, and all their pilots.

"Surround the *Lightning Rod!* Aim your cannons outward to defend the ship. Let her back up to the settlement and take the colonists on board."

The enemy spheres tried to move in, but with all four squadrons working together, the fighter wings held the aliens at bay.

Dozens of people ran out of the colony, but when they got near the *Lightning Rod's* cargo hold, they vanished. They were only holograms.

The *Lightning Rod* lifted off with a cloud of fighter craft hovering around her. The ship climbed into orbit and sailed away. The other squadrons split off and returned to their own ships while English and his crew went back to the *Lightning Rod*.

Chapter 9

Racer stripped off her uniform jacket and tossed it into the mountain of other crap covering the bottom of her locker. She didn't care anymore. She would probably never wear the uniform again and she didn't care if she did. She didn't want to wear the uniform after today.

She still trembled from the dry run, but at least she had the locker room to herself. Wing 17 hadn't come back yet.

What should she do next? She would go up to the bridge and tell Captain Ogden that she was finished. She would resign from the Force and take the consequences.

She would let Captain Ogden bump her down to the Lunar Detention Center. Anything would be better than this.

At least Racer wouldn't have to see Gunny English before she left. Captain Ogden would probably throw her in the brig where she belonged until the *Lightning Rod* cycled back to Earth orbit.

That was best. Racer didn't want to face her crewmates, but facing English would be a thousand times worse.

She stripped off her regulation t-shirt and pulled out the ratty old black shirt she'd been wearing when she first left the Lunar Detention Center to join the Force.

She took a deal from the Youth Detention Officer to join the USF instead of serving her full sentence. Joining the Force was Racer's only chance at freedom.

Now she would never be free. Once she went into the LDC's adult section, no one would ever offer her any more deals. She'd blown her only shot at a decent life. She might as well let herself go and be as rotten as everyone always said she was.

Even Captain Ogden knew Racer was rotten. The captain wouldn't have done this to her if Racer wasn't rotten.

Captain Ogden must have been right about English, too. English was too much of a knight in shining armor to recognize a rotten apple like Racer when he saw one. He actually believed in her. What a sucker he turned out to be.

Everyone else in Wing 17 was a sucker, too. They all thought the sun shone out of English's ass. Racer wouldn't be a chump like that anymore.

She would never believe in anyone again or let them believe in her. She would make sure they all knew she was rotten to the core.

She rifled her old stuff and found a black leather jacket studded with metal spikes. She hadn't worn it since she entered the service. Now she would put it back on to go see the captain.

This jacket represented Racer's personality much better than the uniform. This whole stint on the *Lightning Rod* had just been a detour from Racer's true destiny. Now she was back on track straight into the gutter where she belonged.

She jumped and spun around when the door opened. Her heart stopped when English glared at her from the doorway.

She should tell him to go screw himself. This was the women's locker room. He had no right to come in here, but she was so stunned and frozen in shame that she couldn't say a word.

He walked right in without even blinking. "There you are. What the hell happened down there?"

"I don't know what you're talking about." She turned her back on him and threw the jacket back in her locker. She suffered another pang of shame that he was seeing what a mess her locker was.

"You deliberately missed your targets. You deliberately targeted Manheim—Manheim, Racer! She's supposed to be your friend and you shot at her when she was pinned down by enemy fire. How could you do that, Racer? I don't understand you at all."

"Yeah, that's always your problem," she spat over her shoulder. "You don't understand much of anything."

He stalked up to her, grabbed her shoulders, and jerked her around to face him. "I understand you're one of the best pilots in the whole damn squadron and you pull something like this. You could be as good as Duran if you applied yourself and practiced more."

She gaped at him in horror. He did not just say those words. He did not just say she could be as good as Duran.

He meant it, though. He didn't pull punches like that. She had only known him for a few weeks, but he wouldn't say something like that just for effect.

Was he serious? Could she really be as good as Duran?

She tore herself out of his grip and spun away. "I don't know what the hell you're talking about. I didn't do anything. It was chaos down there. You saw it. I missed. Did you come here to rub my nose in it? Thanks a lot."

He swiveled around her to block her path. "You aren't going anywhere until you give me some explanation. No way did you just miss. I've seen you in the arena, Racer. You don't miss and you sure as hell wouldn't miss to hit Manheim and then again to hit Duran. You could have hit any of the others, but no, it had to be him. That was no accident. Now tell me the truth. What happened?"

"Nothing, okay?!" She heard herself screaming at him, but facing his righteous outrage hurt too much.

She darted around him and headed for the door. She definitely needed to quit now. She couldn't stand English even looking at her.

"What don't I understand, Racer?" he called after her. "You were kicking ass and taking names on the training runs and then you completely rolled over out there. Something happened, so explain it to me. What do I not understand?"

She froze on the threshold. She couldn't tell him. English had enough problems with Captain Ogden. He didn't need this. She had to keep her secret if only to protect him.

She turned around, stalked past him to her locker, ripped out her duffel bag, and started jamming her things into it. "I'm resigning from the Force. I'm going back to the LDC. That's where I belong. Tell the others I'm sorry I screwed up today. I don't belong on this wing."

He watched her in silence for a minute, which somehow made it so much worse. Was she really going to walk out.... on him?

Tears stung her eyes as he just stood there staring at her. She was betraying him.

Leaving the wing betrayed his belief in her so much worse than throwing the dry run. He could forgive that. He wouldn't be able to forgive her if she threw herself away.

He would make her throw herself away under his eye. He wouldn't let her crawl away and hide. He would make her face her shame and see how rotten she was. He wouldn't let her fool herself that she was worthy of the uniform or his consideration or anything else.

She packed everything except her jacket. She finally grabbed a fistful of old family photos from the bottom of her locker, stuffed them in with the rest of her old clothes, and zipped her duffel closed.

"You care, Racer," he murmured under his breath. "You care about this wing and your crewmates. You didn't want to let them down. Something happened. If you tell me what it is, I might be able to help you. That's what I'm here for, you know."

"You can't help me," she croaked. "You can't even help yourself."

He frowned. "What is that supposed to mean? I'm responsible for you. If you're in trouble, it's my job to fix it."

"Well, you can't. No one can fix this except by me leaving the Force. That's all there is to it, okay?"

She sniffed just in case he wasn't quite sure how upset she was, but she couldn't stay here. She had to get out of this conversation now.

"Did someone in the crew say something to you about the dry run? Did someone mention you missing?"

"No."

"If you wanted to leave, why didn't you do it before I came on board? Is it me? Did I say something to piss you off? Did I offend you or something?"

"Shut the fuck up, English!" she snapped. "You don't know what the fuck you're talking about, okay? Just leave me the fuck alone!"

She ripped her duffel off the bench, but when she turned to storm out of the locker room, one of the straps snapped and the bag yanked out of her hand. The bag hit the floor and she stooped to pick it up.

English didn't help her. He just watched her from a distance. "Are you going to see your wingmates before you leave?"

"Of course not. Are you stupid?"

"I'm not so stupid that I didn't see you really trying in the arena. You were proud of your flying. You got snotty when Thorpe implied that you didn't know how to fly. You could be an officer, Racer. You might even make captain, but not unless you tell me what's going on."

"You don't want to know what's going on—unless you already do!" she raged. "Why don't you just go ahead and beat the shit out of me and get it over with instead of hammering me with all these questions? You already know what happened. You were there."

He frowned again. "When?"

"It was Captain Ogden, okay?!" she shrieked. "You know that! Do I really have to say it?"

He froze staring at her and Racer felt the full weight of what she just said fall on her head. Now she did it. Now she was finished for certain.

She turned her back on English, but she couldn't leave the locker room now. She couldn't go see Captain Ogden, now that she told English point blank that Captain Ogden was the one who set Racer up to fail.

Racer couldn't go to the flight deck again. She couldn't go anywhere. She was trapped and now she had no options left at all. Maybe she should end it. Then she wouldn't have to think about any of this anymore.

Racer paced along the lockers breathing fast. Her heart hammered and her hands shook. Cold sweat dampened her palms and she rubbed them against her pants to dry them, but it didn't help.

English didn't move. He stayed quiet for so long that she wondered if he was thinking about attacking her.

She didn't care if he did. She deserved that. She deserved worse.

When he finally spoke, he husked in a barely audible murmur. "What did she say?"

"She said...." Racer choked, "that I had to throw the dry run and let the other wings look good. She said she would stop you from bumping me off the squadron. She said she could bump anyone from the *Lightning Rod* and it was up to her if I stayed or went or if *you* stayed or went."

"I see."

Those words echoed into a bottomless well of horror and meaning. Racer cringed at the finality of it all.

Something thumped on the bench behind her and attracted her attention. She glanced over her shoulder to see him picking up her duffel. He grabbed the broken strap and tied it together with a few quick yanks. A giant knot stuck out of the strap, but the bag was usable now.

He strode over to her and stopped at her shoulder. She couldn't look at him.

"Well, you did what she told you to do. You threw the run, so she has nothing to say about your actions. You followed orders and none of the other pilots know it was deliberate. You can go back to the barracks if you want to."

Her head shot up and she found herself staring at him right in front of her. "What.... you mean it?"

"Sure. You're a damn good pilot. The Force would be the loser if you left. No one knows but you, me, and Captain Ogden. You did what she said and I won't tell anyone. Duran might be pissed off at you for a while, but no one has to know about this. Go back to the barracks."

"But.... what about the captain? What if she does something else? What if she tries to mess with you again?"

"You let me deal with Captain Ogden. I'm sorry you got mixed up in the middle of this. It put you in a very bad position and that wasn't fair to you. I'll deal with her. There's no reason you should leave the Force because of this."

"But....my results.... from the run...."

"We'll strike the two hits you made on Manheim and Duran. That will put your results at zero, but at least this run won't show up on your record as a negative mark. You can work on making up for it in future runs."

She blinked at him in stunned disbelief. Was he really going to do this? Was he really going to wipe her mistake? Could someone really do something like that.... for her?

He strolled over to the door and looked back at her. "It would be a real shame if you left the service because of something that had nothing to do with you. You're an asset to our crew and I would hate to lose you. I really hope you do the right thing and come back to the barracks, but if you do that, you'll need to get back into uniform."

Chapter 10

E nglish dropped into the chair behind the desk in his quarters, buried his face in his hands, and let out a deep, shuddering sigh. This posting on the *Lightning Rod* was turning into a much more exasperating trial than he ever expected.

He ought to do something about Captain Ogden threatening Racer. He ought to report it, but if he did, that would only make Captain Ogden more hostile toward him.

If he reported it at all, he would have to report it to the Command Staff. They would have to investigate the incident. That would take time and it would give Captain Ogden too many opportunities to retaliate against Racer.

English wasn't too concerned about Ogden's treatment of him. He could take it. He didn't blame her for feeling threatened by him. He expected it to go like this when he came back on active duty.

He couldn't turn a blind eye to the captain messing with Racer. She was by far the most vulnerable member of his wing. That must be why the captain targeted Racer and not one of the others. Captain Ogden could threaten Racer with something Racer really cared about—her position on the crew.

He couldn't let something like this happen again, but he had to come up with a way to stop it.

Discussing it with Commander Radcliffe could turn out to be a double-edged sword, too. English didn't want to put Matt's position in danger, either. Turning Radcliffe against Ogden would definitely put Radcliffe's position in danger.

English sighed again, opened his eyes, and turned to his computer screen. He had to work out a simulation practice schedule for his pilots. They were all dangerously out of practice except for Duran. That kid must have been doing simulation practice since he could walk and it showed.

All the others would show marked improvement with a little more practice each week. It would do wonders for their confidence, not to mention their scores.

He put out his hand to switch on his computer terminal when a signal came through it. The screen blinked on to show the USF logo and a line of text at the bottom.

Incoming transmission:

Origin: Earth.

From: Doctor Melanie Ann English.

He flicked the screen on and opened the transmission. A beautiful, fresh-faced young woman with shoulder-length copper-brown hair and laughing brown eyes appeared before him. "Hi, sweetie," English greeted her. "How are things?"

She groaned and her eyes darted off the screen. "Something is going on, Dad. I don't know who to turn to."

English frowned at his daughter. "What's up? I thought you were happy at the Command Center Hospital."

"I am, but something is going on. I don't really understand it. Things have gotten really.... strange here. I thought you were crazy to go out on the *Lightning Rod*, but now I really wish you were here. Then again, I really wish you *weren't* here, you know what I mean?"

"No, darling. I don't know what you mean. What is happening that's so strange?"

"I'm not sure. That's the problem. There's some big shake-up happening with the Command Staff. The whole Command Center is on edge."

"What's the problem?" he asked.

"No one will tell us. That's why everyone is walking on eggshells."

English frowned even deeper. "I don't understand, sweetheart."

"I don't understand it, either. No one does." She ran her hand across her forehead. "I really need to talk to you about this. Dad. I don't know what to do."

"Okay, darling. I'm right here. Talk to me. What do you know so far? I don't see how what happens in the Command Staff can have much effect on the hospital. The hospital staff and administration aren't under the Command Staff."

"I know! That's what's so weird about it. Whatever goes on in the Command Staff shouldn't affect us at all, but it is. No one knows who to trust. Everyone suspects everyone else of everything and...."

"Suspects everyone of what, sweetie?"

"I'm not sure." She groaned again and covered her eyes. "I know it doesn't make sense. It doesn't make sense to me, either. That's what's so bizarre about the whole thing."

English took a second to let his mind catch up with what she wasn't telling him. "Maybe I should call Admiral York and ask him what's going on."

"Would you, Dad? I'd really appreciate it. I've been going crazy. I even called Dan and he doesn't understand it, either."

English stiffened. "Really? That's odd."

"I know. He's in direct daily communication with the whole Command Staff and no one will tell anybody anything. The whole Command Staff is up in the air and no one knows why."

"Dan is captain of the Ufa Long-Range Alert Station," English pointed out. "If something was going on with the Command Staff, he would be the first to know."

"I know, Dad, but he doesn't know anything. He was as frustrated and upset as I was when I talked to him. He's my own brother. If he knew anything, he would have told me. In fact, he was even more pissed off than I was. He thinks something is threatening Earth and no one will tell him what it is."

"So nothing is showing up on the alert system?"

She shook her head. "Nothing.... except the maneuvers on Fenrir."

English hardly heard her. His son Dan had rocketed to the top of the USF chain of command on his own merits. Dan would have gotten assigned to Ufa Station without being Sailor English's son and there never was a more conscientious officer born. If Dan didn't know what was going on, calling Admiral York wouldn't get English anywhere, either.

English scrambled to come up with another option. Part of him wished he had accepted the post at the Command Center that the USF brass offered him, but Melanie was already inside the Command Center.

Dan was one of the most trusted officers in the whole Force. Neither he nor Melanie knew anything, which meant English would have been in the dark even if he had been there.

Just then, a shuddering boom sounded from somewhere and Melanie's image wobbled. English cocked his ear to listen to the noise vibrating through the *Lightning Rod's* walls, but the explosion didn't come from the ship.

Melanie looked up at the ceiling. "Oh, my God!"

"What was that, sweetie?"

"I don't know. It sounds like something just hit the building." Another blast went off—louder this time. Melanie shot to her feet and bellowed into the screen. "I gotta go, Dad. I'll...."

The screen cut out. English stared at it for a second trying to decide what to do. That explosion gave him grave misgivings.

He switched his computer over to check on the USF Command Center, but at that moment, another siren went off inside his quarters.

The same loudspeaker started blaring, "Battle stations! All fighter wings—battle stations! All crew members report to designated defense posts. Maximum alert!"

English charged out of his quarters and almost collided with Charlie Frasier coming from his own cabin. "What the hell is going on?"

"No idea," Frasier replied. "The whole computer and communications system just shut down."

The two gunnery sergeants raced for the stairs. More *Lightning Rod* crewmen poured out of their quarters trying to answer the alert.

English passed another door and Matt Radcliffe came out. "What's going on?" English asked.

"The word just came down. Someone attacked the Command Center. The whole damn Force is on alert."

"Who attacked it? It couldn't be aliens. There's nothing on the long-range alert system."

"We aren't sure who did it, but the shots definitely came from somewhere on Earth. Right now, it looks like it came from USF destroyers."

English halted dead in his tracks at those terrible words. USF destroyers were attacking the Command Center? They couldn't be.

Radcliffe shot English a significant look and vanished into the stairwell, but English couldn't move. Melanie was at the Command Center. She was under bombardment from the Force itself.

This was the worst scenario that haunted English's nightmares. Earth and the United Space Force couldn't go into a civil war against themselves. That was not possible.

Frasier tapped English's elbow. "Let's go. We gotta get down to the flight deck."

English snapped back to his senses and followed Frasier downstairs. The elevators had completely locked down along with everything else on board.

The whole *Lightning Rod* crew was up and moving. Every pilot from all three fighter wings swarmed the flight deck. English and Frasier parted to deal with their crews.

Wing 17 mobbed English the minute he got near them. "What's going on, Sir?" Thorpe asked. "Are the aliens invading again?"

"I wish they were, son. I really wish they were."

"Are we going out against them?" Babbitt asked. "Are we going back to Fenrir?"

"We aren't going to Fenrir. I don't know where we're going."

Duran furrowed his brow at English. "You know something, don't you, Sir? Tell us. We have a right to know."

English took a deep breath. "We don't know for sure yet, but it looks like civil war is breaking out on Earth. We don't know yet. We just have to wait and see, but if we go out against anyone, it will be our own people."

The crew fell instantly silent. Every face stared up at him in horror and English turned away feeling sick. "I'm going to check in with Lieutenant Eismann. Each of you get to your birds and do your pre-flight checks. Make sure you're ready to roll the instant the order comes down. Go on."

They left to follow his order, but Racer hesitated. She met his eye for a second and English's heart twisted. She was still here and she was back in uniform, so that was saying something. He still had a chance to bring her back into the fold.

She finally broke away and vanished behind her own craft. English returned to Eismann's desk and met Frasier and Lloyd there, too.

"What do you know, Brock?" Frasier demanded. "Don't leave us in the dark."

Eismann switched from one computer screen to the next. "Long-range scans show the Command Center under bombardment from fifteen destroyers. Fourteen more are defending the place, but it's impossible to tell which ships are on which side. Our systems aren't designed for this. They all look like friendlies."

"Where did the first shots come from?" English asked.

"I'm trying to find out, okay? I'm as anxious to know what's going on as you are."

English forced himself to remain calm. "Where did the attacking ships launch from?"

Eismann pursed his lips. "It looks like the first shots came from the Tripoli Earth Defense Battery."

"But they would need Command clearance to change their target to another USF station on Earth itself," Frasier pointed out.

"I know that, Charlie!" Eismann snapped. "We're talking about civil war, okay? Someone or several someones inside the Command Staff took over these stations and batteries and ships."

"Who would do this?" Lloyd croaked. "Who would betray everything we've fought and bled for?"

Eismann compressed his lips again and bowed over his computers. "The Gibraltar Battery is bombarding Manchester, Stockholm, and Hamburg. There are more USF batteries turning their guns on other stations. The whole damn world is going crazy."

English gulped and glanced over his shoulder. Each of his pilots stood by their fighter craft and most of them watched him. They were all waiting to see what he would come back and tell them.

An alarm went off on Eismann's computers and he sprang sideways to check it. "Here it comes! Another contingent of destroyers is launching from Adelaide. They're leaving orbit on an intercept course for Fenrir."

Just then, another siren blasted across the flight deck. "Battle stations! All fighter wings—prepare to launch!" the loudspeaker squawked. "Battle stations! All fighter wings—prepare to launch!"

Frasier, Lloyd, Eismann, and English gave each other another sick glance and the three sergeants left for their wings.

"What are we doing, Sir?" Thorpe asked in a quavering voice as he, Duran, Babbitt, and Ritchie gathered around English.

"We're preparing to launch. Load up, all of you."

English shoved his way through the pilots. None of them went anywhere. "Who are we fighting, Sir?" Manheim asked. "Please tell us."

"I wish I knew, sweetie. I really do."

English climbed into his bird before they finally left him alone. His controls switched on and showed him the whole crew loading up. No one talked or joked. They went through their checks and made their adjustments in silence.

English fought down rising panic. How in the name of God was he supposed to fire on USF destroyers and squadron pilots? How could he be responsible for taking another human life? Fighting aliens was one thing. He didn't sign up for this.

"Squadron Command to Wing Leaders 10, 12, and 17," Eismann announced through the communications system. "Stand by to launch."

"Standing by to launch," English replied. "Just give us a clue who the hell we're supposed to fight."

"Transmitting signatures to your controls now. Go with God, Fighter Wings."

A prickle went up English's scalp when he read the information Eismann sent him. English knew every name on the list of enemy destroyers.

Octopus. Restless. Shadrack. Copernicus. Fiji. Buckingham Palace. Golden Hind. Afrikaans. Isaac Newton. Foresight. Robbie Burns. Starlet. Henrietta.

Friends, acquaintances, and many of English's former crew and commanders manned those ships. He had fought and bled and cried and lost with them. He dedicated his whole life to them. Could he really open fire on them?

The bottom dropped out from under his world when he spotted another name on the list. *Dannevirk.*

Sean Duran, Ezra Duran's older brother, served on the *Dannevirk* as a fighter pilot. If Wing 17 went against the *Dannevirk*, Duran would be fighting his own brother.

English glanced over to Duran's cockpit. Duran didn't speak or move. He sat in his seat staring down at his controls.

English looked over at Eismann's desk, but Eismann was too busy to notice. Did anyone on this crew know what was about to happen?

At that moment, Eismann switched on the communications system. "All fighter wings—launch! The *Lightning Rod* is under assault from the *Hermes* and the *Nostradamus*. The *Solar Flare* is taking hits! Full assault! You have your targets!"

The launch bay doors slammed open and Wing 12 launched followed by Wing 10. English launched with his pilots right on his ass. They all dropped out into a massive space battle to end all space battles—except that it wasn't.

This was only two ships against two ships. The swarm of fighter craft buzzing around all four got so confused that English couldn't tell one from the next.

The *Hermes* and the *Nostradamus* flanked the *Solar Flare* on both sides. The four destroyers had migrated into the asteroid belt heading for Mars. The whole contingent must have been on its way back toward Earth in formation when the *Hermes* and the *Nostradamus* attacked the *Solar Flare*.

The two enemy destroyers pounded the *Solar Flare* with their huge range cannons and punched holes in the *Solar Flare's* hull. Catastrophic booms rippled down the *Solar Flare's* sides.

The *Solar Flare's* squadron raced in a figure-eight pattern from the *Nostradamus* to the *Hermes* and back again. The fighter craft sliced their plasma into the destroyers' sides, but nothing stopped their hellish bombardment—until the *Lightning Rod* showed up.

The *Lightning Rod* raced into the battle showering both attackers with shots. The *Hermes* rotated away from the *Solar Flare* and the *Hermes* turned all her venom on the *Lightning Rod* instead.

"Cut it back, Wing 17!" English ordered. "Defend the *Lightning Rod*!"

"What about the *Solar Flare*?" Babbitt asked.

"She's got her own squadron. Surround the *Lightning Rod*!"

Wing 17 wheeled back to the ship. Wing 12 appeared out of nowhere and both wings separated the *Lightning Rod* from the rest of the battle. The *Hermes* stalked the ship with guns blazing. The *Hermes* squadron abandoned the *Solar Flare* to attack the *Lightning Rod* fighter wings instead.

English rocketed forward to engage with them, but as soon as Wing 17 joined him, he wound up with the same problem. His instruments didn't recognize which fighters belonged to the enemy and which were his own—or the *Solar Flare's*. He couldn't tell who to shoot at.

Wing 17 pilots yelled back and forth to each other, but everyone besides the four destroyers had the same problem. No one could tell friend from foe.

English fired at a few fighters only to realize too late that he was shooting at Frasier's crew. English looped back to the *Lightning Rod* and surveyed the battle from a distance, but he still couldn't see who was who.

Lieutenant Eismann's voice squawked in his ear. "*Lightning Rod* squadron, return to the ship."

"We're taking a pounding out here!" Lloyd shrieked. "We're flying blind!"

"*Lightning Rod* squadron!" Eismann roared. "Return to the ship and take up position behind the cargo hold. Respond, Fighter Wing Leaders. I repeat, return to the ship and take up position behind the cargo hold."

"Acknowledged, Squadron Command," English replied. He made sure his pilots retreated as ordered and left the *Hermes* squadron to assault the *Lightning Rod* without limit.

As soon as the *Lightning Rod* squadron pulled away, the *Hermes* and her squadron laid into the *Lightning Rod* with a vengeance. They pounded the ship, but the *Lightning Rod* only turned away. She swiveled to present her back to the *Hermes*.

The *Nostradamus* saw the *Lightning Rod* running scared and broke off assaulting the *Solar Flare*. The *Nostradamus* advanced until she and the *Hermes* ganged up on the *Lightning Rod*.

"This is bullshit!" Thorpe snarled. "They think we're cowards. We should stand and fight."

"You have your orders, Wing 17," English snapped. "Take up your positions behind the...."

The words died on his lips when he moved behind the *Lightning Rod* and saw what the ship's bulk blocked him from seeing before now.

A huge contingent of USF destroyers sprinted through Earth's atmosphere on a dead course for the *Lightning Rod*. The ship was the only thing standing in their path.

Chapter 11

"Fighter wings in position!" Master Chief Terranova reported.

Captain Ogden hunkered deeper in her chair and tightened her grip on her armrests. "Arm all cannon batteries."

"Cannon batteries armed," Commander Radcliffe replied. "All gunners on standby."

"Damage reports coming in from Decks 14 on down," Lieutenant Avila added. "The flight deck has been damaged. It's gonna take an act of God to get our fighter wings back on board when this is all over."

"Let's not put the cart before the horse," Captain Ogden replied. "Any word from the Command Staff?"

"Nothing," Radcliffe told her. "The power is out at the Command Center. They aren't capable of communications. We're on our own."

"All right," she muttered. "Stand fast."

Silence fell over the bridge watching the enemy destroyers crawl closer by the second. The three fighter wings hovered in front of the *Lightning Rod*. They looked so puny in the face of so many destroyers.

Booming crashes rocked the ship as the *Hermes* and the *Nostradamus* laid into the *Lightning Rod* from behind, but no one paid any attention. The bridge and all the cannon batteries faced the oncoming enemy.

The two enemy destroyers left the *Solar Flare* alone and she attacked them from behind them, but the *Solar Flare* had been so severely damaged that she couldn't do much.

Her fighter wings zipped around the *Lightning Rod* and joined the *Lightning Rod* wings. They all stood guard as the rebel destroyers drew closer.

The *Dannevirk* opened fire from a distance. "All fighter wings—attack!" Captain Ogden ordered. "Get in amongst them! Mix it up, squadron!"

The fighter craft zoomed into the enemy with every cannon on fire. They bombarded the enemy in a blinding whirl of plasma and all the enemy squadrons launched to meet them. Enemy birds enveloped the *Lightning Rod's* squadron until Radcliffe couldn't see them anymore, but that meant nothing.

Rebel destroyers charged for the *Lightning Rod's* position and drowned the *Lightning Rod* in shots. A blistering plasma jet blasted the bridge and nearly knocked Radcliffe off his feet.

"We're losing power!" he told Ogden. "The bridge can communicate with Eismann, but Squadron Command can't get through to our birds. The fighter wings are cut off!"

"How many batteries do we still have?"

"No idea." Radcliffe tried to bring up damage reports, but nothing worked.

"Plasma is still coming from our cannons!" Avila reported. "The batteries are firing independently."

"Get us out of here, Matt!" Ogden ordered. "Fall back to the Acheron Colony."

"There is no Acheron Colony!" Radcliffe roared over the noise. "We'll have to settle for the Io Center."

"I don't care! Just get us out of here."

"What about our fighters?" Terranova asked. "We can't abandon them."

"We can't communicate with them. Fire into the field. Target Gunny English."

Radcliffe's head shot up and his jaw dropped. "You can't be serious!"

"Signal him, damn it! Signal him that we're falling back. He must realize communications are down. Fire!"

Radcliffe scrambled on the few instruments he still had and brought up one cannon battery he could still communicate with. He transmitted the identity signature of English's fighter and the order to fire.

The plasma jet erupted from the *Lightning Rod's* battery and Radcliffe seized the helm. He eased the ship backward out of the battle, turned tail, and gunned the engines for Io.

The shot sizzled into the field and grazed English's fighter. He wheeled and then all of Wing 17 hurtled out of the throng followed closely by Wings 10 and 12.

They raced back to the *Lightning Rod*, but the *Hermes* and the *Nostradamus* both split off to attack the ship as she passed. The two rebel destroyers dodged into the *Lightning Rod's* path.

Before anyone on the bridge could say a word, English and four Wing 17 pilots whizzed past the *Lightning Rod* in a dead sprint. They plummeted toward the *Hermes's* bridge and unloaded right into the bridge window.

The window exploded and a cloud of debris and even a few bodies ripped into space. The debris cloud started to spread and then a withering explosion blasted out the whole bridge.

Wing 17 raced past the *Hermes* and bombarded her starboard engine panels. They detonated in flames and the *Hermes* teetered in space.

The *Nostradamus* pivoted to target the *Lightning Rod*, but Wing 17 had already won the ship just enough of a gap to make a break for freedom.

The *Lightning Rod* skidded past the *Hermes* as the ship started to implode, but the *Nostradamus* was too fast. She veered hard in front of the *Lightning Rod*, and when the *Nostradamus* opened fire, the *Lightning Rod* lacked the firepower to defend herself.

Wing 17 made it past, but Wings 10 and 12 got trapped closer to the *Lightning Rod*. The two wings closed in front of the ship trying everything to protect the destroyer from the *Nostradamus*, but nothing could stand against the *Nostradamus's* guns.

"Wing 17 is coming back!" Avila reported.

"No!" Ogden barked. "Signal them to keep going on to Io."

"We can't," Radcliffe countered. "We can't communicate with them."

"English and Duran are attacking the *Nostradamus* from behind," Terranova reported. "They're targeting Deck 8."

Ogden jerked around. "That's the life support system."

"Yes, Ma'am. They've done it! They've compromised the *Nostradamus's* life support system. The crew is evacuating."

"Can we get through now?"

"The *Octopus* and the *Shadrack* are feinting to run us down," Radcliffe replied.

"Come about!" Ogden ordered. "Stand your ground."

Radcliffe pulled the ship backward and the *Lightning Rod's* fighter squadron flowed back to confront the oncoming rebels.

"We can't stand against one destroyer, let alone two," Radcliffe pointed out.

"Wing 10 has already lost four fighters," Avila reported. "They're chipping away at us to weaken us."

"Stand fast," Ogden replied.

The minute she said it, Wing 17 blasted past the bridge and surrounded the *Octopus*. The fighter craft completely ignored the *Shadrack*.

"They're pulling the same trick they pulled on Fenrir," Radcliffe muttered under his breath, but those words spread through the whole bridge. This was English's doing. He was using the same strategy to destroy one ship at a time.

The *Octopus* was better prepared than the *Hermes*, though. The ship opened fire much sooner and plasma erupted into the fighters. Wings 10 and 12 joined in and a royal battle broke out between the *Lightning Rod* squadron and the squadrons of both rebel ships.

Plasma obscured visibility for a second and then the *Shadrack* burst through the confusion. It appeared right on top of the *Lightning Rod*.

"We got nothing!" Radcliffe hollered. "All batteries are out of communication. They're fighting on their own. We're sitting ducks."

"Pull back!" Ogden ordered. "Can we still retreat?"

"Not likely!" Radcliffe replied. "The *Nostradamus* is blocking our way."

"Ma'am!" Terranova cut in. "Another contingent is coming in! They're launching from the Falklands Base. Ma'am—they're firing on the rebels! The Force is coming out to save us!"

Plasma spouted from a hundred cannons and splintered the enemy mob. Half the rebel destroyers wheeled backward, but they had already taken too much damage. The new arrivals made short work of them.

"Get out of the line of fire, Matt!" Ogden ordered. "Can we get through?"

"The *Nightside* and the *Greyhound* are flanking us to attack the *Nostradamus*! I think we can do it."

Radcliffe dragged the sluggish helm into reverse one more time, but the fighter wings didn't see this time. They got so buried in enemy fire that Radcliffe couldn't even tell which ones belonged to the *Lightning Rod*.

He checked his instruments, but he couldn't distinguish which fighters were which. He no longer had any communications with his own batteries to pull the same trick as before. He could only hope the fighter wings noticed in time.

The *Greyhound* and the *Nightside* sandwiched the *Nostradamus* the way she sandwiched the *Solar Flare* with the *Hermes*.

The two destroyers smashed the *Nostradamus* in plasma blasts. Fighters hurtled into the mix and exploding fighter craft dotted the night sky.

Wing 12 raced out of the battle and swirled around the *Lightning Rod* as she made her escape, but neither Frasier's nor English's wings escaped.

Radcliffe cast one backward glance toward the battle. The friendly destroyers engaged in a whole-scale stampede of the rebels.

Destroyer battled destroyer and fighter craft battled fighter craft. It was the most sickening sight of Radcliffe's career, but the *Lightning Rod* couldn't do anything about that now. She couldn't even save her own from this disaster.

He pulled the *Lightning Rod* around the *Shadrack* and picked up speed making for Io. The navigation system was down, too, so he had to steer the ship manually.

The fighters swarmed the ship's lower decks, but they couldn't get inside with the flight deck smashed to pieces.

No one on the bridge spoke, not even Captain Ogden. Radcliffe headed back through the asteroid field to the Io Center, settled the *Lightning Rod* into a stable orbit, and straightened up. "It's done, Ma'am. We're out of danger for now."

"All ship's internal communications are still down," Terranova reported. "Whatever we do, we'll have to deliver messages in person."

"That's fine. We'll do it." Captain Ogden got to her feet and tugged her uniform into place. "Julio, you come with me to the batteries. Santiago, you go get the engineers working on the communications system. Let me know the minute you reestablish contact with Earth. Matt, you go down the flight deck and get every mechanic working on the launch bay doors. Get our birds inside before they run out of fuel."

Chapter 12

E nglish plowed through fourteen fighters packed between four destroyers. Plasma flew in all directions. He couldn't see which fighters or destroyer cannons the plasma was coming from.

Someone screamed in the mayhem and one of dozens of fighters exploded right next to his starboard wing.

"The *Lightning Rod*—!" Babbitt shrieked. "She's flying away! Captain Ogden is abandoning us!"

"We've lost contact with Eismann!" English told him. "Communications is down."

"Take that, you cocksuckers!" Duran plastered cannon shots at some random fighter, took a punishing barrage across his roof, and cartwheeled sideways to pound the *Outrigger's* port engine. "You want some of this, assholes? You asked for it!"

"The *Outrigger* is one of ours, son!" English told him.

Duran looked around him in all directions. "Which one is the *Outrigger*?"

"*Lightning Rod* Wing 17—pull up!" English ordered. "Get above the battle."

He veered his fighter upward, but five enemy pilots hounded him all the way. They stung his tail again and again, but he ignored them.

Sure enough, another wing from the *Vampire Bat* materialized out of the plasma stream. They scattered his attackers before the strangers split formation and vanished back into the mayhem.

Duran, Thorpe, and Ritchie caught up with English and he looked around. "Here comes Racer! Where's Janacek?"

"I think I saw him over by the *Riordan*," Racer panted. "He was taking a licking, that's for sure."

"You four beat it back to the Io Center. You can rendezvous with the *Lightning Rod* there."

"What makes you sure the *Lightning Rod* was heading for Io?" Ritchie asked.

"Because the Acheron Colony is gone and Cyllene is uninhabited. The Io Center is the only colony left. Get moving and don't look back. You hear me, Thorpe? I'm putting you in charge. Don't let any of the others come back for us." No one answered. "Thorpe?"

"Yes, Sir," Thorpe grumbled and the four of them limped away toward the asteroid belt.

English waited a second longer and Manheim staggered out of the battle. Her agonized wheezes came through his communications system. "Follow Thorpe and Racer, Ada," English ordered.

She didn't answer and she didn't leave. He noticed her staring at nothing with the same look of glazed shock she had in the arena.

English couldn't wait any longer. He rocketed back into the battle calling at the top of his lungs. "*Lightning Rod* Wing 17! Do you read?"

"Gunny!" Janacek yelped. "Help me!"

"Where are you, son?"

A torturous bellow answered him and English burst through a curtain of plasma. He almost collided with four fighters all gathered around a small cluster of Wing 17 pilots.

Janacek occupied the very center of the ball while Babbitt and Stoval defended him. All three of them spat plasma shots with ferocious speed. They showered their enemies with ten shots to one and held the rebels at bay, but none of the three could break out.

English reacted without deciding first what he would do. He took a page from Duran's book, slammed his fighter into reverse, and skidded in a long, sideways curve. He pulled up alongside the enemy and opened up with all his cannons.

He punched the throttle and zoomed across their line raining hellfire on the enemy fighters. He punched three of their hulls and left a trail of fire behind him.

The others spun around to confront him, but he was flying too fast for them. "Get out, boys! Fly straight up and rendezvous with Manheim."

"What about you, Sir?" Babbitt asked.

"Get out, I said! Beat it back to Io with the others—now! Go, Janacek!"

The three of them sprinted upward while the remaining rebels hounded English into the battle, but he buried himself in plasma and lost them in no time.

He revolved through a few more slalom runs between friendly destroyers. He made sure no one followed him and finally vaulted upward into empty space.

The remaining destroyers and fighter craft were too busy attacking each other to notice a few stragglers making their escape. English gunned his engines and caught up with Janacek.

The boy's fighter limped at half-speed. Babbitt and Stoval flanked him to guard him. Manheim had already gone ahead.

A few minutes later, their grouping met the rest of Wing 17. The pilots hovered in orbit around the Heinrich Satellite located between Mars and the asteroid belt.

English pulled to a stop next to Duran. "What's going on? Why didn't you go through to Io like I told you to?"

"Look," Duran told him. "It looks like there was another battle here. There's too much crap in the way and some of the engine debris is still venting plasma. We didn't want to risk it without talking to you first."

English checked his fighter's instruments. Duran was right. Random pieces of ships' fuselages and combusting gas and plasma flooded the asteroid belt. It was way too crowded with junk to risk crossing and combusting the gas.

English scanned the area. "We'll have to land on the satellite. We barely have enough fuel to make it to Io anyway. We're dead in the water until we can reestablish communications with the *Lightning Rod*."

He turned back to call to Babbitt and Stoval....and his guts wrenched when he spotted six destroyers coming straight for them.

The *Riordan* and the *Copernicus* traded shots with the *Foresight* and four other enemy destroyers. Plasma jets and explosions flashed in the darkness and two enemy ships fired on Wing 17.

"Get down on the satellite—now!" English ordered.

"How do we......?" Manheim began before a wayward shot zipped past her cockpit. She screamed again.

"Follow me!" English ordered. "Racer—fall back and help defend Janacek!"

"What about......?" The enemy destroyers sprinted for the Heinrich satellite. Maybe they had the same idea about landing on it.

English hit the throttle. "Wing 17—with me!"

He dove for the satellite running at full speed. He peeled his craft sideways to skate between two giant refinery towers.

"Sir....!" Thorpe began, but at that moment, Duran burned past him to catch up with English.

Duran hovered at English's elbow all the way. English torched a path through the satellite's residential section making for the Tecrium reactor.

The enemy destroyers advanced and pounded the satellite trying to hit Wing 17, but they broke off when English approached the reactor. He and Duran circled it just to make sure.

"Land your people here, Ezra. Take them all inside the reactor."

"You got it, Sir." Duran started to descend.

"Follow Duran, all of you." English pulled up. "I'm going back for the others."

Thorpe, Ritchie, and Manheim drifted down onto platforms surrounding the reactor and English lost sight of them.

He overtook Stoval under heavy fire from the *Foresight*. English rocketed toward the ship's rear end and unloaded on Deck 8. The *Foresight* rounded on him.

"Get your boys back to the satellite, Auggie! Take them down to the Tecrium reactor. Beat it, son!"

"I'm trying, Sir," Stoval called. "Janacek—I think he's foundering. He isn't making any progress."

English twirled around the *Foresight* and checked his readings on Janacek's fighter. "Shit!"

Babbitt and Racer stood guard over Janacek. He kept firing and furious bellows came from his fighter, but his ship no longer moved, not even to turn from one side to the other.

English bolted for Janacek's position ready to stand and fight with the rest, but at that moment, the *Riordan* caught up with them and bombarded the *Foresight* with fresh volleys.

The *Foresight* tried to hit both Janacek and the *Riordan*. The *Riordan* launched her squadron to overrun the *Foresight's* fighters and the *Foresight* squadron abandoned Wing 17 for the larger battle.

English veered in close to Janacek. "Deploy your grappling hook, Auggie! Catch Janacek's port wing and I'll take the starboard. Racer, you and Babbitt defend us against all comers."

"Yes, Sir," Racer replied.

She and Babbitt fell in on either side. English and Stoval strapped their grappling hooks around Janacek's ruined fighter and started the slow, painful crawl back to the Heinrich satellite.

Racer and Babbitt closed ranks. They took hits from the *Foresight* squadron, but when the *Copernicus* finally showed up to help the *Riordan*, all the fighters broke away.

English scanned the skies while he and Stoval lowered Janacek's fighter into position with the others already on the ground. Janacek popped his cockpit and Racer laughed cruelly when he fell flat on his ass jumping to safety.

English bit back a grin. He could enjoy their narrow escape through her.

He made sure Stoval, Babbitt, and Racer got down on the satellite before he landed his own bird. Duran and Thorpe came out to greet them and the whole group hunkered down inside the reactor housing.

Janacek collapsed against a low wall panting, gasping, and whining for breath. "I.... can't.... breathe.... I.... can't.... breathe...."

English rested his hand on the boy's shoulder. "You're okay. Just take it easy and calm down. You did great out there. I'm proud of you." He looked around at eight pairs of huge eyes reflected up at him in the dim light. "You all conducted yourselves superbly out there. I couldn't ask for better. You all deserve decorations for your conduct. That was absolutely outstanding flying and exceptional shooting—the best I've seen in my career."

"Now what do we do, Sir?" Ritchie asked. "How do we hook back up with the *Lightning Rod* after this?"

"We're safe in here for now. No one will shoot at the reactor."

"Are you sure?" Janacek asked. "They blew up the reactor at the Acheron Colony. What makes you think they won't do the same thing here?"

"We don't know who blew up the Acheron Colony," Thorpe replied. "That could have been an accident."

"None of this does anything except fuel our fears," English told them. "The rebels won't blow up this reactor because the shockwave would destroy any ships close enough to shoot at the reactor. Did you see how the rebels cut their fire when we came over here? We're safe here for now."

"How do you know they were rebels?" Duran asked. "How do we know who's a rebel and who's friendly?"

English sighed. "Unfortunately, we don't know. We only know about our wing so that means me and you have to get ourselves out of here."

"How do we do that?" Manheim squeaked. "We're trapped here."

"We aren't trapped here," Ritchie pointed out. "We all still have fuel—except Janacek."

"We don't have much," Racer added. "We barely have enough to get to Io—assuming we could get through that debris field. We don't even know if the *Lightning Rod* is on Io or somewhere else. We could get all the way to Io and find out we're stranded there with no fuel at all."

"Stash the wild speculation," English cut in. "We have our own business to attend to. First off, all our communications are working which means the communications problem was on the *Lightning Rod's* end. The ship took a pasting from the *Hermes*. Most of the flight deck was caved in, so we'll just have to hold our own until the ship undergoes repairs."

"What does 'hold our own' mean?" Thorpe asked. "What can we accomplish *here*?"

English peeked through the doorway. Artificial atmosphere enveloped the satellite. The eight remaining fighter craft lined up outside, but beyond that, he couldn't see anything but more and more pipes from the refinery.

"Like I said, the communications problem is on the other end. I'm going back out to my fighter to see if I can raise the *Lightning Rod*. The ship might have restored communications. I doubt she has, but I'll try and then we'll...."

He started to move toward the exit, but when he got near it, someone swiveled into the doorway from outside. A grey-haired man with a long beard blocked the light and pointed a handgun in English's face. "Hold it right there! Don't move!"

English raised his hands. "Easy, man. We're from the *USS Lightning Rod* and we're grounded here. We just want to...."

Splitting pain and exploding stars burst in English's brain as the stranger slammed his gun into English's nose. English staggered backward and the guy kicked him square in the chin.

English's head snapped back a second time, and before he could think twice, the guy was on top of him.

Racer screamed behind him. "Gunny....!" The next second, more colonists poured into the reactor housing and tackled English to the floor.

Punches, kicks, and blows rained on his head, back, and sides. He curled into a ball to protect himself. He heard the sounds of a scuffle nearby and the pilots yelling. Manheim screamed much louder than Racer did. Manheim's voice kept getting farther away.

The crew's voices gave English superhuman strength and he forced himself onto his hands and knees. The blows kept falling, but he raised his head to see where his people were.

A dozen colonists were dragging the Wing 17 pilots out of the reactor housing. Duran, Stoval, and Babbitt put up one hell of a fight. English couldn't see Thorpe, Ritchie, or Janacek anymore.

One beefy colonist had picked up Manheim around the waist. He clasped her against his body and carried her backward toward the door. She kicked and flailed, but she was too small to overcome his strength.

"Gunny!" Manheim shrieked. "Gunny—no! Let me go!"

Two guys had taken hold of Racer's arms. They were trying to haul her toward the exit, but she gave them so much trouble that they had to stop there to consolidate their grip.

She tore away from them and charged English. "English!" she roared. "English!"

The guys beating up English stopped immediately. The whole group froze on the spot and all eyes turned to English. A husky voice asked, "You're Sailor English?"

English staggered to his feet. His head spun and he felt blood running down his face. "Yes!" he gasped. "I'm posted to the *USS Lightning Rod*. We were in orbit around Fenrir when the battle broke out. We're loyal to the Force! I swear it!"

He hauled his vision into focus to face the grizzled old guy who first attacked him. The colonists let go of his pilots. Manheim and Racer bolted over to English and Racer planted herself between English and the attackers.

English started to push her behind him when Duran, Stoval, and Babbitt barged in and did exactly the same thing. They surrounded English and blockaded him from the colonists. A second later, the last three charged in and formed ranks with their wingmates.

The old guy surveyed the pilots squaring up to defend English from another assault. The guy's eyes traced the blood streaking English's face and then the old colonist nodded.

"You must be Sailor English if these kids care about you so much." He stuck out his hand. "We didn't know who you were. We thought you were rebels. I'm Galvion Ayama. I'm the senior sergeant-at-arms in charge of security for the satellite."

English shook the guy's hand, but he had to wedge his arm between the pilots' bodies because they wouldn't let him near the guy. "We're Fighter Wing 17 from the *Lightning Rod* squadron. You can check the USF roster if you don't believe me."

Galvion eyed him more closely. "I don't have to check. Sailor English's word is good enough for me."

English ran his wrist across his eyebrow and it came away bloody. "We don't want to leave the reactor in case the rebels come back and try to shoot at us, but we need to contact the *Lightning Rod*. I would say we should contact the Command Center, but I don't know about that."

"We have communications equipment and we're in contact with Earth. We can take you to use our equipment....and you don't have to worry about the rebels attacking. Our cannon batteries are keeping an eye on the battle. We'll shoot down anyone who comes near the satellite."

"Why did you let *us* land, then?" Thorpe blurted out. "If you can shoot down anyone who comes near the satellite, why didn't you shoot *us* down?"

"We thought we could capture you and torture you for information about the rebellion happening on Earth."

"What do you know about what's going on down there?" English asked. "We don't know anything."

"It's all-out civil war. A whole group of Command Staff senior officers is trying to overthrow the rest of the Command Staff. They've commandeered ships, stations—the works. They bombed out the Command Center. The whole center is flattened. There's nothing left."

English's blood ran cold. Melanie. Was Melanie dead?

Galvion waved toward the door. "Those rebel destroyers out there were supposed to neutralize every other ship still on maneuvers in the system. The rebels already had the *Hermes* and the *Nostradamus*, so that left the *Solar Flare* and the *Lightning Rod*, but a bunch of loyal ships launched to stop them. Now all hell is breaking loose in the system."

"What about the defense batteries on the planet?" Duran asked. "How many of them do the rebels have? If they have too many, we'd never be able to get back to Earth."

"I hate to say this, kid, but I don't think any of us is getting back to Earth any time soon. We all have enough to deal with right now with rebel ships trying to take the rest of the system. We're going to have our hands full just securing our own satellites, stations, and colonies to stop the rebels from taking those, too." Galvion nodded at English again. "You better come with us. We'll clean you up and you can see about contacting your ship."

Chapter 13

English expected the Heinrich colonists to go back outside the reactor housing, but they didn't.

Galvion Ayama pushed past Wing 17, shouldered English out of the way, and led the group deeper inside the reactor.

Ayama climbed onto a catwalk and opened a door inside the structure. From what English could see, the door led straight into the Tecrium chamber itself. No one could go in there and survive.

The pilots all looked at English, but he only shrugged. If these colonists were as friendly as they made out, Wing 17 might as well go along with them. English didn't want to think about the alternative.

The other colonists hung back, no doubt to guard the wing's rear and stop them from escaping if they tried anything. English climbed the ladder and followed Galvion inside the reactor.

Another ladder plunged into total darkness and Galvion's footsteps echoed from below. "Come on!" he called up the pitch-black shaft. "Our command center is down here."

English started to descend. Babbitt's voice muttered behind his back. "Are you sure about this, Gunny?"

"It's better than getting shot at." English slowed to let the young man catch up. "Is everyone here? Do a quick head count."

"I'm here," Thorpe replied.

"Here," Duran added.

"I'm here and so is Racer," Manheim chimed in.

"Janacek!" English called into the darkness. "Where are you?"

"I'm coming!" Janacek panted. "I can't see a thing in here."

"Stick together. Hold onto each other if you have to. Don't get separated."

A light flicked on and beamed in English's eyes. It made him squint. "What's the hold-up?" another colonist boomed behind Janacek's back.

"Where are the rest of my people?" English called. "Auggie! Where are you?"

"Ritchie's tying his goddamn shoelace or some shit," Stoval growled.

"I wasn't!" Ritchie protested. "I was just...."

"Move it!" Stoval snapped. "You're holding up the whole damn train."

Ritchie and Stoval finally caught up. Stoval shoved Ritchie and glared at him while Ritchie tried to fend Stoval off.

The colonists made room for the last two pilots, but not without plenty of dirty looks.

"Stick together," English ordered again. "Don't anybody fall behind."

Their escort switched off the light and English started down again. He kept slowing to make sure his pilots all stayed with him. He finally descended to a horizontal passage dotted with electric lights.

Galvion waited for them there and then the whole group moved off in a mixed body. English didn't have to worry now that all his people were with him. He could see them all and they stuck close to him.

Galvion opened one last door at the far end of a corridor lined with doors. This one led into a large chamber built under the reactor housing. "This is the satellite security command center." He crossed to a bank of communications equipment. "You can see the battle going on outside."

English and all the pilots gathered around to stare at the image in front of them.

The *Lightning Rod* was nowhere in sight, but English already knew that. The other destroyers kept bombarding each other between Mars's orbit and the Strategic Lunar Base.

A greyish smear of debris, ship parts, vented gas and plasma, burning rubble, and explosions blocked English's view of the battle. He still couldn't tell who was friendly and who might belong to the insurgency—not that it mattered.

The United Space Force was at war with itself. Earth was at war with itself.

There would be no winners in this and any alien attacker might decide that this was the perfect time to strike. The whole solar system was totally defenseless as long as this civil war was going on.

The Heinrich satellite's long-range scanners read the situation on Earth, too. More battles, colossal explosions, and confusion reigned down on the ground. Most of it centered on USF bases, stations, and installations dotting the planet's continents.

North and South America faced the satellite, so English couldn't see what was left of the Command Center or the Ufa Long-Range Alert Station. He didn't want to see them.

Just then, an alarm went off at a different station. "Incoming transmission!" the technician called. "It's coming from the NORAD station at Point Hope, Alaska."

Everyone walked over to his station and Galvion bent close to the display. It switched on to reveal a middle-aged man. His hair stuck out at odd angles and blood stained the collar of his torn uniform. "Heinrich satellite, come in! Heinrich satellite, do you read?"

"We're here, General!" Galvion called. "What's the situation down there?"

"The insurgents are overrunning our position! We've lost contact with the ships who were supposed to be defending us. I'm not even sure there are any left. You have to listen to me, Galvion! They're coming out of the Strategic Supply Base at Harare! That's their headquarters. They're using the Supply Base as a launching point! That's how they're getting all these ships! They've been planning this for months—maybe even years!"

English leaned in. "Is there anything we can do, General? We have a few ships—not much—but we might be able to do something. Should we attack the SSB? Would it help to cut off the insurgents' supply?"

The general's expression changed. "Sailor? Is that you?"

"Yeah, it's me. I was on the *Lightning Rod* and now I'm here at Heinrich."

The general's eyes misted over and he sniffed. "Thank God you're there! Don't come near Earth. Keep as much of the Force outside the combat zone as you can. If the insurgents take the outer system, we're sunk. We have to keep the outer system in loyalist hands no matter what."

"All right, Sir. I understand."

"How many....?" An explosion interrupted him. The general ducked and a shower of dirt and dust covered him.

He straightened up squinting into the screen. "See if you can contact Admiral Hearst at the Seychelles Naval......"

Another shuddering boom rocked the image and then it blipped out. English and Galvion stared at the blank screen.

"He's gone," the technician murmured.

English puffed out his cheeks. "This is bad. This is so much worse than I feared."

Galvion bumped the technician's shoulder. "Can you raise the Seychelles Naval Yard at all?"

The technician shook his head. "Nothing."

"What about the *Lightning Rod*? Can you locate her?"

"She's in orbit at the Io Center docking station, but communications are still down. She's taking on plasma."

"So the Io Center is still intact?"

The technician nodded. "None of the fighting has made it out that far."

"Which means the Io Center is still loyal," Galvion pointed out. "That's something. It means we have a line between ourselves and the Outer Rim colonies."

"The *Lightning Rod* won't be able to stop a fleet this big from getting through if they want to. We need more ships." English looked around at the pilots facing him. "We need to get back to the *Lightning Rod*. Can you give us any extra fuel?"

"We can, but it will be risky."

Half an hour later, Wing 17 crouched in the reactor entrance where they first arrived. The Heinrich colonists had given the pilots food and they'd given English medical attention. Now English and his pilots were back on deck and not in a nice way.

"As soon as you get in the air, the rebel ships will come and try to stop you from leaving," Galvion told English. "You'll need to fly fast."

"We can do that," Duran replied.

"We'll open up with our big guns," Galvion went on, "but it will still get hairy out there. You might not succeed."

"If we can't get to the fuel depot," Thorpe replied, "we can just beat it out to the Io Center. We aren't totally out of fuel yet. We can still make it."

"The only problem with that is we might draw the enemy out to the Io Center," English pointed out. "The *Lightning Rod* is out there because she can't fight. She won't be able to defend us or the Io Center."

"I have a plan," Galvion told him. "As soon as you get near the asteroid belt, we'll fire into it and ignite all the plasma floating around. We'll make sure no ships follow you, including friendly ones. You'll make it....as long as you get off the satellite all right."

"Then that's what we'll do." English straightened up. "You heard the man, Wing 17. Get to your birds and get airborne as quick as you can. Get over to the fuel depot, tank up, and beat it through the asteroid belt."

"Just make sure you go through it at the same time," Galvion told him. "If you go through one at a time, either I'll have to let the destroyers through or some of you will get trapped over here."

English blew out a shaky breath. "All right. New plan. Once we get over to the fuel depot, we'll assemble and see if it's clear enough for us to refuel. If it is, we'll refuel. If it isn't or if things go to shit, we leave. Simple."

The pilots nodded. English clapped Thorpe on the back. "Go!"

The whole wing burst into the open and raced for their birds. Janacek ran to Manheim's fighter. She was the lightest and he was the heaviest, so carrying two people would affect her craft the least.

Everyone piled on board and English fired up his engines. All the other fighters switched on. English launched and blasted across the satellite making for the fuel depot, but he didn't get further than a few miles before he spotted the enemy moving in...or maybe it was his friends. He couldn't be sure.

Fighter squadrons hurtled from the battlefield to attack the satellite again. English dodged lower and wove his way through pipes and towers.

The satellite's big cannons opened up and the cannons knocked fighters out of the air, but more enemy birds assembled from nowhere.

They whizzed around the satellite trying to acquire a target. They hovered over the cannons for a second and then noticed Wing 17 making a break for the fuel depot.

English took a position above the depot as Babbitt and Stoval came pelting in. "Down you go, boys! Fuel up as quick as you can!"

Both pilots plunged into the maze of pipes and English lost sight of them. He didn't lose sight of the enemy fighters converging from every direction.

He chose one at random. If they were shooting at him, they were his enemies, no questions asked. He crushed his firing mechanism and plastered four of them. Racer zoomed in, turned a pirouette around English, and started pounding.

Manheim and Duran showed up a second later and Wing 17 plunged into a massive gun battle. Another muddle of plasma and explosions distracted English for a second.

Stoval's voice cracked in his ear. "All clear, Sir! We're fueled!"

English started to order the next two down when all the enemy fighters whizzed away and vanished. "What happened?" Manheim asked.

English looked around and gulped. "Clear off! Everyone to the asteroid belt! Abandon the satellite!"

"What about......?" Racer began and then her voice broke. "Oh, shit!"

The wing pivoted as one and took off for the asteroid belt. English glanced back to see three destroyers advancing on the satellite. The enemy ships bombarded the satellite with plasma from beyond the defense guns' range.

"Faster!" English ordered. "Lay it down, boys!"

He crawled up on Thorpe and Ritchie, but it wasn't enough.

"Someone's coming out from the satellite!" Manheim called.

English made one more check of the situation behind him. The destroyers stationed themselves around the Heinrich satellite and hammered its superstructure with deafening shots.

Explosions ripped out of the refinery, and when they hit the defense guns, columns of fire rippled into the night sky.

A single fighter craft vaulted out of the flames on a dead course for Wing 17. English dropped back just in case someone was coming to threaten his people, but as Wing 17 got nearer to the asteroid belt, Galvion called to him. "Keep going! Break through now!"

"What about......?" English cut himself off when the three destroyers left the ruined satellite and sprinted for the asteroid belt. They were coming after Wing 17.

English slammed his throttle to the wall and Galvion matched him step for step. Wing 17 raced into the asteroid belt, but the enemy destroyers gained by the second.

"Keep going!" Galvion roared. "Don't stop and don't look back!"

"What about you?" English asked.

Galvion didn't answer. He flanked English all the way until they got halfway through the field.

English strained his eyes to miss every floating rock, but Galvion didn't. He jerked his stick hard to port and smashed his fighter dead into an asteroid in the center of the plasma cloud.

Fire erupted from his fuselage and ignited the plasma. A bone-shaking boom slammed English's bird in the tail. The shockwave caught Wing 17 and flung all eight fighters clear on the other side. The enemy destroyers stayed behind that wall of flame while Wing 17 made the last run for Io.

Chapter 14

E nglish landed his fighter on the *Lightning Rod's* flight deck and went over to Manheim's bird. Janacek got down first and then all the pilots gathered around. "We made it!" Ritchie breathed. "I'm never flying again."

"You better," Racer told him. "We got a war to win, son."

"You were all outstanding," English said again. "I'm proud of you all."

"What do we do now, Sir?" Thorpe asked.

"You folks are all dismissed until further notice. Go get yourselves some well-earned rest."

Just then, Gunny Frasier charged over and seized English's hand. "Jesus! You made it! We all thought you were dead."

"We almost were," Manheim quavered. "I thought we were dead for sure when Galvion blew the asteroid field."

The rest of the pilots fell silent. "He gave his life to save us," Janacek husked. "I never thought I'd ever see anything like that."

"He was a great man," Thorpe added. "I'll never forget him."

"That's all right." English gripped Thorpe's shoulder and then patted Manheim on the back. "That's the way it is in war. Good people die so we can keep fighting the good fight. Now get up to the barracks. We aren't finished yet and you people need food, sleep, and rest."

"Yes, Sir," Thorpe replied and the pilots headed for the elevator.

As soon as they walked away, they all started talking about everything that happened. They relived their most terrifying moments and every detail of the great battle of USF destroyers fighting USF destroyers.

English and Frasier watched them go. "What the hell did you do to them?" Frasier whispered.

"Huh? Nothing. I didn't do anything to them. They were great out there. I've never served with better."

Frasier cocked an eyebrow at him. "How did you get them all home? We thought you were all finished."

"No such luck. We lost Janacek's bird, but that wasn't his fault. He fought like a lion. They all did."

Frasier studied him. "You're different. What happened?"

"Nothing." English looked away. "I'm just worried about what's going on down on Earth. My family is down there."

Frasier squeezed his elbow. "You better go check in with Eismann. We were just discussing recruiting another wing of pilots from the Io Center, but now that you're back, I'm sure Captain Ogden will have a thousand questions."

English grimaced and then laughed. He was actually looking forward to dealing with Captain Ogden's defensive attitude. That whole problem seemed almost delightfully insignificant compared to thinking about his family being trapped on Earth.

He headed for Lieutenant Eismann's desk. Eismann hopped off his stool and pumped English's arm off his shoulder. "It's a miracle! What did you do? How did you do it? God, no wonder you have so many decorations!"

"Give me a break, Sir," English growled. "If anyone deserves decorations, it's my wing, not me."

"Will you stop calling me that? You're embarrassing me."

English nodded toward Eismann's desk. "What's the story?"

"We're still working on the communications system, which means none of the fighter wings will be going anywhere until we fix it."

"How long will that take? The enemy won't stay on their side of the asteroid belt forever. They know we're out here."

Eismann shrugged. "I don't make command decisions. I'm just a clerk."

"Hardly."

Just then, an alert came through Eismann's many computers. They couldn't have been too damaged.

Eismann made a face. "Captain Ogden is calling you up to her ready room."

"Why?" English asked.

"She doesn't tell me shit. You better go."

English glanced down at his uniform. It wasn't as tidy as it could be, but it would have to do.

He got into the elevator, and when he exited on the bridge, everyone present turned around to stare at him approaching the ready room.

He rang the bell and Captain Ogden's voice called, "Come in!"

Captain Ogden sat behind her desk with her three bridge staff standing around her. Their expressions gave nothing away.

English pulled up to attention and found a spot on the wall behind her head to stare at. "You asked to see me, Ma'am?"

"That's right, Gunny. Your wing did very well in the battle."

"Thank you, Ma'am."

"Now I want to know why you took so long to catch up with the *Lightning Rod*."

Commander Radcliffe spun around. "What?"

Captain Ogden glanced at him and then returned to studying English. "Well, Gunny? What's your excuse? Did you see the *Lightning Rod* retreating?"

"Yes, Ma'am."

"Did you understand Commander Radcliffe's signal that you should fall back with the ship?"

"Yes, Ma'am."

"I know you did because you started to fall back with the ship and then you broke off and returned to the battle. Now I want to know why."

"Excuse me, Ma'am," Commander Radcliffe cut in again, "but that should be pretty obvious, shouldn't it? Some of his pilots were stranded in the swarm. Gunny English went back to get them out. We all saw that."

"Well, Gunny?" Captain Ogden asked again. "I want to hear the reason from you. Why didn't you fall back with the ship?"

English swallowed. "Because some of my pilots were stranded in the swarm, Ma'am. I went back to get them out."

Captain Ogden snorted. "You could have gotten them out and then fallen back with the ship. What have you been doing all this time when you should have been defending the *Lightning Rod*—which is your duty, Gunny. Your duty is not to make a name for yourself by playing heroics on the battlefield. Do you understand that?"

"Yes, Ma'am."

"Excuse me, Ma'am...." Commander Radcliffe's voice started to rise. English realized with a pang that it wasn't rising in agitation or anxiety but in anger. Matt was losing his grip on himself. "Our long-range sensors clearly showed Wing 17 in combat with enemy ships and taking refuge on the Heinrich satellite. Even then, the satellite was under bombardment right up until Wing 17 broke away. It's a damn miracle Gunny English made it back with all his pilots alive. Not many gunnies could do that. He should be commended, not reprimanded."

"I'll be the one to decide who gets commended and who gets reprimanded, Commander," Ogden snarled. "You were in communication with Earth mere seconds before the battle broke out, Gunny. You were on a secure channel with the Command Center itself. Explain yourself."

English's eyes snapped to the captain's face. Just for a second, he forgot all about keeping himself distant and formal. He gaped at her in shock. She had access to every communications log on the ship. She had to know who he was talking to before the battle broke out.

"I'm waiting, Gunny. Explain this to me in a way that doesn't make it look like you were involved in coordinating this insurgency. Explain it to me in a way that doesn't make it look like you aren't a rebel plant on board this ship to sabotage us and weaken the loyalist resistance."

"Ma'am!" Commander Radcliffe barked. "This is highly out of line. I sincerely doubt you intend to make communicating with relatives an impeachable offense on this ship. If you do, you better start by impeaching yourself and every other member of the bridge staff first."

English cringed. Now Radcliffe was really crossing the line, but his behavior obviously relayed to Captain Ogden and everyone else that he wasn't prepared to back down.

Captain Ogden rounded on him. "If you can't stand by and do your duty, Commander, I'll have you removed from the ready room....and from active duty. Is that what you want?"

"You've been dangerously hostile toward Gunny English since he first set foot on this ship, Captain, but this is taking it too far," Radcliffe went on. "You know as well as I do exactly why Wing 17 didn't rejoin the *Lightning Rod*. Wing 17 couldn't have rejoined the *Lightning Rod* at the time anyway because the flight deck was damaged."

"Easy, son," English interrupted. "You don't have to defend me. I can take care of myself. Just keep your post and...."

"I'm defending the Force, Sir. I didn't sign up to stand by and watch this treatment."

Captain Ogden gasped. "You call him 'Sir'? Is this your way of upholding the chain of command, Commander?"

"It's a term of respect, Ma'am, and if you don't understand by now that Sailor English deserves all our respect, then I don't want to serve under you. The Uniform Code of Conduct requires every member of the Force to speak up and report conduct unbecoming, and if this doesn't qualify, I don't know what does. Gunny English did absolutely nothing wrong by communicating with his daughter and we all know she's a doctor at the Command Center Hospital. There's no way she or he could have been coordinating the insurgency attack during their call, especially the Command Center was under bombardment at the time and we heard firsthand that the insurgents were coordinating out of Harare."

Radcliffe broke off trembling with rage. Ogden gaped at him. Every hint of color drained from her cheeks. Terranova and Avila stared at Radcliffe in blank horror.

Ogden's voice shook when she finally found her voice to speak. "I think you better go to your quarters, Matt."

He didn't flinch once. "I have a better idea. How about I get Terranova, Avila, and Lieutenant Eismann to come in here and give a ruling on your fitness to command the *Lightning Rod*? How about I call a hearing right now and have you removed from command? You've violated the Code of Conduct countless times where Gunny English is concerned. I can call up witnesses from the crew to testify that you refused to relieve him when he was seriously injured from the Acheron fire. You kept him on duty out of some vindictive lust for revenge and that is a gross violation of your duty to command.... Ma'am."

Ogden sank into her chair and her eyes slid out of focus. She stared straight in front of her and her whole aspect went dead.

English struggled to get his voice working. "You shouldn't have done that, Matt."

"Yes, I should have, Sir." Radcliffe straightened up and every trace of the young man English used to know evaporated. "Go to Sick Bay and get your wounds seen to, Gunny, and then go downstairs to the barracks. You've had a hard couple of hours and you need to recharge. I'll let you know when you're scheduled to go back on duty and I'll also reassign Janacek to one of our backup birds."

English sighed heavily. "Yes, Sir."

Radcliffe clamped English on the shoulder. "That was great flying out there, by the way. You have the gratitude of your crew and captain. Welcome home."

English left the ready room and across the bridge. He didn't relax until the elevator doors closed and he was alone.

Now that the shooting stopped, everything that happened in the last few hours started to catch up with him. Melanie. Radcliffe. Galvion. Each one tugged him in a different direction and he couldn't do anything about any of them.

The elevator doors opened and he stumbled into the corridor. He should have turned off toward Sick Bay, but he wound up going into the locker room instead.

Frasier and Lloyd both started talking fast about what English did on the battlefield and about everything that happened afterward on the satellite. They exclaimed over the explosion when Galvion sacrificed himself so Wing 17 could escape.

English couldn't answer. He opened his locker and stared into it trying to decide what to do next.

Just then, the locker room door opened behind him. Radcliffe took one look at Frasier and Lloyd, who buttoned their lips immediately.

Radcliffe crossed to English's side. "I told you to go to Sick Bay."

"Yes, Sir," English muttered. "I was just about to."

"Are you okay? I'm sorry you had to hear that."

"I'm sorry, too." English felt exhausted, especially after what he just witnessed in the ready room. "I'm sorry I put you in this position. It wasn't fair of me to interfere with your career. Are you gonna be able to keep your post? I hate to think what she does after this."

"Don't worry about her. I'll handle her....and don't worry about yourself, either. She won't bother you again. I'll make sure of it."

English looked up. Radcliffe stood over him exactly the way English had stood over countless junior officers in his career. His position with Radcliffe had completely reversed. Now Radcliffe was the one reassuring and protecting English.

Radcliffe gripped his shoulder again and gave him a slight shake. "I meant what I said. Get to Sick Bay. Don't do anything else until you get your head treated. I just saw Thorpe and he told me what happened. We need you operational."

"Yes, Sir."

Radcliffe headed for the door. English turned around. "Matt.... thank you."

"Forget it. It's nothing you haven't done for me a hundred times."

Radcliffe let himself out of the locker room and both Frasier and Lloyd rounded on English. "What happened?"

English passed his hand across his eyes. "You don't want to know."

"You better go to Sick Bay like he said," Frasier prompted.

"Yeah. I'm going." English slammed his locker shut and staggered toward the door. He wasn't sure how much longer he could stay on his feet.

Frasier and Lloyd moved out of his way, but as soon as English got near the door, the siren went off. "Battle stations! All fighter wings—prepare to launch! Battle stations! All fighter wings—prepare to launch!"

Chapter 15

E nglish charged onto the flight deck. The whole deck teemed with pilots, mechanics, and officers going every which way.

Frasier, Lloyd, and English pulled up in front of Lieutenant Eismann's desk. "What's going on? How many are coming after us? What's the communications system looking like?"

Eismann held up both hands. "Slow down, boys! The communications system is up and running, so I'll be in touch with all your birds as usual. So far, we can only see one destroyer crossing the asteroid field, so arming to defend ourselves is just a precaution at this point."

"Which destroyer is it?" English asked.

"It's the *Dannevirk*."

English froze, and like something out of a long-forgotten nightmare, Duran burst out of the stairwell and rushed onto the flight deck at that exact moment.

English dove for him and caught him. "Hold up, son."

Duran glanced across the deck. The other Wing 17 pilots were already loading up and Duran had his jacket unbuttoned. "You heard the call-up, Sir. I have to...."

"Go back upstairs, Ezra. You're sitting this one out."

"Huh?" Duran hauled his attention back to English. "Why?"

"Because we're going out against the *Dannevirk*. We faced them before, but that was with more than thirty other ships around. She's crossing the asteroid field alone this time, which means it will be the *Lightning Rod* against the *Dannevirk*. Go back upstairs and stay in your quarters until this is over."

Duran blinked at him and then glanced over at Eismann. The other two sergeants listened in silence. Duran gulped, turned on his heel, and vanished into the stairwell.

English couldn't wait any longer. He stalked over to his fighter and climbed in.

The communications system switched on and voices assaulted his ear. "What's the lay of the land out there, Sir?" Babbitt asked.

"The lay of the land is we're about to get shot at," Ritchie replied. "We tumble out and roll 'em up like pigs in a blanket. What could be simpler?"

"How many are coming in, Sir?" Janacek asked.

"Only one so far that we know about. The *Dannevirk* is crossing the asteroid field which means more could be crossing behind her. I guess we won't know until we get out there."

"Why isn't Duran coming with us?" Racer asked.

"He's sitting this one out. Orders from higher up."

"I saw him right before the siren went off," Manheim chimed in. "He was fine then."

"There's nothing wrong with him. It's a command decision."

The conversation turned to a few crude jokes. English let his mind wander while he went through the automatic routine of powering up his engines.

He didn't want to go out against the *Dannevirk*, either. He knew Sean Duran only too well. Would English be the one to kill a pilot as talented as that?

English knew quite a few other pilots on the *Dannevirk* squadron. He couldn't excuse himself just because he might wind up killing someone he knew. He shouldn't have excused Duran, either—not technically. This was war and no one could pick and choose their battles.

English wasn't prepared to pit brother against brother in a head-to-head fight. One Duran killing another in a confused, chaotic battle of multiple destroyers against multiple more destroyers was one thing. Fighter against fighter—no way.

The minutes ticked by. English finished his pre-flight checks and sat idling on the launch pad. The other pilots made faces at him from their cockpits. They tried to crane their necks to see if anything was going on at Lieutenant Eismann's desk.

Nothing happened. Lieutenant Eismann didn't look over at them or at any of the other fighter wings. English caught Frasier and Lloyd looking in that direction, too. What was going on?

Would this whole thing turn out to be a false alarm? If it did, English was going to have to talk to Duran about whether he should be in the service under the circumstances.

English settled into his seat and went back to tinkering with his controls. He had nothing else to do.

Without warning, Eismann's voice barked in his ear. "Squadron Command to all Wing Leaders—launch! All fighter wings—launch!"

Everyone jumped. The launch bay doors still weren't even open yet. Three of English's pilots gunned their engines and immediately had to pull back to wait while Eismann opened the doors.

English dropped out into the clear black sky. He and Racer zoomed around the *Lightning Rod* and the rest of the squadron swarmed to the ship's nose.

The *Dannevirk* loomed overhead drawing closer to the Io Center. Her squadron wheeled around her and came screaming out to meet the *Lightning Rod* fighter wings.

English punched his engines and his whole wing copied him. They met the *Dannevirk* squadron head-to-head and cannon-to-cannon. English stared at his controls in rising excitement. His instruments showed up which fighters belonged to which destroyer.

His targeting system picked out the *Dannevirk* squadron in green while it highlighted the *Lightning Rod* squadron in red.

All confusion evaporated and a thrilling whoop pealed down the communications system.

Wing 17 went at it with a vengeance. The two squadrons twirled around each other in a hectic dance of rolls, somersaults, and wild dives. English hammered his enemies with shots and left the *Dannevirk* fighters in flames. Several went down over the Io Center.

The *Dannevirk* plowed a path through both squadrons and opened fire on the *Lightning Rod*. The *Lightning Rod* detached from the Io Center docking station and throttled away from the moon to engage the *Dannevirk* in a raging battle.

The two destroyers rushed each other spouting plasma everywhere. The clouds ignited amongst the fighter craft, but Wing 17 only used the explosions as diversions to confuse the *Dannevirk* squadron.

Thorpe and Babbitt teamed up and flanked a single fighter between them. They slammed their victim back and forth driving the pilot into a desperate race to escape.

Thorpe veered hard to starboard to herd the enemy into Babbitt's guns. The pilot turned his cannons on Babbitt, but Babbitt feinted and dodged away.

The enemy pilot saw an opening and plunged through it to get away. He wound up running straight into a plasma stream from the

Lightning Rod's cannon batteries. Thorpe and Babbitt both opened fire, combusted the plasma, and the fighter exploded.

"Oh, you thought you could fly better than us?" Thorpe crowed. "You thought you were a badass? I beg to differ."

"Right behind you, fat head!" Ritchie called. "If your head gets any bigger, you'll blow your own bird."

Thorpe spun around. "Where?"

Two *Dannevirk* fighters snuck up behind him, but at the moment when they would have pummeled him into next week, Stoval pounced. He hammered the first one, blew it up, and used the burning fireball as cover to blow the second one.

"Silent but deadly!" Janacek shrieked. "Do NOT mess with my boy!"

"You know all about silent but deadly, don't you, Janacek?" Racer teased.

"Heads up!" English called. "The *Lightning Rod's* in trouble!"

The *Dannevirk* had taken advantage of the *Lightning Rod* clearing the docking station. As soon as the *Lightning Rod* got away from the docking station, the *Dannevirk* darted behind her to cut the *Lightning Rod* off.

Continuous shots pounded both destroyers' hulls, but anyone could see the *Lightning Rod* suffering. The *Dannevirk* drove the *Lightning Rod* farther and farther away from the Io Center.

The fight escalated to an all-out battle and the *Lightning Rod's* damage from the previous battle started to tell. She couldn't maneuver as fast as the *Dannevirk* and the *Dannevirk* exploited her advantage to the maximum.

The *Lightning Rod* charged the *Dannevirk* trying to reestablish her position over the Io Center. The *Lightning Rod* slammed the

Dannevirk back toward the docking station, but instead of fighting back, the *Dannevirk* just let her come.

The two ships locked in a death struggle and the *Dannevirk* fired all her cannons straight into the *Lightning Rod's* lower decks.

The ship shuddered and groaned under the bombardment. Explosions and venting life support gases escaped into space surrounding the *Lightning Rod*.

"Wing 17—wheel back and assault the *Dannevirk*!" English ordered.

"We're with you, Wing 17!" Frasier called and Wing 10 fell into formation with English.

He swooped low over the *Dannevirk's* hull pounding the cannon batteries, but nothing worked. "Target her bridge, Wing 10! Wing 17, with me!"

"Are we going for life support again, Sir?" Ritchie asked.

"Target Deck 15—Section 45!" English replied.

"That's the plasma core!" Racer pointed out.

"Fall in single file behind me and hit Section 45 one after the other. Concentrate all your firepower on that one section so we bust through the hull and hit the core."

"Right behind you, Sir!" Janacek replied.

English banked and cut in close to the *Dannevirk*. The enemy squadron buzzed all around him, but he held his course. He dealt Section 45 a punishing blow and rocketed away to leave room for the rest of Wing 17 to do the same thing.

Racer and Ritchie followed with Manheim and Stoval right behind them. Thorpe, Babbitt, and Janacek angled into position. The *Dannevirk* squadron couldn't stop what was about to happen.

English skated around for another pass. Wing 17 shadowed his every move, but when Thorpe dodged in close to the *Dannevirk's* sides, she gave an almighty lurch and broke away from the *Lightning Rod*.

The *Lightning Rod* decoupled from the enemy and the *Dannevirk* unloaded with crushing force. Her batteries smashed the *Lightning Rod* back even farther and the destroyer staggered.

"We got a massive problem!" Frasier yelled. "Four more destroyers crossing the asteroid field!"

English tore his eyes away from the stricken *Lightning Rod* and his blood ran cold. Four of the destroyers that Wing 17 battled earlier advanced through the asteroid field on an intercept course for the *Lightning Rod*. The *Lightning Rod* couldn't hold her own against one destroyer, let alone five of them.

She started to limp away heading deeper into space, but the *Dannevirk* only fired her engines to hunt the *Lightning Rod* down.

"*Lightning Rod* squadron—full assault on the *Dannevirk*!" English ordered. "Wing 10, bring it into formation with Wing 17. Full assault on the plasma core!"

"You bet!" Frasier replied.

English peeled sideways and throttled for the *Dannevirk*. Wing 10 dropped in line behind Wing 17, and a second later, Lloyd's wing joined them.

English plummeted much closer to the *Dannevirk's* hull. The *Dannevirk* squadron realized what the *Lightning Rod* fighters were trying to do. Fighters swarmed in thicker than ever, but they hesitated to fire on English when he was this close to their own ship.

English struck his target with deadly accuracy and the rest of Wing 17 piled in making run after run. The *Dannevirk* turned her cannons on the *Lightning Rod* squadron, but she couldn't hit them as long as they hugged her sides and never left her.

English came in for his fourth pass. "The hull is cracking! All in, boys! Give her everything we've got to cover the *Lightning Rod's* escape."

Word must have spread to the incoming destroyers. They pivoted to head for the *Dannevirk*. The *Lightning Rod* crawled out of range en route to the Europa Environmental Zone.

English came in hot and fast, unloaded on the *Dannevirk's* hull, and it buckled beneath his cannon. "Get out!" he roared. "*Lightning Rod* squadron—clear out! Get to a safe distance before......!"

The *Dannevirk* listed and another section of hull caved from the inside. The whole aft starboard section crumbled and brilliant flashes blinked inside the ship.

English punched his throttle. He didn't have time to retreat with the rest of his wing. He rocketed toward the Io Center and took a turn around the moon's other side.

He blasted out just in time to see the *Dannevirk* implode and then a colossal outward-sweeping mushroom cloud detonated against the stars. It knocked the *Lightning Rod* farther toward Europa and the four enemy destroyers slowed to a halt.

The *Lightning Rod* squadron zoomed away toward the ship with English bringing up the rear. The *Dannevirk* squadron remained scattered with nowhere to go.

Chapter 16

D r. Eva Cassidy pressed a square of gauze to Captain Ogden's head and shone a flashlight into her eyes. "Are you having any trouble focusing?"

Captain Ogden shoved Dr. Cassidy's hand away. "Will you leave me alone? I'm only having trouble focusing because you keep getting in my face. I'm sure there are plenty of other crewmen who are more seriously injured than I am. Go take care of them. I'm fine."

Dr. Cassidy straightened up and let her hand fall to her side. She rolled her eyes at Commander Radcliffe. "I swear they issue extra doses of attitude with every promotion in rank."

Dr. Cassidy tossed the bloody gauze in Captain Ogden's lap and walked away. Dr. Cassidy's long white braid swayed down her back as she headed for the mechanics working on the *Lightning Rod*.

Dr. Cassidy moved with the strength, speed, and agility of a woman half her age. Everyone looked up to her as almost a surrogate captain.

"Well, this is one hell of a pickle, Matt," Captain Ogden muttered. "It's only a matter of time before the insurgents come to find us here and we won't be able to defend ourselves with the *Lightning Rod* damaged."

"Don't count us out yet, Ma'am. We still have pretty much a full squadron."

Captain Ogden shot a look sideways across the Europa Environmental Zone. The artificial sunshine inside the terraform bubble gleamed on broad grassy fields with wildflowers swaying in the breeze. Horses, sheep, and deer grazed in the peaceful atmosphere.

Captain Ogden grimaced at the fighter craft dotting the landscape. They arranged themselves in no particular order at a distance from the *Lightning Rod*. Pilots and mechanics worked around them and Radcliffe could see the three gunnery sergeants liaising with their wings.

Captain Ogden never again mentioned Radcliffe's threat to get her removed from command. After he came back from seeing English, she pretended the exchange never happened and then this battle started.

Radcliffe sincerely hoped she never brought it up again. He was fully prepared to follow through on his threat if she didn't start seeing reason pretty damn quick where Sailor English was concerned.

Lieutenant Eismann hustled over to them just then. "All fighter wing pilots present and accounted for, Ma'am. Wing 10 took some damage, but the pilots are working on their birds. That should free up the mechanics to repair the *Lightning Rod*."

"Thank you, Lieutenant. What's the situation upstairs, Matt? Are those destroyers hanging around waiting to ambush us?"

"Last I checked, they were setting up a perimeter around the Io Center. Would you like me to go up the bridge and get you a more recent update?"

"Not now." She looked down at the gauze in her hand, sighed, and got to her feet. "I better go see how bad the damage is. The mechanics can give me a timeframe on the......."

She trailed off as someone came striding toward her from the squadron. The whole bridge staff stiffened for another showdown when Gunny English walked right up to the captain, snapped to attention, and saluted. "Forgive the intrusion, Ma'am."

"What is it, Gunny?" she asked in her frostiest tone.

"One of my pilots just picked up a signal from the other side of the Environmental Zone, Ma'am. Some fighters from the *Dannevirk* squadron have landed beyond the woods over there. We weren't sure if the *Lightning Rod's* sensors picked them up since the enemy is nearer to Wing 17's sensor range."

"What does that have to do with anything, Gunny? We have a much more serious situation trying to get the *Lightning Rod* off the ground and some of our cannon batteries are non-operational. If the *Dannevirk* squadron isn't threatening us, we can leave them alone."

"Yes, Ma'am," English replied. "It's just that.... well, Ma'am, Sean Duran is with them. I know him personally, Ma'am. He's notorious in the Force and bound to be loyal. He would have come out against the *Lightning Rod* under orders from his captain, but he's always been dedicated to the Force and he's been decorated at least four times. His wingmates are bound to be as sturdy as he is. We might be able to turn them and bring them over to us.... Ma'am."

She studied him for a minute. "Are you volunteering to go over there and talk to them, Gunny?"

"Yes, Ma'am...and I would take Ezra with me.... if you approve, Ma'am."

"I see." She thought it over for a second. "Very well, Gunny. If you can turn them, do so.... but take more than just Ezra....and arm yourselves."

"Yes, Ma'am. Thank you, Ma'am."

"I'll come with you, Gunny," Radcliffe offered.

Captain Ogden spun around to stare at him, but she didn't argue. English left and Radcliffe bent over to tie his boot lace. "Keep an eye on that man, Matt," Captain Ogden muttered. "Report to me if he does anything suspicious."

"You can NOT be serious!" Radcliffe declared. "Did you just hear him? He wants to turn the *Dannevirk* pilots to our side. Do you actually believe he could be doing anything underhanded by volunteering to put his life in danger like this? What is the matter with you?"

She smacked her lips and whirled away. "Fine. Just don't let any of our people get hurt."

Radcliffe stalked off and met English at the cargo hold weapons locker. The whole ship was in a state with the mechanics working all over the damaged hull.

English took one look at Radcliffe's face and grinned. "Let me guess."

"Don't even talk about it, okay? Don't say a damn thing."

English chuckled. "Okay. I won't say it."

"Have you spoken to Duran yet—our Duran?"

"Not yet. He wasn't with us during the battle. When Eismann scrambled us against the *Dannevirk*, I stood Duran down because I didn't want him going out against his brother."

Radcliffe nodded. "Smart. I still say you should be in charge of this ship."

"That's about as likely to happen as Hell freezing over, son. Now do me a favor and go out to my wing pilots. We'll take a few of them along with us."

"Yes, Sir," Radcliffe replied.

English exploded in laughter. "Very funny."

They parted ways and Radcliffe crossed to Wing 17. They all stood milling around Babbitt's bird and talking while Babbitt welded a damaged hull section.

Thorpe snapped to attention. "Sir! Is Gunny English under disciplinary action?"

"Of course not," Radcliffe countered. "Why on Earth would he be under disciplinary action?"

"We just wondered...." Janacek began. "After the way Captain Ogden was acting toward him......and then him going over there to talk to her, Sir...."

"She'll bite his head off every chance she gets," Ritchie added. "She's got one hell of a burr under her saddle about him. You'd think she was worried because she recognized a real captain when she saw one."

"Keep that shit to yourself, Airman," Radcliffe interrupted. "Gunny English isn't under disciplinary action with the captain and he isn't going to be."

"What did he go talk to her about, then?" Racer asked. "Why didn't he come back? We all saw him go into the ship and he hasn't come out."

Radcliffe made a split-second decision not to reprimand these kids for sticking their noses into command business. They'd been watching English's every move since he walked over to the captain.

It really was touching how much they cared about him. They were all worried about him and they obviously wanted him as their CO.

He really worked wonders with this crew, but that was always English's way. The man could soften the coldest heart. Radcliffe only hoped English would be able to work the same magic on Captain Ogden.

English was the perfect person to send over to the *Dannevirk* pilots. He was a hero to everyone in the Force and everyone knew him.

"Don't worry about English," he told the pilots. "He's coming back and...."

"There he is!" squeaked Manheim. "He's bringing Duran with him."

They all craned their necks to stare at English and Duran striding toward them. Both of them were armed and English carried a bunch of extra rifles.

"What's going on, Gunny?" Ritchie asked. "Are we mounting our own insurgency?"

"That isn't funny, Airman," English fired back. "Thorpe, you and Stoval come with me. Commander Radcliffe and I are going on a little mission."

"What's the mission?" Racer asked.

"We're going to pay a social call on the *Dannevirk* squadron."

Racer started forward. "Great. Give me a rifle."

"You're staying here. All of you are."

"Aw!" Ritchie complained. "This is so not fair!"

English shoved a rifle into his hands. "The rest of you guard our birds. Make sure no one slips out of those trees to ambush us and give Babbitt enough cover to finish repairing his craft. I want every fighter in this wing fit and ready to fly by the time I get back."

"Yes, Sir," Ritchie grumbled.

English caught Radcliffe's eye and the five of them moved off into the trees. Thorpe, Stoval, and Duran all checked their rifles on the way.

"Keep your guns over your shoulders, boys," English murmured. "Don't threaten the other pilots. They're our friends. Duran, you come up here with me and Commander Radcliffe."

They crossed the woods and emerged into another field. Ten fighters glimmered in the sunshine. "Is Sean really over there?" Duran murmured.

"His wing landed here after the battle," English replied. "You let me and Commander Radcliffe do the talking at first. Just let Sean see you before you try to convince him."

Duran nodded, but he wouldn't stop staring into the distance. A tense silence hung between the fighter wing and the watchers hidden in the bushes. The *Dannevirk* squadron didn't notice the *Lightning Rod* party approaching.

English and Radcliffe started forward with Duran between them. Thorpe and Stoval stayed behind them as they crossed the field.

The *Dannevirk* pilots woke up to the *Lightning Rod* party's approach. Most of the *Dannevirk* pilots carried weapons. The pilots moved closer together and faced off against English's party.

Radcliffe spotted Sean Duran right away. He wasn't as tall as the others, but he took a central position in their formation. He had to be the leader.

English had been right about him, but Radcliffe already knew that. Everyone in the whole Force knew about Sean Duran. The Duran family didn't earn their reputation for nothing.

Sean narrowed his eyes at the *Lightning Rod* crew, but he immediately relaxed when he recognized English. He burst into a huge smile and saluted. "Captain English! What an honor! It's so good to see you again."

English saluted him back and then shook Sean's hand and hugged him in sight of everyone. "It's good to see you, too, son, but I'm not a captain anymore. This is Commander Matt Radcliffe. He's the XO of the *Lightning Rod*, which is parked right over there beyond those trees."

Sean's countenance darkened. "Is that so?"

English stood back and addressed the whole *Dannevirk* crowd. "I don't know what your COs told you, but there's a civil war going on all over the system. A bunch of USF Command Staff out of Harare attacked the Command Center and, as far as we know, they destroyed it. The insurgents have captains and USF brass planted all over the place. It looks like they had your captain on the *Dannevirk*, too, which is why you were ordered to come out against us."

Murmurs went through the *Dannevirk* squadron and a few people scowled at English, but he plowed right on ahead.

"No one is blaming you boys. I know each of you is loyal to the Force, which is why I'm here. It isn't too late for you to do the right thing. Our captain is prepared to offer each of you a post on our ship. You can uphold your oath and do your duty to Earth and the Force. I know each of you is loyal and you'd never do anything to turn against your own people. The *Dannevirk* is gone. Come over to the *Lightning Rod* and you can keep serving the way I know you all want to."

Mutterings broke out behind Sean. He and most of the other *Dannevirk* pilots scowled at English and then Sean looked down at his brother.

"I don't know about any civil war and no one told us why we were going out against our own sister ships," he began, "but if Sailor English is on the *Lightning Rod*, that's good enough for me."

A few people nodded behind him.

"Great. I'm delighted to hear it." English sliced his forefinger behind the *Dannevirk* squadron. "You boys take your birds over to the *Lightning Rod*. You can park with Wing 17, which is the one nearest to these trees on the other side. Commander Radcliffe and I will meet you there and we'll take you before the captain."

"Yes, Sir," Sean replied and he turned away to give orders to his fellow pilots.

English shot Radcliffe a significant look and they started back the way they came. "That went down a lot easier than I expected," Radcliffe murmured when they got under the trees.

"I knew they'd come over," English replied. "They're good men. They would never knowingly turn against the Force."

"They came over because of you."

English didn't answer. Their party returned to Wing 17 just as the *Dannevirk* pilots zoomed their fighters over the trees. Their engine wash kicked up the grass.

Wing 17 squinted up at them and shielded their eyes watching the *Dannevirk* squadron come down to land.

English sent Ezra, Thorpe, and Stoval back to Wing 17 and English and Radcliffe approached the *Dannevirk* pilots. They disembarked and clustered tighter together now that they were surrounded by strangers.

"Come with me, boys," English told them. "As soon as you see the captain, she can assign you to the squadron and you can all get back to work."

He led the way over to the *Lightning Rod* where Captain Ogden was reviewing the hull repairs.

The *Dannevirk* pilots saluted her. "Ma'am!" Sean Duran clipped. "Wings 18 and 11 reporting for duty, Ma'am. Thank you for the opportunity to serve under you, Ma'am."

She inspected them closely. "At ease, Airman. Would you mind telling me what your COs told you to convince you to attack one of your sister ships and fire on your fellow pilots?"

"They didn't tell us anything, Ma'am. We didn't know anything about any civil war or anything until Captain English told us just a few minutes ago."

Ogden stiffened visibly and lowered her voice to a snarl. "*Gunnery Sergeant* English is NOT in command of this ship, Airman. You better learn that real quick if you think you're going to serve on the *Lightning Rod*. There is only one captain on this ship and that's me."

"Yes, Ma'am," Sean choked and held himself even more firmly at attention.

"Very well," she went on in that deadly undertone. "I'm assigning Wing 18 to Gunnery Sergeant Frasier and Wing 11 to Gunnery Sergeant Lloyd. Commander Radcliffe will show you where to go. You're all dismissed."

"Thank you, Ma'am," Duran replied and the whole crowd dispersed.

Radcliffe took the *Dannevirk* pilots over to Wings 10 and 12. By the time he finished explaining the situation to Frasier and Lloyd, English had disappeared into the woodwork.

Chapter 17

English found Duran, Thorpe, and Stoval surrounded by the rest of Wing 17. "Is it true, Sir?" Babbitt asked. "Did the whole *Dannevirk* squadron come over to the *Lightning Rod*?"

"All of them that survived the battle, yeah. Commander Radcliffe and I just went over there to talk to them."

"How are we gonna stand up to pilots as experienced as that?" Ritchie asked. "How are we supposed to fly next to them?"

"You're in luck, son. I just saw Commander Radcliffe taking the *Dannevirk* pilots over to meet Frasier and Lloyd. It doesn't look like any of the new guys will be in our wing. In fact, I think we can stop calling them the *Dannevirk* pilots now since they aren't anymore." English looked around. "Where's Racer?"

"She's over there." Janacek pointed beyond the line of fighter craft.

"What's wrong with her?" English asked.

"No clue."

"Maybe she's sulking because she can't touch up her makeup," Ritchie suggested.

"Are all your birds ready to fly?" English asked and the pilots nodded. "Get up to the mess and get yourselves something to eat. You can all stand down until we know what's going on."

He waited until the wing left and then he went over to Racer. She stood behind the fighters where they concealed her from her fellow pilots' view. She stared off in another direction toward the trees.

Some strange stillness surrounded her and English hesitated before going over to her. Maybe he shouldn't go over there at all. Maybe she wanted to be alone. If she did, that only proved that something was wrong.

"Are you hungry, Airman?" he began when he sauntered up. "The rest of the wing is going inside to get something to eat."

"Naw," she muttered. "I'm not hungry."

He leaned forward and studied her profile. "You okay? What's on your mind?"

"Nothing."

"Talk to me," he insisted. "You're high on life as long as you're flying around blowing things up. Now you're on the ground and you get all down in the mouth. What's up?"

"Nothing," she said again. "It's just.... this place. It reminds me of the place where I grew up. It brings back a lot of bad memories."

"Oh." English cast a fleeting look at the sun-washed fields and lush forest. It was one of the most beautiful landscapes he could remember, but maybe it wasn't to everyone.

"I did a lot of stupid things back then," she murmured under her breath. "I went out of my way to piss everyone off and I did a really good job of it. I spoiled everything and now I can never go home. My parents never want to see me again. My dad even said so when I went up to the Lunar Detention Center the last time."

"What exactly did he say?"

"He said he never wanted to see me again. He said as long as I was *this*, he didn't want to know me or even to know that I was still alive."

She gulped and turned her head even farther away so English couldn't see her. "I did something.... something really stupid."

English didn't ask what it was. He didn't need to know.

"Anyway, that's all in the past now." She let out a shaky sigh. "I'll be all right again as soon as I get out of here. You don't have to worry about me."

English took a deep breath. This wasn't his first rodeo. He'd seen so much of this in young recruits when they first entered the service. He'd seen far too much of it.

"Do you want to know a secret?" he told her. "Do you want to know a secret almost no one knows about me?"

She spun around to stare at him. "What is it?"

"I went up to the Lunar Detention Center when I was young."

Her jaw dropped. "No way."

He nodded. "I got busted for setting a house on fire. There was a kid at school that I hated. He used to beat up my best friend and I decided to pay the guy back by torching his house with him and his whole family inside. I had gotten into trouble before, so the judge decided this latest incident was a sign of serious anti-social problems or some shit like that. I spent three months in the LDC."

Racer burst into a wicked grin. "Just wait 'til I tell the others!"

"You tell them whatever you want. I just want you to know you aren't the only one. I made the decision while I was inside the LDC that I was going to join the Force and become a pilot. I signed up the day I got out. My parents were furious. They didn't want me to join the military. They wanted me to go to college and become a professor like my dad." He laughed. "They said some pretty bad things about the military and the kind of people who joined."

"I can't believe this!" She blinked at him. "You? I can't imagine you as a rowdy teenager locked up in the LDC."

"Well, I was. I want you to know you're one of the best pilots I've ever seen. You're making me and the whole wing proud. Your dad told you he didn't want you to be *this*, but you aren't anymore. You're changing into something else. You're changing into someone he would be very proud of. Take my word for it. I have kids and I would be very proud if one of them turned out like you."

He saw his words hit home and he knew he said the right thing. Her expression cleared. She turned back to the trees, but that oppressive air didn't hang over her anymore. He walked away and headed back to the *Lightning Rod* to get himself something to eat.

The elevator wasn't working so he took the stairs. The mess was in an uproar with practically every watch gathering there while the ship was under repair.

Talk flew thick and fast about the civil war, the state of battle beyond the Europa Environmental Zone, which ships might be on which side, and everything that happened since it all went down this morning.

English got himself a tray of food and sat down with the Wing 17 pilots. Racer entered a moment later and disappeared into the crowd around the service bench.

"How do we know who's our enemy and who's our friend?" Janacek asked. "I mean, it's great and all that we have these signals coming through our controls to tell us who to shoot at, but how do we really know? What if the signals are wrong? What if someone makes a mistake and we wind up shooting a friendly pilot?"

"We just have to trust that the captain and Lieutenant Eismann know what they're doing," Thorpe replied. "Hell, the captain and the XO might be wondering the same thing. How are they really supposed to know which ship is on which side?"

"That's the problem," English agreed. "Shooting at aliens is easy compared to this."

Just then, Ritchie came over and slung his leg over the bench. "Hey! One of the new pilots from the *Dannevirk* is named Duran, too. What are the odds?"

"He's my brother, dipshit," Duran fired back.

"No way!" Ritchie countered. "You both joined the Force? That's amazing."

Duran's eyes darted to English and then Duran looked away. None of the rest of the wing knew about Duran's family and English planned to keep it that way until Duran spilled the beans first.

English put a spoonful of macaroni in his mouth and scooted down the bench to make room for Racer to sit down just as Matt Radcliffe came over to the table. "What's up?" English asked.

Radcliffe jerked his head over his shoulder. "Do you mind if I have a word with you in private?"

"You're busted again, Gunny," Ritchie mused. "You really aren't setting a good example for the crew, you know."

"Keep it civil, Airman," Radcliffe told him.

English stood up and stepped over the bench. He pointed at his tray and then at his pilots. "Anybody touches my apple cobbler and they'll be shining the whole wing's birds for the rest of the week."

They all exploded in laughter and Ritchie and Duran pretended to wrestle each other to see who could reach English's tray first. Even Radcliffe laughed…. until he and English walked away.

Radcliffe led the way across the corridor to the recreation office. It was deserted and he shut the door behind English.

"You okay?" English asked. "Is everything all right with the new pilots?"

"Forget all that. I need to talk to you about Ogden."

"What about her?"

Radcliffe lowered his voice to a conspiratorial whisper. "Do you think she might be working for the other side? I mean, could she be one of the rebel captains?"

English raised his eyebrows. "You're joking, right?"

"I'm serious! She was acting squirrely when you first came on board. She was all worked up about you because she thought the Command Staff planted you on the *Lightning Rod* to spy on her." English burst out laughing. "What's so funny? Don't you get it? That's why she went after you. She thought you were here to bust her for doing something untoward."

English couldn't stop laughing. "That's great! Now it all makes sense."

"How can you not take this seriously? Don't you see? Why would she even think that unless she was up to something? If she was completely above board, she never would have thought of something like that. If she did think of it, she wouldn't have cared that the Command Staff was checking up on her because there would be nothing to find."

"What are you telling me this for?" English asked. "Even if you're right, there's nothing I can do about it. Why don't you tell Eismann or Terranova or someone higher ranked?"

"I'm telling you because I trust you, all right? If I told Eismann or Terranova, they might tell the captain and then the jig would be up."

English laughed again. "There is no jig, Matt. Ogden isn't a rebel captain. Trust me."

"What makes you so sure?"

"Look. If she was a rebel captain, she would have turned the moment the *Hermes* and the *Nostradamus* attacked the *Solar Flare*. The *Lightning Rod* is in this condition because Ogden has been fighting the rebels. I shouldn't even have to tell you this, Matt."

Radcliffe pulled his head down between his shoulders. "You might be right about that."

"I am right about it. You might not like the way she's been acting toward me, but that only proves she isn't one of the insurgents. If she was and she suspected I was out here to trip her up, she would have gotten rid of me. She would have denied my request to join her crew. She would have been too anxious to keep her treachery hidden until she couldn't and didn't want to hide it anymore. She wouldn't keep me around where I might see what she was doing."

Radcliffe shrugged. "Still...."

English squeezed Radcliffe's shoulder. "Give her a chance to come around about me. Now I understand why she felt so threatened by me, but it doesn't change anything. We're all in this mess together and we all have to pull together to get out of it. She's the only captain we have, so stick with her. She's all right in my book as long as she's fighting on the right side."

"I'll take your word for it."

"You don't have to take my word for it. Just look at her behavior."

"I *am* looking at her behavior, Sir. That's exactly what I am looking at."

English only beamed at him. He didn't tell Radcliffe not to call him 'Sir'. Old habits died hard and English's habits died even harder. "I meant her behavior on the battlefield, son. She isn't a rebel captain. We would know by now if she was."

"All right. If you say so."

"I do." English pulled the door open. "By the way, you might want to suggest to her that she sends the fighter wings out of the atmosphere first so we can clear a path for the *Lightning Rod* to launch. You could suggest that the *Lightning Rod* stays powered down to make it look like she's still under repair. That way, if any enemy ships are hanging around waiting for her, the fighter wings can draw them away for the *Lightning Rod* to get airborne."

"Good idea. I'll suggest that....and I won't tell her it was your idea."

English laughed again. "You're learning. Now I gotta go. If those kids ate my apple cobbler, I'm coming to find yours."

Radcliffe laughed with him and English went back to the mess. All the pilots sat in the same places. Nothing on English's tray had been touched and they all smirked up at him with cheesy, challenging grins.

He sat down, picked up his apple cobbler container and his spoon, and pulled off the container cover. They all watched him take a bite and then the conversation started bubbling again. These kids were really starting to act like a crew.

Chapter 18

A familiar voice cracked in English's ear. "Squadron Command to Wing Leader 17—stand by to launch."

"Damn, it's good to hear your voice, Lieutenant," English replied.

Lieutenant Eismann laughed. "Stay in contact this time, Gunny."

"Yes, Sir. I'll do my best."

"Long-range scans show Europa, the Io Center, and the whole Jovian system clear for you. You've got a straight run all the way to the Heinrich satellite."

Janacek groaned from his launch pad. "Sweet Jesus, Sir! Don't say the words 'Heinrich satellite' again. I can't take it!"

"I was just about to tell Gunny English not to go near the satellite, Airman," Lieutenant Eismann replied. "Once the *Lightning Rod* leaves Europa, she's on her way to the Mars repair shop to rendezvous with the other friendlies."

"Friendlies," Ritchie chimed in. "I'm liking that word more and more."

"Where are the enemy ships?" English asked. "Don't tell me they pulled back to Earth."

"It looks like it. Maybe they encountered more resistance on the planet than they expected. All the bad guys have withdrawn, but we can't expect it to stay that way."

"I'll believe it when I see it," English muttered to himself.

"Wing 10 standing by," Frasier chimed in from across the flight deck.

"How are your new boys, Charlie?" English asked.

"They're great. I couldn't ask for better. They're all hot to trot and very well trained."

"Wings 10 and 17—you are clear to launch," Eismann cut in.

"Wing 17—launch!" English ordered and his pilots rocketed away. They swooped off the flight deck, over the Europa Environmental Zone, and punched through the terraform bubble into orbit.

They skimmed past the Io Center and English looked around. "The lieutenant was right," Racer remarked. "The whole area is deserted."

"Stay frosty," English ordered. "I don't like this. It can't be this easy."

"Don't tell me you actually want to make it harder." Charlie Frasier took a tour around the Io Center, but there was nothing to see. "Be grateful we don't have to fight our way out."

"The enemy wouldn't just leave. They risked a lot to capture the system. They wouldn't just turn tail and abandon it."

"What about what the lieutenant said?" Ritchie asked. "Maybe things went south on Earth and the rebels needed those ships back there."

"It sounds too good to be true," English replied. "I'm going over to Saturn to make sure."

"Don't break formation!" Lieutenant Eismann cut in. "The *Lightning Rod* is launching. We need all fighters in position to cover the……"

A crash drowned out what Eismann said next. English had been about to turn toward Titan when a fountain of plasma smashed into Stoval's bird.

The blow knocked Stoval into English and then shots enveloped the whole squadron. A bunch of fighter craft swarmed out from behind Titan and pounded Wings 10 and 17.

Manheim shrieked and the whole area erupted in mayhem. English struggled to pull his head back into the game. Stoval scrambled to get his craft moving. He sat still while the enemy surrounded him.

English ripped his guns around to drive them off. He gunned it into the mob and skidded to a halt next to Stoval. "Auggie! How bad is it?"

"She's lost power, Sir! I got nothing!"

"Thorpe—anybody!" English called as the enemy pounced on him and Stoval.

English slammed his guns right and left to carve a space around Stoval. English barely drove the enemy away before they destroyed both fighters, but the enemy only took up a position farther off and hammered English from out of range.

He heard his pilots yelling in the background, but he couldn't see them beyond the ring of enemy cannons. He also didn't see any ship the enemy fighters might be attached to—not that it made much difference.

All at once, another fighter blasted into the throng, but she didn't come to his side. She sliced a path through the enemy spitting plasma everywhere. "Stand your ground, Sir!" Duran yelled. "Help is on the way!"

A second later, Racer plowed into the mix from the opposite side. She and Duran shattered the enemy formation and made the attackers easier to hit.

English's spirits soared when a third fighter sprinted through the gap and skated to a halt next to him. "You all right, Sir?" It was Sean Duran. "These pesky bastards got the jump on us, too."

"I'm all right. Stoval is the one in trouble."

"Hold hard, Gunny," Lieutenant Eismann called. "We got our eyes on you."

Sean and English kept up a steady torrent of shots to defend Stoval. Racer and Ezra Duran cut wide circles to flank the enemy and break up their formation, but it still wasn't enough.

Racer kept screeching around the perimeter and Ezra blasted through the enemy to get closer to the stranded fighters. He pulled up next to his brother, glanced over, and Ezra's cheeks colored. "I heard you might need a little help."

"That was some serious badassery out there, little brother," Sean countered.

Ezra blushed again, but at that moment, an enemy blast hit Sean's bird. "Sean!" Ezra bellowed and he leaped out of position.

He gunned his engines and wheeled his fighter between Sean and the enemy. Ezra unleashed a hellish barrage to drive the enemy away from Sean.

"I'm all over you, buddy!" Racer called and dove in from the other side. She and Ezra sandwiched three fighters between them and blasted them to pieces.

Sean limped back to English's side and corrected his aim. "Who the hell is this kid?"

"Just some punk I picked up from the gutter," English replied. "He's been blowing the lid off everything since he got here."

"I think I'm gonna have to have a word with my dad when this is all over."

Ezra got pulled back out into the fight. He and Racer stationed themselves together deep inside the enemy throng. Plasma spouted from their guns holding the enemy at bay while Sean and English went back to keeping the attackers away from Stoval.

The enemy closed tighter on all sides. Where did they all come from?

A second later, a searing jet of plasma punched through the enemy formation and torched ten fighters. Racer and Ezra had to get out of the way in a hurry as the *Lightning Rod* advanced into the battle.

Her giant sides sent the enemy fleeing, but not without multiple cannon barrages cutting their numbers down as they beat it back toward Titan.

The *Lightning Rod* loomed over the five fighters remaining on the battlefield. English hailed Lieutenant Eismann. "We got a stranded fighter out here, Sir."

"Transmitting to the bridge," Eismann replied. "Stand by and we'll bring you in."

English waited while the *Lighting Rod* wheeled and pointed the cargo hold at Stoval. "I'm taking a tour over to Titan to see where those weasels are hiding out."

"Take Wing 10 with you, Wing Leader 17."

"You got it. Let's go, Charlie."

Wings 10 and 17 fell in with English. Sean stayed close English's side while Racer and Ezra joined the rest of their crew. Both wings flew in a jumble with no one paying much attention to formation.

The two wings advanced to Titan and surprised fifteen fugitive rebels hiding behind the moon. The enemy spun away and sprinted for the Saturn colonies. Frasier took a page out of English's book and hailed them.

"*Lightning Rod* squadron to unidentified fighter wing. It isn't too late to do the right thing and show your loyalty to the Force. Come over to the *Lightning Rod* and join our crew. Our captain will give you amnesty and you can continue to do your duty and serve the Force."

No one answered him.

"Nice try, Gunny," Sean remarked.

"It was worth a shot. Let's beat it back to the ship."

"Hold on," Ezra called. "What if those fighters are attached to another destroyer? It could be hiding farther out in the system. We should go check."

"We can't check," English replied. "We'd be getting too far away from the *Lightning Rod*. If we got in trouble, the ship would have to put herself in danger to save us. Come on, son. We can fight another day. Long-range sensors will tell us if there's a ship out there. If there is, one ship can't do much damage against the Force from so far away."

Ezra rejoined the squadron on the way back to the *Lightning Rod*. Wings 10 and 17 separated to land on their pads. English went over to Stoval, who was helping the mechanics work on his bird.

"You all right, son?"

"Yeah," Stoval replied. "Thanks."

English clapped him on the shoulder and started toward Lieutenant Eismann's desk when he spotted Sean Duran coming toward him across the desk.

Sean walked straight past English, marched up to his brother, and embraced him in a huge hug in front of all his crewmates. The Wing 17 pilots stood around staring at them, and when the two brothers parted, Ezra's cheeks flamed.

Sean grinned at him and squeezed the back of Ezra's neck. "I'm proud of you."

Ezra kept blushing like a fiend until they both walked off together. English watched them go with a pang. At least someone on the *Lightning Rod* knew where one of his loved ones was.

Chapter 19

E nglish stepped into his cabin and crossed to his desk. He considered for a moment and then switched on his computer. He sent a signal to Earth and it connected.

A young man with curly brown hair appeared on the screen. He wore an immaculate USF uniform and every detail of his appearance had been meticulously attended to.

"Dad!" he exclaimed. "Damn, it's good to see you! I was so worried when I heard the *Lightning Rod* had been in combat and taken damage. How bad is it? Are you all right?"

English's heart twisted. "It's good to see you, too, Dan. I was worried Ufa might become a target for the rebels. The *Lightning Rod* is fine. We did some repairs at the Europa Environmental Zone. Now she's en route to the Mars repair shop to rendezvous with the other loyalist destroyers." English frowned at his son. "How are you holding up?"

Dan threw up his hands and gasped in exasperation. "It's been absolute bedlam down here. No one knows who's loyal and who's a traitor. I'm one of the lucky ones. I trust everyone under me and the station is secure. It's all the bastards outside it I have to worry about."

"Have you heard anything from Melanie?"

"Yeah, she's fine. The Command Center Hospital is still intact. The rebels hit the communications system. They wanted to stop the Command Staff from coordinating any response, but all the hospital staff are alive and as well as can be expected."

English covered his face. "Thank God! I was worried sick."

"I should have contacted you before to tell you. She's working around the clock dealing with the wounded and coordinating civilian refugee aid, but she's fine. The Command Staff has negotiated an agreement with Harare not to attack the hospital or any other non-combatant target."

"That's a relief. What about Andy?"

Dan went serious. "I haven't heard from him. He was in command of the *Buckingham Palace* when the fighting broke out."

"What? No!" English cried. "He was on the *Obsidian*!"

Dan shook his head. "He transferred. You were on your way out to the Acheron Colony to rendezvous with the *Lightning Rod,* so I guess you didn't hear. It was sudden. Captain Henley died. Did you hear about that? The Command Staff had to find a replacement real fast so they promoted Andy. He was on the *Buckingham Palace* during that first attack."

English's blood ran cold. The *Buckingham Palace* had been among the enemy ships that attacked the *Lightning Rod* and the *Solar Flare.* Could English's youngest son have gone over to rebels?

English didn't want to believe it, but from the look on Dan's face, English could see that Dan believed it. English shivered. What would it mean if English started to think of his own son as one of the enemy?

The *Lightning Rod* had fought against the *Buckingham Palace* in that battle. Where was the *Buckingham Palace* now?

Eismann said the rebel destroyers pulled back to Earth, but what if all that intelligence was wrong? What if the *Buckingham Palace* was

out here in space just waiting to ambush the *Lightning Rod* again....
or vice versa?

"Listen, Dad...." Dan turned to something off the screen. "I've been
thinking a lot about that lake we used to visit when we were younger....
you remember which one I'm talking about...."

Dan faced the screen and his eyes took on a hard, distant, coldness
English had never seen before. He knew his children better than anyone in the world. English spent decades looking into those eyes.

Now he had no idea who he was talking to. This man in front of
him was not his son. He became someone completely different. Could
being the captain in command of the Ufa Long-Range Alert Station
change a man that much?

"Anyway," Dan went on in the same casual tone that left absolutely
nothing between himself and his own father. "I wrote something
about it that I want to send you. I'd really like to get your feedback
on it."

"Uh.... okay," English stammered. What could he say to this
stranger?

"I'm sending it now. I'll talk to you later, Dad."

Dan cut English off without even saying goodbye. English stared at
the screen. What the hell was that all about? He never took his kids to
any lake when they were younger.

Another transmission came through from Earth. The headline
read, *Memoirs, Captain Daniel Caleb English, Ufa Long-Range Alert
Station, Ufa, Russian Federation.*

English opened the transmission without thinking. His mind remained fixated on that terrible blank look in Dan's eyes. Something
was wrong—seriously wrong. Did Dan turn, too? Was he working for
the other side?

English couldn't believe that. Dan had been the most enthusiastic of all English's kids about joining the Force and following in his father's footsteps.

Dan joined the USF the day he graduated from high school. He worked his ass off to become a captain just like his father. Dan would never turn.... would he?

English started reading and instantly understood.

Dear Dad,

I can't stop thinking about the lake we used to visit in Antigua Guatemala. It reminds me so much of the cabin where we spent the summer in the Pyrenees National Park. We had so much fun there, didn't we? I remember how we took our canoes out on the lake and we caught fourteen fish. That was nothing compared to the forty-eight we caught in the Pyrenees, but it was still pretty good. Those are such wonderful memories, Dad. I'll always be grateful to you for giving us that.

Then there was the time we went stargazing and looked into space with our telescopes. I'll never forget it. It was October 17 and I was one week away from turning twelve. I saw twenty stars and I even saw a shooting star going down over Greenland. That was the night you told me all about the USF and the bases all over the world.

Melanie saw forty stars that night, but Andy only saw eight. He was so mad.

Anyway, I just wanted to remember all the good times we had together when we were younger. I hope you're settling in on the Lightning Rod. *I'll talk to you soon. Love you always, Dan.*

English stared at the text. On its surface, it looked like some random letter between a son and his father. Now English knew exactly what Dan was doing when he changed his tone so drastically. He was sending English a message.

English never took his children to Guatemala or to the Pyrenees and he definitely never took them stargazing.

English had enough on his plate commanding ships in the Force while his children were growing up. He struggled back then to make it home often enough to stay involved in their lives and keep up with all their activities and milestones.

This letter had nothing to do with anything he and Dan did when Dan was younger. Dan had embedded some kind of code in this letter. He must be worried about someone intercepting the information. Dan didn't want anyone to find out he was sending English this message.

English went over the letter piece by piece. October 17 was one week away just like Dan said. That had to be significant. Antigua Guatemala and Pyrenees National Park.... English knew those names.

The Antigua Guatemala base hosted dozens of destroyers and thousands of personnel. The Force had another base almost as big in the Pyrenees just next to the national park, but there was more here than met the eye—a lot more.

Dan said they caught fourteen fish on the lake at Antigua, but that was nothing compared to forty-eight fish at the Pyrenees. Those numbers must mean ships.

Then there were the stars. Dan saw twenty stars and Melanie saw forty stars, but Andy only saw eight. These must mean ships, too.

Dan was the captain of the Long-Range Alert Station. He had almost two hundred destroyers in the Early Warning Response Fleet at Ufa. The Early Warning Response Fleet in residence at the Command Center usually had four hundred. English divided the number by ten to give the number of stars.

English already knew all that, so why was Dan telling him in code? Dan went to a lot of trouble to tell English this.

Dan obviously thought Andy was on the other side or at least suspected it. That meant the rebels had eighty ships.

It all came down to the date. October 17. Something was going to happen. The Force had six hundred ships and the rebels only had eighty. That was a pretty big difference so the rebels must not be all that interested in striking back.... unless they had a plan.

Why did Dan mention Greenland? The Force only had one base there and it was tiny—hardly worth the insurgents' notice.

The Arsuk base was the Force's northernmost installation left over from the war between the Western Hemisphere and the Eastern Hemisphere.

The fledgling Force needed an early warning station back then. They needed a base to alert the Western powers if an attack came in from the east, but the Force hadn't used Arsuk in centuries.

Some of the Command Staff even talked about decommissioning Arsuk, but they always decided against it. Decommissioning Arsuk would cost more than keeping it active.

It must be active now.... or someone wanted to think it was.... or maybe someone didn't want someone else to know it was.

English printed the letter on a piece of paper. He hadn't done that in years. Then he deleted all record of the letter off the *Lightning Rod's* database.

He tapped out a quick message.

Dear Dan,

I really loved your memoir about your childhood experiences. I'm glad I could give you those memories to carry with you into adulthood. I'm glad they give you the same feeling of love and happiness now that they gave you then.

I'm so proud of you, son. You're doing great work there at Ufa. I know you'll continue to be an asset to the Force for a long, long time. I love you more than anything, Dad.

The minute he hit send, he picked up the paper copy of the letter and walked out of the cabin.

Chapter 20

C ommander Radcliffe checked and rechecked the chart for the thousandth time. "The route to the Mars repair shop is all clear."

"Any sign of the enemy?" Captain Ogden asked.

"There are fifteen destroyers patrolling Earth's atmosphere, but they aren't venturing out this far. Those fighter craft are still orbiting Titan where we left them. They aren't attached to any destroyer. We're the farthest destroyer out with nothing between us and Mars."

"How many destroyers are at the repair shop?"

"Ten from the battle. The *Earl of Wessex*, the *Outrigger*, the *Sea Lion, Battle Hardened, Marigold, Boer, Lone Ranger, Flint, Vampire Bat*, and *Catherine the Great*."

Captain Ogden groaned. "That's nowhere near enough."

"It's all we got, Ma'am." Radcliffe threw his device on her desk. "At least we'll be able to get fully repaired on Mars."

She started to say something when her doorbell rang. "Come in."

Radcliffe stiffened when Sailor English walked in. He couldn't be here to tell Captain Ogden about Radcliffe's suspicions of her loyalty. English wouldn't do that.

Radcliffe relaxed when he saw English's expression. The sergeant set his face in a mask of grim determination and he held a piece of paper in his hand.

He came to attention, but unlike all the other times he entered Captain Ogden's ready room, he didn't fix his eyes on the wall behind her head. He looked directly at her and didn't look away once. He didn't even look at Radcliffe. "Ma'am."

"Can I help you, English? It's late."

"Yes, Ma'am. I have something to tell you." He held up the paper. "I just received a communique from my son, Dan."

She leaned forward in her chair. "So you've been in contact with Earth again, Gunny?"

"My son," he went on, "is captain of the Ufa Long-Range Alert Station, Ma'am. He sent me an encrypted message because he's obviously worried about the rebels monitoring his communications. I believe he's trying to warn us of an attack either against the loyalist force or a preemptive strike by the loyalists against the insurgency. He specifically states that the attack will take place in a week."

Ogden frowned. "Is that so?"

"Take a look." English set the paper down on Ogden's desk and swiveled it around so she could read it. "This letter lists three different locations, a date, and several numbers that don't correspond to any events that happened in real life. He mentions trips we took to Guatemala and the Pyrenees, but we never went there. We never went fishing and we never went stargazing."

Radcliffe leaned over the captain's shoulder and peered down at the letter. He skimmed through it and instantly saw what English meant. "What do you think these numbers mean?"

English straightened up, threw back his shoulders, and hardened his features even more. "My son Andrew is the captain of the *Buck-*

ingham Palace. Dan thinks Andy might be working for the other side....and I agree. The *Buckingham Palace* came out against us in that first battle. I didn't know he was in command of the ship at the time—not that it matters—but Dan is obviously using Andy as a code word for the rebels."

Ogden leaned back and pushed the letter away. "This is interesting, Gunny, but we have our work cut out for us handling the rebels. They're trying to take the solar system and the *Lightning Rod* needs repair. If something is going on down on Earth, it's completely out of our hands."

"But don't you see, Ma'am?" English pressed on. "We can help them. If the loyalists are planning a knockout strike against the rebels, these numbers indicate that the Force is planning based on the number of ships they have on Earth. They aren't counting on us—all eleven of us. We could make the difference."

"How?" Radcliffe asked. "The Force has six hundred ships. We're only eleven. We can't even make a dent in the rebels even if they only have eighty."

"We can do it by striking different targets. Look." English pointed back down at the Greenland reference. "He wants me to understand something's going on at Arsuk. The Force has completely discounted it, but what if the rebels haven't? What if the rebels have set up a new position there that the Force doesn't know about? Eleven ships could hit it hard and destroy it before the rebels make a surprise attack."

"That's stretching it a little, don't you think, Gunny?" Ogden asked. "First of all, we don't even know when the attack will take place on October 17. We'd be shooting in the dark—assuming this attack is really going to take place."

"Then we strike Arsuk on the 16th. Our long-range sensors should tell us from here whether there's any activity at Arsuk."

"If there is, don't you think the Command Staff would have noticed it by now?" Radcliffe asked.

"Not if they're too concerned with rebel activity in other parts of the planet." English started talking faster and his countenance came alive. "The rebels have set up their main center of operations at Harare. The Force is planning to strike Antigua Guatemala and the Pyrenees bases, which means the Force will be monitoring those locations closely.... which explains how Dan knew what force the rebels have there. He must be involved in keeping track of rebel movements."

Ogden rotated her chair from side to side. She set her fingertips together in a steeple and rested the tips against her chin. She turned her eyes away and they lost focus. "All right, Gunny. I'm listening. Let's hear your recommendations."

"We're going into the Mars repair shop. That gives you time to coordinate with the other loyal captains—which you were going to do anyway. We just have to make sure none of them communicates with Earth—or better yet, that they communicate faulty information. They can tell the Command Staff that we're all a lot more severely damaged than we actually are and that we aren't fit to fight back."

Radcliffe had to laugh. "Oh, dear."

English cracked a wild grin and then immediately buried it. "We can all stay in the repair shop right up until the 16th. We can check out the situation at Arsuk and maybe see about any other targets we can find."

"Assuming the crew at Arsuk doesn't put up any resistance," Radcliffe pointed out.

"They will," English replied, "but we won't be there to take any damage. The *Lightning Rod* will slip away while the other ten loyal ships carry out the attack on Arsuk."

"We won't slip away," Ogden growled. "We wouldn't do anything so cowardly."

This time, English grinned right down at her and his eyes twinkled. "I have a better idea, Ma'am. I can contact Andy on the *Buckingham Palace*. I'll tell him the *Lightning Rod* wants to turn to the rebel side, but I'll tell him we can't meet as long as everyone is at the repair shop."

"You would do that?" Radcliffe gasped. "What if you're wrong about your son? This could sour your whole relationship with him."

English only shrugged. "What difference does that make as long as we weaken the rebels before the attack? The rebels will send out at least one ship to rendezvous with us. They might even send out several. We can use the pretext to lure enemy ships away from Earth and leave the rebels more vulnerable to the attack. In fact, I think this might be why Dan sent me this message in the first place."

Radcliffe stared at the man in stunned disbelief. Everything he knew and admired about English was nothing compared to this. He would actually break ties with his own son if it benefited the Force.

Ogden swiveled her chair back to the front. "All right, Gunny. I will take this on board and discuss it with the other captains when the *Lightning Rod* gets to the repair shop. I'll let you know when we're ready for you to contact your son. You're dismissed."

"Yes, Ma'am." English saluted and turned to leave.

Ogden swept to her feet, took one look at the paper, and called out, "English!" He stopped on the threshold to turn back. "Thank you," Captain Ogden said.

English dipped a single nod. "Yes, Ma'am. I'm just doing my duty." And he walked out.

Ogden sank into her chair and relaxed back. She gazed into empty space and didn't speak. Radcliffe watched her. English was right. She was finally coming around.

Radcliffe's heart skipped a beat and he picked up his device to hide his agitation. English didn't say a word about Radcliffe's suspicions. Of course he didn't.

English was too true for that—too solid. Nothing existed for English but whatever was best for Earth and the Force. Nothing else even entered his head.

Chapter 21

The *Lightning Rod's* hull clanged against metal and the ship vibrated as she locked into place at the Mars repair shop. English stepped out of his cabin to find the whole ship in an uproar. He hadn't seen or heard this kind of activity since that first emergency call-up.

The whole *Lightning Rod* crew poured out of their quarters heading for the elevator. A massive logjam blocked most of the corridor.

Instead of everyone rushing to battle stations, they laughed and talked excitedly while they waited their turns to go downstairs to the cargo hold.

Many couldn't wait and filed into the stairwell. English found himself between Charlie Frasier and Matt Radcliffe again. "What's on the agenda for you, Charlie?" English asked. "Are you hitting the whore houses to blow all your pay?"

Frasier colored and looked away. "Are you kidding? My wife would tan my hide if I did that."

English laughed and clapped him on the back. "You're too much of a prince, aren't you?"

"Charlie will be too busy tailing his pilots around the station to make sure none of them steps out of line," Radcliffe teased. "No one can get away with anything with Bloodhound Frasier on the prowl."

All three of them laughed. "What about you, Matt?" English asked. "Don't tell me you're going to the races like you did when you were seventeen."

Radcliffe colored, too. "You're gonna give away all my secrets, Gunny."

"I won't tell the Station Constable where the bodies are buried."

Radcliffe caught English's eye for a second and they both looked away. They both knew where the other was going while the *Lightning Rod* crew was on shore leave at the repair shop, but neither would tell anyone else.

Another load of crewmen got into the elevator, and then English, Radcliffe, and Frasier got in. They rode down to the cargo hold and had to wait again while another huge crowd headed for the blast doors to get off the ship.

The *Lightning Rod* sat docked in an even bigger hold with ten other ships. The other docking stations stood empty. These eleven were the only ships in residence at the Mars repair shop.

The towering parapets and superstructure of the Olympus Station rose as far as the eye could see above the docking station. The *Lightning Rod* crew streamed down the concourse and dispersed inside the station.

Laughter and excited talk echoed in front of and behind English. He smiled at the happy, carnival atmosphere greeting everyone to their well-earned shore leave, but he didn't join in.

Charlie Frasier slapped him on the shoulder. "You two stay out of trouble or I'll have to bust you downtown, too." He sped up, shot English and Radcliffe a crazy grin over his shoulder, and disappeared into the crowd.

"See you around, Charlie," Radcliffe called after him.

English slowed his pace. He was in no hurry to get off the *Lightning Rod*. Every minute brought him closer to the task he himself suggested to Captain Ogden. Would she take him up on it?

If she did, the eleven captains on this station would call up English to betray his own son so the loyalist destroyers could carry out this surprise attack against the insurgency. Was English really ready to do that?

He raised all three of his children to value loyalty to Earth and the Force. They all took the USF mission seriously.... except Andy, apparently.

He wasn't just on the *Buckingham Palace*. He was the ship's captain, which meant that everything the *Buckingham Palace* did came down to Andy's orders.

If Dan was right and Andy turned the *Buckingham Palace* to the rebel side that quickly, he must have been working with the rebels for a long, long time.

He must have betrayed his oath months or even years ago. How could English's son go so wrong? English didn't understand it at all.

He would have liked to talk to Andy about it. He would especially like to talk to Andy before carrying out this surprise attack, but English wouldn't be able to do that. It wouldn't be a surprise attack if he did.

English became aware of Radcliffe walking at his side. Radcliffe matched his pace to stay there. English didn't want to talk to Radcliffe. If English talked about it, he might have to face the truth of what he was about to do.

He'd been waiting all this time for Captain Ogden to realize that he wasn't out to get her or to challenge her authority. If she took his suggestion seriously, it could mean the turning point in his position on the *Lightning Rod*.

Her taking his suggestion to the other captains would be the best possible scenario he could ask for, but he dreaded it. He almost wished she mistrusted him too much and would just ignore it. Then English wouldn't have to deal with Andy at all.... except on the battlefield.

Radcliffe broke in on his thoughts. "Where are you gonna go? Do you have any plans?"

English shrugged. "Not really."

He turned away from Radcliffe, mostly so he wouldn't have to see the understanding in Radcliffe's eyes.

English found himself in front of the giant windows in the concourse wall. They looked out over the docking stations to the repair hold.

The *Lightning Rod* crew had all made their way onto the concourse. No more crewmen came out of the cargo hold.

Mechanics, welders, and engineers streamed the other way and flooded the ship. They used hover lifts to position themselves on the outer hull and started welding, grinding, and adjusting the ship to repair the damage.

"I guess she'll be ready to rock and roll in no time," Radcliffe murmured at English's side. "She'll be right as rain in a few days."

English nodded at nothing. He didn't want the *Lightning Rod* to be ready for anything if it meant going out against his own people, his own Force, his own family.

Radcliffe didn't say anything for a long time. English wished Radcliffe would leave. English wanted to be alone, but Radcliffe didn't leave.

Radcliffe finally bumped English's elbow. "Why don't you come down to the Quad? I'll buy you lunch."

English nodded again. He wasn't hungry, but he couldn't exactly stand here staring at the *Lightning Rod* until he got word from Captain Ogden—much as he'd like to.

He and Radcliffe started walking again, crossed the concourse, and entered the station itself. Scaffolds, terraces, hanging gardens, and shopping malls rose in hundreds of stories farther than the eye could see.

The whole superstructure surrounded a long shaft with light shining down from above and from windows on all sides.

People streamed in and out of stores, sat at cafés, and visited all the entertainment establishments lining the shaft on every level.

English and Radcliffe made their way downstairs to a huge court packed with people. Eateries, theaters, and cabarets occupied every corner.

Uniformed USF crewmen walked, talked, ate, drank, gambled, and lounged in every doorway and at tables on the terraces.

Circus acts floated in the center of the shaft with acrobats spinning on ropes, swinging on trapezes, blowing fire, and dozens of other spectacles. They distracted English from his thoughts.

Radcliffe headed for an Italian restaurant and English tagged after him. Radcliffe was his only companion right now. Radcliffe was the only other person alive besides Ogden who knew the doubts nagging at English's mind.

Radcliffe kept not bringing it up which, English realized, actually did make him feel better. Someone knew, and even more importantly, Radcliffe knew enough not to mention it. He just knew and stuck by English's side.

Radcliffe was young enough. He could have gone off to enjoy himself anywhere and everywhere. Radcliffe might even have a sweetheart somewhere on the *Lightning Rod* that English didn't know about, but Radcliffe didn't leave. He stayed with English.

It meant a lot even if it only forced English to think about it even more. He wished he could stop thinking about it, but Radcliffe leaving wouldn't change that.

Radcliffe took a place in the queue of USF personnel waiting to get into the restaurant. The two men took a few steps when a commotion drew their attention across the court.

A bunch of USF crewmen surged and struggled near another eatery. The tumult escalated to such a pitch that a few people even fell over.

They hit the floor and English saw arms and fists flying in the center of the crowd. Uniformed crewmen were having a knockdown-dragout fight over there.

English strode over and waded into the mix with Radcliffe right next to him. They yanked people out of the way and hurled them out of the line of fire.

English shouldered his way to the center of the scuffle and grabbed one of the main combatants. He yanked the young man back and stared down at Ezra Duran.

"What the holy hell do you think you're doing?" English bellowed.

Ezra struggled against English's hold. Ezra had a bloody nose and his sweaty hair stuck to his face and got in his eyes. He bared his teeth in an animal snarl and tried to tear himself out of English's grip to get back into the fight.

Another seven guys pounded, kicked, and wrestled a few feet away. A bunch of pilots from the *Lightning Rod* squadron stood around yelling and pumping their fists to cheer on the combatants.

English and Radcliffe forced their way between the attackers and tore them apart. English forced them to the limits of his own arms to stop them from lunging back in to tear each other to pieces.

"Hold it!" he roared, but the combatants paid no attention.

They charged in again and English jammed his body between them. It took all his strength to wedge them apart. "I said hold it!"

His voice finally penetrated the fog of war and the attackers paused with English's palms flattened against their chests.

He looked from one to the other and found himself staring at Sean Duran. Radcliffe and a few other random officers managed to separate the rest of the combatants. English's heart dropped when he saw that at least four of them were pilots from his own wing.

Thorpe, Babbitt, Janacek, and Ritchie were all bloody and bruised, but they were also still seething with rage and snarled in fury at their enemies.

The pilots on the other side glared back at them with equal venom. Some tried to fight their way around English and Radcliffe to restart the fight. English had to let go of Sean to stop Ritchie and then Janacek from doing the same thing.

"What the hell is going on?!" English bellowed. "You're supposed to be on shore leave. What the hell are you doing fighting in the damn street?"

"He's a piece of shit traitor!" The guy Sean had been fighting tried to charge him again. "He killed my best friend! I'll tear him to pieces!"

Sean crashed into English at the same time and an unholy din broke out with everyone yelling at once. Sean's face was already covered in blood and his uniform had been ripped down the front. He looked like an animal, too.

Sean yelled something about following orders and Ezra erupted out of control trying to claw his way toward the other pilot. "How dare you call my brother a traitor?!"

English seized the boy by the jacket and sent him staggering back into the crowd. Racer, Stoval, and Manheim all grabbed him to stop him from attacking again.

English, Radcliffe, and the other officers finally managed to separate everyone again. English rounded on the pilots he didn't know, the ones who must have attacked Sean. "Which ship are you boys on?"

Sean's opponent muttered something under his breath, spat a wad of bloody saliva on the floor, and turned away.

English snatched the guy's collar and jerked him around fast. "I asked you a question, Airman. Which ship are you on?"

The guy started to struggle and then held himself stiff. "I said we're from the *Vampire Bat*."

"Excuse me?!" English bellowed in the guy's face. "You better watch your mouth, Mister, or you'll be out of the squadron so fast it will make your head spin."

"The *Vampire Bat*, Sir!" the guy yelled back.

English let go of his jacket with a sudden, disgusted jerk. "Take your crew and get the hell out of here. Go back to your ship and report to your captain and XO. I'll be checking up on you within the hour. If you don't report this incident right away, I'll see you bumped out of the Force for good. Understand?"

The guy muttered, "Yes, Sir," and a bunch of the other pilots did the same thing before they wandered off.

English watched them out of sight and Radcliffe came over to him. "We should have seen this coming."

English sniffed and turned back to Wing 17. They stood around shuffling their feet and casting questioning glances at Sean and English. The rest of Wing 10 had gathered around Sean and were talking to him.

English pulled himself up to his full height. "Now listen up, all of you punks. You've got at least a week on this station, and if even one of you puts a foot out of line, you'll never see the inside of a cockpit again as long as you live."

His crew shrank from him and several looked at the floor.

"This is conduct unbecoming, Ezra," English told the young man. "You of all people should know what that means. You shamed your family and your crew with this behavior....and don't give me that shit about defending your brother. None of you was in any danger from those guys, but fighting in the street sure puts your career in danger."

Ezra wouldn't look at him.

English rounded on Sean. "And you! This is a fine way to set an example for the younger pilots. You're making me seriously regret ever bringing you over to the *Lightning Rod* if this is the way you act. Maybe I should have let you rot with the rebels. Maybe that's where you really belong."

Sean stiffened and gritted his teeth, but he didn't reply.

English squared his shoulders and raised his voice even more. "You punks just wasted your last ounce of goodwill on this crew. You just pissed away every scrap of respect you earned with everyone on our crew, especially mine. Do you get that? I thought you might actually be shaping up to be decent crewmen, but I was obviously wrong. I'll be keeping an eye on you all for the rest of the week, and if I see so much as a smudge on one of your uniforms, I'll bump you all out of the service with dishonorable discharges. You can all go back to Earth and herd sheep for the rest of your worthless lives! Do you got that?"

Ezra muttered, "Yes, Sir," down at the floor and the other Wing 17 pilots said it, too.

English rounded on Sean. "I asked you a question, Airman. I said do you got that?"

Sean straightened up, but he only made the most fleeting eye contact with English before Sean said, "Yes, Sir."

"Get the hell out of here," English snarled. "Don't let me see your worthless faces again until we get the order to deploy."

Racer and Stoval pulled Ezra away. Wing 10 gathered around Sean and drew him away, too.

A giant crowd had gathered around to see English humiliate his own crew in front of the whole damn station. His pilots kept glancing up at him and looking away, but the crowd blocked them from leaving. It took them a long time to get away from him.

His pilots whispered to each other and a few patted Ezra on the back. Janacek and Ritchie were both bleeding. English pretended not to notice Manheim handing Ezra a piece of gauze that he pressed to his nose.

Radcliffe appeared at English's side again, but Radcliffe still said nothing. He was just there. He of all people knew how agonizing it felt to reprimand his subordinates, especially somewhere so public.

English forced himself to turn away. He hated dressing anyone down, but he never did it to anyone who deserved it more than these punks did.

He felt sick to his stomach. He was really starting to think highly of his crew and now this happened.

Radcliffe was right. English should have expected this when he invited the *Dannevirk* pilots to join the *Lightning Rod*.

He followed Radcliffe back to the restaurant. Enough of the patrons had left to watch the excitement, so he and Radcliffe got a table right away. Now English had no choice but to face his young friend.

Radcliffe smiled at him and glanced toward the door. "They're good kids. They'll shape up in time."

English gnashed his teeth. "That might not be soon enough."

"If it wasn't your crew, it would have been someone else. This whole war is going to be brother against brother and friend against friend. It's inevitable. We're going to see a lot more of this."

English growled under his breath. He didn't want to think about it, but he supposed he had to. It wasn't going to go away anytime soon, if ever.

Chapter 22

The doorbell rang and Captain Ogden called out, "Come in!"

The door hissed open and Sailor English walked into the conference room. He stiffened on the threshold when his sharp eyes darted around at eleven captains and their XOs staring back at him.

Commander Radcliffe stood at Ogden's elbow and his nerves stood on end when English entered. This was it. This was the moment of truth.

Ogden and the other officers had been discussing English's report and his proposal for more than two hours. Now it was go time. None of their talk meant anything without English.

Radcliffe had spent as much time as he could with English over the last few days. Radcliffe didn't want English to be alone with the course he'd chosen.

English brooded much more than he normally did. He wasn't his usual chipper, friendly self, but Radcliffe didn't mind.

Radcliffe didn't even mind when English stalked the Olympus Station ambushing his pilots to make sure they didn't step out of line again, but they never did. They took his threat seriously and for good reason. He never threatened anything like that unless he meant it.

Radcliffe and English even ran into Charlie Frasier a few times. He was doing the same thing with his own pilots. English told Frasier about Sean and the others fighting and Frasier agreed to go extra hard on the pilots if they ever slipped up again.

So they spent the rest of their stay haunting the halls and establishments putting the fear of God into their crewmen. None of that eased the tension, though, and now it all came to a massive head. No one could hide from reality anymore.

"Come in, Gunny," Ogden told him. "I've briefed my fellow captains and their XOs on your proposal."

"Thank you, Ma'am." English came forward and Radcliffe made room for him at the table.

English stood at attention, but he didn't shy away from making eye contact with the other captains. Most of them knew him personally and several expressed incredulity behind closed doors. They didn't want to believe he could seriously go out of his way to destroy his relationship with his son to benefit the loyalist cause.

"None of us has any problem with your proposal, Sailor," Captain Fletcher Detrick of the *Lone Ranger* began. He was about English's age and just as burly. "Our only concern is for you and your wellbeing. I think I speak for us all when I say we aren't comfortable with you manipulating your son to carry out this attack."

"Thank you, Sir," English replied in a flat undertone. "I'll be totally honest with you and say I'm not entirely comfortable with it, either."

"We've searched the Arsuk base like you said," Captain Ogden told him. "You were right. The rebels are using it as a staging area for ships, supplies, and personnel, but they haven't mobilized. From what we can tell, the ships are all being kept in a state below combat readiness. The personnel are all either decommissioned or discharged. None of them is active duty."

English spun around. "How is that even possible? How can the rebels be bringing in discharged and decommissioned personnel?"

Ogden completely ignored his lapse in protocol. "Most of them are dishonorable discharges or decommissioned without cause, which means they were never officers or even enlisted in good standing. It looks like the insurgents have been recruiting former servicemen who have training but not the temperament to hold proper USF rank."

"We can still carry out a surprise attack on Arsuk, Sailor," Captain Gustav Colby of the *Marigold* interjected. He was much younger, but no less steady than English. "If you aren't absolutely committed to this course with your son, you shouldn't carry it out. We can still use Captain English's information from Ufa to benefit the loyalists. You don't have to do this."

"I want to do it, Sir," English replied. "I want to see Andy. I want to see for myself if he's really on the other side....and if seeing him will draw the *Buckingham Palace* and a few other rebel ships away from Earth, so much the better. The *Lightning Rod* might even be able to destroy a few of them into the bargain."

"It means putting the *Lightning Rod* in danger," Captain Caroline Kimmel from the *Battle Hardened* pointed out. She was at least twenty years older than English with short, curly white hair, but she was still active and as vital as ever. "The *Lightning Rod* will be alone against however many ships the rebels send out to meet you. We're already dangerously short of destroyers. We can't afford to lose another one."

"The *Lightning Rod* would be in danger if we *didn't* carry out this plan," Ogden replied. "She'd be facing an even bigger potential threat in the Arsuk attack. I'm with English on this one. I want to look these bastards in the face and see how they stand up to justify their actions."

"You won't be able to ask them about that," Radcliffe pointed out. "The whole point of this mission is to make them think the *Lightning Rod* wants to turn."

"We'll only have to pretend until we get on board," English pointed out. "Once we confront the *Buckingham Palace* staff, our fighter wings and the *Lightning Rod* will launch the attack and it will be all on."

"But you'll be ON the *Buckingham Palace*!" Captain Detrick exclaimed. "You'll be trapped on board with the enemy."

English shrugged. "It's the only way to trick them, Sir."

Detrick shook his head and looked away. "I don't like this, Sailor. I don't like it at all. It's a suicide mission."

"Don't count us out so easily, Sir," English replied. "I'd say it's more a high possibility rather than a certainty."

Detrick smacked his lips, but Captain Colby interrupted. "Exactly who are you planning to take over to the *Buckingham Palace* with you? You can't go alone if you want Captain English to believe this ruse."

English counted on his fingers. "There'll be me, Captain Ogden, Commander Radcliffe, Lieutenant Avila, and Master Chief Terranova. That should convince him."

Captain Detrick gasped so loud that half the assembled officers jumped. "You're out of your natural mind! That's four of our top officers—and you, Sailor—all in the line of fire. It's out of the question! Captain Kimmel is right. We can't afford to just throw away good people."

"Actually," Captain Ogden chimed in, "I support Gunny English's proposal completely. I think this is our best bet to weaken the rebels in a way they'll never expect. I think it's worth the risk."

"This is absolute madness, Georgia!" Captain Detrick rounded on Radcliffe. "For the love of Jesus, Matt! Talk some sense into these people."

"I agree with Gunny English and Captain Ogden," Radcliffe replied. "This plan is risky, but it's also a perfect way to hit the rebels where it hurts. Their whole insurgency depends on ship numbers. We already have them at a disadvantage. If we can whittle their numbers down even more, I think it will be worth it."

Detrick threw up his hand and spun away from the table. He stormed over to the big windows overlooking the Quad. He kept shaking his head and he didn't come back.

"We don't have to agree on the *Lightning Rod's* course," Captain Ogden went on. "You ten can carry out the attack on Arsuk according to our agreement. The *Lightning Rod* will go her own way."

"I don't like you going alone," Captain Leonard O'Shea of the *Outrigger* remarked. "It would be just as easy for another ship to go with you. Then you wouldn't have to face the *Buckingham Palace* alone. It would go a lot easier for you when the shooting starts."

"If we tell Andy we have two ships that both want to turn," English pointed out, "it means the rebels will probably send out even more ships. They'll want to make sure they have enough in case we pull something exactly like this."

"But that means we'll have the chance to destroy or damage more of them," Captain Colby countered. "Isn't that what we want?"

English and Ogden both looked at each other at the same time. "Which other ship would come with us?" Ogden asked.

"*Battle Hardened* could come with you," Captain Kimmel volunteered.

"Are you sure, Caroline?" Ogden asked. "I hate to put you in danger."

Captain Kimmel burst into a big, bright smile and her eyes sparkled. "It's really kind of you to say that, but we're at war. We all have to make sacrifices." Her gaze darted over to English and she smiled at him, too. Her face softened even more looking at him. "Like you said, *Battle*

Hardened will be in danger attacking Arsuk anyway. One risk is as good as another."

"I don't suppose any of us will be in any better position once the shooting starts," Captain Colby remarked. "As soon as we hit Arsuk, every man and his dog is gonna know what we're up to."

"That just means the rebels will have to send out more ships to stop us," Radcliffe told her. "It will weaken the rebel force so the insurgents can't defend themselves against the loyalists on Earth.... which is also what we want."

"Then we're all agreed?" Captain Kimmel called over her shoulder to Captain Detrick. "Are you going to talk to us at all, Fletcher? We still need to coordinate the attack on Arsuk."

He came back to the table, but he didn't look happy. He kept glaring at everyone and fuming. "I just want to register my objection to this. I mean, I don't mean any disrespect for you and your plan, Sailor. It's just.... it's too risky."

"None of us wants to risk you, Sailor," Captain Colby added. "You're a national treasure."

English blushed and lowered his eyes to the tabletop. "Thank you, Sir."

"It's because of stunts like this that we respect you so much," Captain Kimmel replied. "You wouldn't be the Sailor English we all know and love if you didn't come up with risky projects like this."

"But his projects always seem to work, don't they?" Captain O'Shea chimed in. "If he can't pull it off, no one can."

"There's a first time for everything, Sir," English replied. "Any objections you have to this plan are more than welcome. I'm grateful for them."

He addressed this directly to Captain Detrick, but Detrick didn't respond.

"In that case, we can get to planning. The *Lightning Rod* and *Battle Hardened* will go out to meet the *Buckingham Palace* and whoever she brings with her." Captain Kimmel turned to English. "Which means, Sailor, that you'll need to contact your son."

Chapter 23

E nglish entered his quarters, sat down at his desk, and stared at his computer for a long time, but he didn't turn it on. Something terrible happened every time he turned it on.

This time was bound to be the worst yet. He finally got what he wanted. Now he had no choice but to contact Andy.

English stared at the blank screen for what seemed like hours. He told himself a thousand times to just do it and get it over with, but he still couldn't force himself to turn on the damn computer.

What should he say to Andy? English would have to choose his words very carefully.

For a start, Andy would never believe that English wanted to turn to the rebel cause—not ever. That was too far-fetched. Andy just wouldn't buy it under any circumstances, so English would have to come up with some other elaborate fiction.

This would be the first time in thirty years that English ever lied to one of his kids, but not even that particularly bothered him. If Andy turned to the other side, English would do a lot worse than lie to him.

He would lure Andy into a trap where Andy, his ship, and all his crew would be utterly destroyed. That was the very least a traitor like him deserved.... if it was true.

That was the real problem. English wouldn't know it was true until *after* he lured Andy into a trap. English wouldn't know until he looked into Andy's eyes.

That wouldn't be until English and the other officers were already on board the *Buckingham Palace*.

None of that really meant anything, though. The *Buckingham Palace* came out from Earth to attack the *Lightning Rod* and the *Solar Flare*.

Andy knew by then that English had been posted to the *Lightning Rod*. He knew he was attacking the ship where his father served and Andy did it anyway.

No one could deny that the *Buckingham Palace* was in the enemy ranks, so why didn't English spring his trap—the trap he set based on Dan's information? He planned this. He wanted this, but he still didn't act on it.

If he kept thinking about it, he never would. Time was running out. He had to do it now or the whole plan would fall through.

He didn't give himself a second to think about it. He thrust out his hand and hit the power button. The computer switched on and booted up.

Once he got started, English went through the time-worn routine without considering again. He hailed the *Buckingham Palace*, which was in orbit at the Chronos Docking Station attached to the Borealis Satellite.

English scowled at the screen when he read the names of the other rebel destroyers docked at the station along with the *Buckingham Palace*.

Afrikaans. Isaac Newton. Fiji. Octopus. Copernicus.

The whole rowdy gang had taken over the Borealis Satellite. The bastards must be planning to use it as a jumping-off point in their quest to conquer the wider solar system.

That meant they planned to come out against the destroyers at the Mars repair shop at some point. The rebels might be arming for that very thing right now.

The communications system blinked on and English entered a communique for Captain Andrew Carter English.

Andy flashed onto the screen. He couldn't look more different from his older brother, Dan. Andy had bright red hair and deep green eyes. His skin was much paler than Dan's and the carpet of freckles across Andy's nose and cheeks hadn't faded with age.

Not that Andy was old. He was only twenty-five. He'd only been a captain for a year, so why did the Command Staff promote him to the *Buckingham Palace*?

The Force had plenty of much more seasoned captains and Dan said the Command Staff promoted Andy suddenly.

Appointments like that usually took weeks or even months of accepting applications for transfer or promotion. Then the Command Staff took even longer while they considered all the applicants and selected the most qualified candidate.

English could only think of one reason why the Command Staff would bump Andy up the chain of command so quickly. The rebel officers embedded within the Command Staff must have pushed him up. They must have orchestrated his assignment to get one of their own on the *Buckingham Palace* at the last minute. It was the only logical explanation.

English and his son regarded each other for a long, silent moment as soon as the link established. English did his best to read Andy's expression, but Andy kept his countenance absolutely neutral.

He didn't go cold and distant and unreachable the way Dan did. Andy just looked back at English while Andy waited for English to say something.

Andy finally said, "Hey, Dad."

"Hey, son," English replied.

"How's life on the *Lightning Rod*?"

English shrugged. "Pretty standard. Nothing to report."

"Except that we're at war with each other on opposite sides, right? What's on your mind, Dad?"

English sighed. He should have known Andy wouldn't beat around the bush. He never did. "My captain asked me to contact you. She wants to turn."

Andy's eyes shot wide open. "Is that so?"

English looked away from the screen. He didn't have to pretend very hard how uncomfortable this conversation made him. "Yeah. The *Battle Hardened* wants to come over, too."

Andy frowned. "This is highly out of order."

"Yeah, I know. Maybe you could put them in touch with the right people."

"Ogden wasn't acting like she wanted to turn when she destroyed the *Hermes*."

"I don't make the rules, son. I'm just a lowly gunnery sergeant on the flight deck. I just do what I'm told."

Andy burst out laughing. "Since when?"

"Since I got out here. I wouldn't be contacting you at all if she didn't tell me to. I don't think I have to tell you that."

Andy's smile drained and his features went hard and mean. "So she told you to contact me?"

"Do you honestly think I would be saying this if she didn't?"

Andy wrinkled his nose and looked down at something on his desk. "No, I don't. I'm surprised you agreed to it at all."

"Well, you know what ship captains are like. She can be very persuasive when she wants to be."

"I don't know Ogden at all. What about Kimmel? What made her decide to turn?"

"Neither of them gave me their reasons. They want to meet you at the Io Center in three days."

Andy frowned again. "That's October 16."

English kept his tone flat. "Do you have plans for then?"

"No. We can do that."

"Don't you need to check with your superiors first?"

Andy turned to something else off the screen. "I'm just checking the roster now. I can come out with the *Foresight* and the *Starlet*....and maybe a few others." His eyes kept darting around at different things reading something. "What about the other destroyers who are at the Mars repair shop with you? Won't they try to stop Kimmel and Ogden from leaving?"

"No one knows about this. There's just me and the two captains. They've kept it secret from everyone else."

Andy made another face. "Of course they have. Don't tell me Matt Radcliffe is going along with this. He would remove Ogden from command before he let her turn."

"She plans to remove him first." English anticipated this and came up with a plausible excuse days ago. "She plans to transfer him to another ship before we leave the shop."

Andy furrowed his brow even deeper. "I'm surprised *you* don't try to remove her from command. That's the kind of thing I would expect from you."

English looked away again. He couldn't hold his son's gaze. "I'm not that man anymore, son."

Andy's voice betrayed the slightest bite. "I can see that."

"There are a bunch of rebel fighters lurking around Titan," English went on. "Why don't you get them to come into the Io Center at the same time?"

Andy nodded. "We could do that. We'll escort the *Lightning Rod* and the *Battle Hardened* back to Earth under guard so those chumps at the repair shop don't get any ideas about stopping us."

"Sounds good."

Andy fell silent again. He didn't speak for so long that insatiable curiosity drew English's gaze back to the screen.

"Have you heard from Dan and Melanie, Dad?" Andy asked.

English hesitated. Should he say he'd heard from Dan? Did that question mean Andy knew about the information Dan sent in his letter?

"I've spoken to Dan," English finally said. "I haven't heard from Melanie. Have you?"

Andy shook his head. "Communications with the Command Center are still down, but the word on the street is that the Command Center Hospital is still undamaged and operational."

"That's what Dan said."

This conversation was becoming mechanical and meaningless. English wanted to cut it off. He wanted to be anywhere and doing anything other than talking to his son, now that English finally did what he said he would do.

He forced himself to make eye contact with his son. "Thank you for doing this, son."

Andy held English's gaze and didn't look away even for a second. "I know you don't approve of what I'm doing, Dad. You don't have to pretend."

English heaved another almighty sigh. "I wish I could say I did, son."

"I hope someday you'll understand why I'm doing this. I hope when this is all over, you'll understand enough to be proud of me again."

English's throat constricted. He could barely make himself heard getting the next words out. "I want that more than anything, son."

Andy didn't even blink. He showed no emotion. "I'll see you in a few days, Dad. Hopefully then we'll be fighting on the same side."

Andy cut the line and English stared again into the blank screen. His son was gone, probably forever. English would never be proud of Andy ever again. His own son—a traitor.

Chapter 24

"I'm telling you I've searched everywhere," Janacek insisted. He and the other pilots assembled on their side of the *Lightning Rod's* flight deck. "Gunny English is nowhere on the whole damn station."

"He has to be somewhere, dumbass," Babbitt countered. "The man didn't just up and vanish."

"You heard what Gunny said," Thorpe added. "He said he'd be keeping an eye on us this week and he hasn't been back on the station for three days."

"I swear to God, if they did something to him, I'll tear somebody apart," Ritchie snarled, "Captain Ogden better not have done anything to him or by Christ I'll find a way to make her pay."

"Do you think he reported us to her?" Manheim squeaked. "Do you think he reported that fight and got us in trouble?"

"No one got *you* in trouble," Racer told her. "You weren't involved in the fight."

"If he didn't report us, why is Commander Radcliffe hanging around all the time? He's been watching us a hell of a lot more closely than Gunny English ever did." Ezra Duran turned to Stoval. "Have you seen Gunny English anywhere, Auggie? You've been all over this station. You've seen more than any of us."

Stoval shook his head. "No, I haven't seen him anywhere."

"Someone reporting that we got in a fight doesn't explain why Gunny English just disappeared off the face of the Earth," Janacek pointed out. "He should have at least been around keeping an eye on us. He said he was going to get a lot tougher on us, not disappear."

"He would only disappear like this if something happened to him," Thorpe replied. "I'm with Ritchie. I say we find out if the captain removed him or something. That's exactly the kind of bullshit she'd pull on him. She hates him."

"So what do you think you're going to do, asshole?" Racer countered. "You can't just barge into her office and start demanding answers. Besides, if we had a new CO, we would know about it."

"How could we have a new CO if we didn't even have one before English came?" Ezra argued. "If she removed him, we'd be back to being on our own."

"So, if we're on our own, how are we supposed to fight the enemy?" Manheim asked. "What are we supposed to do if we get the call-up?"

"I think we should talk to Lieutenant Eismann," Racer suggested. "He'll tell us what's going on and what we're supposed to do."

"Yeah! Great idea!" Janacek pointed at Racer. "You can talk to him, Racer."

"Yeah," Ritchie agreed. "Go on. Then you can tell us what's up."

"Me?!" Racer exclaimed. "I'm not going to talk to Lieutenant Eismann. Are you out of your minds?"

"You're the most confident," Manheim pointed out. "You're the best choice, Racer."

"No way!" she countered. "I'm not the most confident. Send Thorpe or Duran. I'm nobody."

An argument started to break out when the elevator opened. No one noticed until Gunny English halted right behind Janacek. "Howdy, folks."

"Gunny!" Racer gasped. "Where the hell have you been?"

"I've been right here, Airman. Where did you think I was?"

"We were worried sick about you, Sir," Manheim piped up. "We thought you'd be out for blood after the boys got in that fight, and then, when we didn't see you and Commander Radcliffe kept hanging around...."

"So you wanted me to ride your asses?" English laughed. "Okay. Your wish is my command."

The other pilots relaxed, but Racer couldn't stop frowning at him. He looked haggard and tired. Where had he really been during the last three days?

He always hung around the mess, the flight deck, and since the crew went on shore leave, he'd been shadowing them everywhere. He didn't just vanish for no reason and now he turned up looking ten years older.

"Are we deploying, Sir?" Ezra asked. "The whole station is crawling with rumors."

"Yeah, we're deploying. That's why I'm here. You need to know the plan."

Racer frowned even deeper. "So you just came down here to talk to us because we're about to deploy?"

He didn't even look at her. "Here's what's going to happen. I'm going off the ship for a while. You folks are going out under Gunny Frasier. I won't be with you."

More gasps went through the group and several jaws dropped including Racer's. "Why not?" Duran asked. "Why aren't you going out with us?"

"Because I'm going on another mission. I'm helping Captain Ogden and Commander Radcliffe with something."

"What is it?" Thorpe asked.

"I can't tell you. It's classified."

Janacek stiffened and Ritchie shut his mouth to glare at English. "You better damn well tell us why you aren't going out with us. We have a right to know."

"You watch your tone, Airman," English countered. "Keep it respectful."

"He's right, Sir," Ezra argued. "If we're going out with another gunny, we have a right to understand why."

English tried to scowl back at them and then wilted. He didn't snap with his usual authority and his eyes had lost their luster. Racer started to have a very bad feeling about what he was going to say.

"If I tell you," he began, "it means you have to stay on board for the rest of your shore leave. We can't run the risk that you might let something slip to the wrong person. Are you all prepared to cancel your shore leave if I tell you what's really going on?"

The pilots exchanged glances and then Thorpe nodded. "Yes. We'll stay on board until we deploy."

English heaved a shaky sigh. He looked more drained by the second. "It's like this. We cooked up this plan.... actually *I* cooked up this plan. We signaled the rebels that we wanted to turn to their side...."

"What?!" Ezra bellowed. "You what? You didn't!"

English held up his hands. "Just listen to me for a second, okay? This is hard enough as it is."

Ezra muttered a few curses under his breath.

"We aren't turning, okay?" English went on. "It's a ruse. It's a trap to lure the *Buckingham Palace* and a few other ships away from Earth.

There's a big loyalist offensive going on and us loyal ships at the repair shop are jumping in."

"We better be," Babbitt chimed in.

English let out another long breath. Every word seemed to cost him more than he could stand. "Once we get them in position at the Io Center, the *Lightning Rod* and the *Battle Hardened* will attack and destroy or damage as many of them as we can."

"Yes!" Ritchie punched his fist into his palm. "That's what I'm talking about!"

A few more people nodded and whispered to each other, but English held up his hands again. "The *Buckingham Palace*....my son is the captain. That's how we communicated to the rebels that we wanted to turn."

Dead silence fell over the group and Racer's heart sank. That explained why English was so off his game. Any sane person would be.

"Captain Ogden and I are going over to the *Buckingham Palace* with a couple other bridge officers—supposedly to negotiate our betrayal of the loyalist cause. Once we get over there and make our appearance, the *Lightning Rod* and the *Battle Hardened* will attack along with both squadrons...."

"Hold it right there, Gunny," Racer cut in. "Just hold the goddamn phone. Are you seriously saying we have to attack the *Buckingham Palace* while you and the bridge staff are still on board?"

"Yes. That's what I'm saying."

"No goddamn way!" Racer snapped. "Forget it! We won't go out."

The rest of the pilots started protesting, too. Their voices rose until English raised both hands this time. "Quiet!" he roared.

The crew fell silent instantly, but Racer's mind kept coming up with one excuse after another why she wouldn't let this happen.

No way would she fire on a ship with him on it. She would resign first. Firing on the enemy was one thing. She wouldn't fire on him. Nothing could make her.

English straightened up. He didn't look as friendly and approachable as he did before. He looked terrible and dangerously determined.

"Now listen up. This is war. Understand? These people are our enemies. They're trying to destroy everything we hold dear and everything we swore to protect. Do you hear me? Aliens aren't as bad as these people. These assholes are destroying our world from the inside. The rebels swore an oath to protect Earth against any enemy and then they were the ones who attacked us. They deserve to die—every last stinking one of them. Understand?"

No one answered. A few of the pilots shuffled their feet and Manheim looked down at the floor.

English's voice started shaking. "My own son is on that ship. I would shoot him in the face if it meant stopping these bastards, and if I can do that, you can damn well fire on the ship from the outside. Don't you even dare go out there and pull any punches on the *Buckingham Palace* just because I'm on board. Understand? To hell with me! I don't give a damn about me! You shoot and you shoot to kill. Is that clear? You go out there and blow the ship straight to hell if you can."

His whole body trembled now. Racer's eyes hurt from looking at him, but she couldn't look away. His eyes had gone bloodshot and his lips went white. He looked like some kind of angel of vengeance on Earth's enemies.

Ezra broke the silence by murmuring under his breath. "Yes, Sir. If you're doing all that, we'll do our duty on the outside. You don't worry about us."

"I expect each and every one of you to give Gunny Frasier your very best service," English went on. "If you all do your jobs, the captain and I will have the best chance of getting off the ship alive. Understand?"

A few people nodded and Thorpe, Stoval, and Ritchie all said, "Yes, Sir."

Racer's eyes stung and she felt herself shaking, too. She couldn't cry—not now—not when English was holding himself together so well under the worst conditions imaginable.

She couldn't imagine anything worse than what he must be going through. Ezra had his brother on the same ship, but this....

English deserved her best. She couldn't run away and quit, not when he was doing this for the cause. If he could put himself through something as awful as this, she could definitely fire on the enemy That was the least she could do.

The others all gazed up at him and the cloud hanging over their crew lifted. They all knew what they had to do.

English passed his hand across his eyes. "Anyway...now you know. Now you all better go back upstairs. I don't know when the call-up will come to deploy. Just remember your promise and don't go out onto the station again. Stay here, okay?"

A few people said, "Yes, Sir." He nodded and walked back to the elevator.

"Damn!" Thorpe breathed as soon as English was gone.

"God! Poor Gunny!" Janacek exclaimed. "This is off the chain."

"Did he really say he was the one who came up with the idea?" Manheim piped.

"That's what he said," Babbitt replied. "God damn, that man is staunch! I never met anyone as staunch as him."

"He's a goddamn hero!" Ezra added. "He's got a list of decorations as long as my arm. He's a damn legend in the Force."

"He is?" Thorpe asked. "How come we never heard of him before?"

"Everybody's heard of him," Ezra replied. "My brothers grew up worshiping the guy. Sailor English is like some kind of saint in the Force."

"I guess now we know why," Janacek remarked. "Who would come up with a plan to trap their own son? Gunny English is a freakin' monster!"

"Why the hell didn't you tell us, Duran?" Thorpe countered. "How could you keep this from us all this time?"

Ezra shrugged. "I guess I thought everybody already knew. You can't spit in the Force without hitting someone who worships the ground he walks on."

"Captain Ogden doesn't worship the ground he walks on," Racer pointed out. "She hates his guts. I wouldn't be surprised if she has something to do with this."

"You just heard him say he came up with the idea himself," Babbitt replied. "If you believe him, she's the one going along with what he already wants to do. Maybe she's coming around about him."

"You can't blame her for resenting him." Everyone turned around to stare at Stoval. This was the most anyone could remember hearing him say in one sitting. "Can you imagine being captain of your own ship and then he shows up posted to fighter wing gunnery sergeant? She probably thought he was here to take her command."

Janacek frowned and rubbed his chin. "I guess it would kinda throw her off."

Ezra turned to his fighter craft. "It looks like we're going out against the *Buckingham Palace*."

"I'll blow 'em to kingdom come!" Ritchie snarled. "I'll kick some people's ass if it means it gives him a chance to come back."

"He wants us to do more than kick some people's ass," Racer replied. "He wants us to destroy the ship....as in, blow it up. Ka-boom."

No one laughed. Ezra nodded. "That's right. We'll give that ship hell for him."

"No way!" Manheim yelped. "How can you guys even talk like this? How can you even think about destroying the ship with Gunny English on board?"

"You heard what he said, Manheim," Babbitt argued. "He wants us to."

"I don't care what he wants!" Her voice rose to a shriek. "I'm not leaving him over there. I can't believe you're even thinking of going along with this."

"So what are we supposed to do?" Thorpe asked. "He'd be the first to bump us out of the service if we don't follow orders."

"We're going to rescue him!" Manheim squeaked. "Of course we're going to rescue him. We aren't leaving him over there to die! I'm not, at least."

She shot such a venomous glare at her crewmates that even Racer cringed.

"How can we rescue him when we're the ones who are supposed to destroy the ship?" Thorpe asked. "If we don't attack the *Buckingham Palace* according to orders, she might destroy the *Lightning Rod*. We couldn't let that happen."

Manheim squared her shoulders. In a way, straightened up and flashing her eyes at her comrades made her look ridiculous, but no one laughed.

"I'm going to talk to Gunny Frasier," she snapped. "I'm going to make him see sense. He won't let Gunny English die over there, and if

Gunny Frasier agrees with this plan, we won't be disobeying orders at all."

She stalked off toward the other side of the flight deck. Frasier and some of the Wing 10 pilots were working over there and Manheim disappeared behind the ranks of fighter craft.

Chapter 25

Commander Radcliffe gazed through the window at four enormous destroyers hovering in space. "Is it me or do they keep getting bigger by the day?"

"I guess the rebels aren't taking any chances," English replied.

"Four against two. Not the best odds I can think of."

"Better than ten against two. It could be worse."

Radcliffe burst out laughing. "I remember you saying that a lot when you were captain of the *Siskiyou*. That was your damn catchphrase." He put on a low, gruff voice and made a ridiculous face. "'Count your blessings, Lieutenant. Things can always get worse.'"

English had to laugh along with the joke. It was the first time he had felt like laughing since he talked to Andy to arrange this meeting.

English had locked himself in his quarters and barely come out to get food. He didn't want to see or talk to anyone. He barely managed to get through briefing his fighter wing pilots before going back to his hole.

English started to feel more human now that he was here talking to Radcliffe. Things couldn't possibly get any worse than they were right now. It gave him hope.

Even knowing that his pilots would be targeting the *Buckingham Palace* trying to destroy the ship made him feel better. He trusted them to do their duty. They knew what was at stake.

He and Radcliffe turned together and gazed out at the four destroyers. The *Foresight*, the *Starlet*, and the *Restless* all accompanied the *Buckingham Palace* to the Io Center.

The four enemy ships made the *Lightning Rod* and the *Battle Hardened* look puny by comparison even though all six ships were the same size.

"Do you think you'll make it back alive?" Radcliffe asked.

"I doubt it, but if we destroy a few of them, it will be worth it."

Radcliffe stuck out his hand. "It's been an honor to serve with you, Sir. It's been the honor of my career."

English shook his hand and genuinely smiled at his young friend. "The honor is all mine, Matt. You're one of the finest officers I've ever served with. I wish you were going over there with me. I wouldn't want anyone else at my side today."

Radcliffe's cheeks glowed with pride and he opened his mouth to say something else when the conference room door opened. Captain Ogden came in followed by Avila and Terranova.

"Are you ready to go, Gunny?" the captain asked.

"Yes, Ma'am."

Ogden went back outside and the four men followed her to the elevator. They rode downstairs in silence.

Radcliffe went with them even though he wasn't going to the *Buckingham Palace*. Captain Ogden and the other loyalist captains had doctored their duty rosters to make it look like Ogden had transferred Radcliffe to another ship when he'd still be on the *Lightning Rod* and commanding the destroyer in Captain Ogden's place.

The five of them stopped when they came to the flight deck. All three squadron fighter wings and dozens of other crewmen lined the deck. "Attention!" Charlie Frasier bellowed and everyone present snapped upright.

English's pulse skipped a beat when he saw his pilots dressed in impeccable uniforms and standing ramrod straight with their crewmates. None of them breathed.

Captain Ogden stepped forward. She, English, and the two bridge officers had to file between the ranks to get to Captain Ogden's transport craft, the *Aftermath*. "Salute!" Frasier roared and all the assembled crewmen saluted.

English stood up straighter. The whole crew was betting on him.

Captain Ogden climbed through the *Aftermath's* rear hatch and the three men boarded after her. Avila took the helm and started to close the hatch while English, Ogden, and Terranova buckled into their seats.

English heard Frasier give the order, "Deploy!" just before the hatch clanged shut. The next instant, Avila fired the engines and the *Aftermath* lifted off the deck.

English fastened his safety harness. He couldn't see what was going on back on the flight deck and he didn't want to see. His heart was having trouble keeping a steady rhythm and he had to continually remind himself to breathe.

He was on his way to the *Buckingham Palace* to see Andy. What happened after that was anybody's guess, but he knew one thing for certain now. He wouldn't be coming back to the *Lightning Rod* alive.

That presentation he just witnessed was the crew's official farewell to him. He did his best to prepare them for the battle ahead. Now they had to fight it on their own.

Andy was waiting for him. English's battle would start when he came face to face with his traitor son. Nothing mattered before or after that moment.

Avila did something on the controls in front of him and, against his will, English saw people racing all over the flight deck behind him. Pilots charged to their birds to load up and stand by to deploy. Heat and venting gas blasted across the desk.

Mechanics rushed from one craft to the next making last-minute adjustments. English's eyes migrated to Wing 17. All his pilots were already loaded up and ready to rock—all except him.

His own fighter sat cold and dead on its pad. He wouldn't be going out with his crew the way he should be. He should be with them. He should be leading them into battle instead of sitting here doing nothing.

Avila floated through the launch bay doors and the *Lightning Rod* dropped away. The *Aftermath* drifted past the *Battle Hardened*. Captain Kimmel's transport came out to join the *Aftermath* and both ships headed for the *Buckingham Palace*

The next minute, the *Battle Hardened* vanished and nothing remained but the *Buckingham Palace*.

The *Aftermath* migrated toward the destroyer. Avila steered around her to the flight deck and the destroyer swallowed both transports.

Fifteen people stood across the empty deck with Captain Andrew Carter English at the very center. His XO stood behind him on one side and his Master Chief stood on the other. Every single one of the *Buckingham Palace* staff was armed.

The whole world vanished except for English and Andy. An invisible force stronger than gravity pulled them toward each other. Time stood still as the *Aftermath* came to land in front of the *Buckingham Palace* staff.

Captain Ogden unbuckled her harness, stood up, and stared through the *Aftermath's* front window. "Well, this is it," she breathed. "I guess we have no choice but to go out there and talk to them."

English's fingers automatically unclipped his buckle. He couldn't hear or see anything but Andy's eyes burning into his soul from a dozen yards away. In a few short seconds, English would be standing right in front of his son.

He startled out of his skin when Ogden touched his arm. English spun around to find the rest of the party waiting for him. English had to tear his gaze away from Andy to walk out of the hatch with the others.

Avila and Terranova positioned themselves behind Ogden and English. Now nothing stood between English and Andy. English lost awareness of Ogden at his side and of Captain Kimmel and her staff joining them.

English advanced to meet his son. They were completely alone in the universe.

"How you doing, Dad?" Andy asked.

English nodded. "Good enough. You?"

"Pretty good." Andy looked away toward Ogden. "Captain."

"Thank you for meeting me, Captain English," she replied. "I realize this is unusual."

"This whole situation is unusual." Andy's eyes flicked through the *Lightning Rod* group. "You came unarmed. I'm surprised."

"We had no reason to come armed," Ogden replied. "Your father told me you planned to escort us back to Earth, so we'd be perfectly safe. Am I right?"

Andy nodded. "Right. What made you decide to turn?"

Ogden did something next to English that he didn't see. He couldn't look away from Andy.

"Someone on Earth contacted me—someone I trust," she said. "That first battle took us all by surprise, but after it was all over.... when we were on Europa.... someone contacted me. I won't say who, but I changed my mind about the whole thing. It got me thinking....and then, when I was at the repair shop, Caroline and I had a few conversations.... I guess you could say it was an ongoing process, but it made sense."

English had to marvel at her nerve. She must have expected this question and put a lot of thought into how she would answer it.

English never had to think about that because Andy would never believe English wanted to turn. Andy had to keep believing even now that English was against this whole move and that he was just going along with his captain.

Andy turned to Kimmel. "What about you, Captain? What made you decide to turn?"

Kimmel shrugged. "It's like Georgia says. Certain people.... you could say they can be very persuasive."

"Well, I guess we don't need to stand on formality," Andy went on. "If you come on board, I'll brief you and then we can arrange how we're going to...."

A low boom rocked the destroyer and everyone looked around. A second and a third blow struck the ship and then the deafening siren blared overhead. "Battle stations! All fighter wings—prepare to launch! Battle stations! All fighter wings—prepare to launch!"

Andy's head snapped around and his eyes locked straight on English. Now Andy knew.

English reacted on pure adrenaline. He charged a young woman at the far end of the *Buckingham Palace* group, punched her square in the face, and she buckled at the knees.

English caught her weapon as she fell, pivoted the rifle to his shoulder, and wheeled around to aim the weapon straight at Andy.

Andy grabbed for the sidearm at his hip, but at that moment, another gun went off somewhere and someone charged between English and his son.

A different man tackled Andy out of the way, and a second later, dozens of pilots burst out of the stairwell. They covered the whole flight deck with more mechanics, officers, and maintenance crewmen rushing everywhere.

The flight deck dissolved in chaos as fighter craft fired up their engines and gunshots erupted all over the place.

Half the *Buckingham Palace* staff scrambled to get through the mob to the stairs. The other half yanked their weapons to gun down the *Lightning Rod* and *Battle Hardened* staff, but nobody could hit anyone with all the fighter wing personnel running around.

English lost sight of Andy in the chaos. English searched everywhere, but he didn't see his son anywhere until he spotted Andy's red hair flash in a sea of bodies.

Andy's XO and another officer were trying to hustle Andy to the stairs, but more pilots coming down blocked their path.

English charged forward cramming his rifle into his shoulder. He took aim, but other people kept interfering.

He stalked closer by the second, but the next time he got a clear shot, a devastating impact rocked the *Buckingham Palace*. The ship lurched and English stumbled to catch his balance.

In that moment when he took his eye off his target, Andy and his staff disappeared into the stairwell.

English hesitated. Fighter craft kept launching all around him. Some of Andy's bridge staff stalked through the flight deck searching for the loyalist officers who betrayed them.

Another concussion shook the *Buckingham Palace* and a high-pitched scream of a woman's voice set English's hair on end. He glanced toward the sound to see Captain Ogden ducking behind an unused fighter craft.

Three *Buckingham Palace* officers surrounded the bird trying to trap her. One of them fired and the shot pinged off the bird's landing gear.

English made a split-second decision, shouldered his rifle, and fired on the man. The guy toppled and the other two officers rounded on him.

English got off one more shot before they came after him. He bolted for another row of unused fighters and the two officers hounded him all the way with repeated gunshots.

He fired behind him and skidded from one fighter to the other, until he came to the end of the row. The launch bay stood open to the stars with just the EM field protecting English from the vacuum of space. He had nowhere left to run.

He stole a peek behind the last fighter and his heart sank. Dozens of security guards flooded the flight deck. They spread out and more of them came toward him. He couldn't get away.

He fired a few more times and took cover behind the craft again. He was just thinking about how he could get in it and fly away when someone opened fire from his other side.

Captain Ogden stormed across the deck laying down a carpet of shots. She drew the enemy away from English and they all went after her again. She veered back into her hiding place, but there was nowhere to hide.

English took his chance, scrambled up into the cockpit of the nearest bird, and fired up the engines. The security guards didn't notice another fighter preparing to launch.

He wound up the engines and lifted off the deck just a few inches before he opened up his cannons. He wheeled the bird in all directions, mowed down security guards, and detonated the last few fighter craft on the other side. He sent the enemy running, but he still had one last job to do.

He cleared the deck and stood guard with his cannons aimed at the squadron commander's desk. The man huddled behind his computers not daring to look out. Bodies covered the flight deck.

Captain Ogden peeked out of her hiding place and English waved to her. He pointed to the *Aftermath* and looked around for Captain Kimmel, but he didn't see her anywhere.

Lieutenant Avila snuck out from somewhere, too, and under English's protection, he and Ogden charged for the *Aftermath*.

Chapter 26

The *Aftermath* eased off the flight deck and drifted toward the launch bay doors to leave the *Buckingham Palace*. English gunned his engines, but at that moment, another batch of security guards charged out of the stairwell.

They brought cannons with them this time and leveled them at the *Aftermath*. The first shot hit the starboard wing and tore it off. The little transport staggered and its starboard side crashed down on the deck while the port side stayed aloft.

English ripped his stick sideways. He hammered the security detail with plasma, but before he could get over there to defend the *Aftermath*, another punishing jet of fire hit his bird from behind.

He tried to correct and face the three fighter craft hovering beyond the launch bay doors. The enemy fighters whirled in the stars outside and more plasma erupted from blazing guns all over the place. Was the *Lightning Rod* foundering under the rebel counterassault?

He wheeled to defend himself when another blow struck his bird's underside. The ship flipped up and a third shot smashed his wing to pieces. The fighter crashed down on the deck and the emergency overload alarm screeched in his ears.

He scrambled to get out of his cockpit. One enemy fighter bombarded him with shot after shot while the other two turned their guns on the *Aftermath*.

English sprang to the floor just as his craft exploded. He took off running, but he had nowhere left to run. The security detail hammered the *Aftermath* and she slumped the rest of the way to the floor. The hatch didn't open and no one came out.

The security detail split in two with half advancing on the *Aftermath* and the other half going after English. He tried to pull the same trick, but he was all out of ideas.

One enemy bird peeled off to return to the battle. The other two stayed in position while the security detail covered the flight deck. No sound or engine noise came from the *Aftermath*.

The security detail approached the hatch. Six guards covered it with their weapons while another unlocked it from the outside.

The hatch purred open, and at that moment, a catastrophic explosion ripped through the flight deck. Four more fighters unloaded from outside the launch bay. The two enemy fighters went up in flames as Thorpe, Ezra Duran, Racer, and Stoval crawled inside.

The security detail swung their guns toward the noise, and at the same instant, gunfire belched from inside the *Aftermath*. It cut the security guys down and left the deck clear.

English sprinted for the *Aftermath* and waved Ogden and Avila out. "Let's go! Move out!"

All three took off running for the fighter craft coming in to land. The pilots wheeled and cracked their cockpit covers to take the three passengers on board.

English boosted Captain Ogden into Thorpe's bird and then English climbed in behind Stoval. "Go, Auggie! Beat it back to the *Lightning Rod* on the double."

"We got a minor problem, Captain," Thorpe announced. "We're getting slaughtered out here!"

Captain Ogden took over his communications system. "Get us out of here, Matt! Break off, *Battle Hardened!* Fall back on Plan B!"

The four fighter craft tumbled out into space and English saw right away what Thorpe meant. The *Lightning Rod* and the *Battle Hardened* engaged in a pitched battle against the four enemy destroyers.

All their squadrons wheeled, somersaulted, and cartwheeled around each other in a blaze of plasma. None of the loyalist fighters could get near enough to the enemy to destroy even one of their ships.

The *Buckingham Palace* and the *Restless* pinned down the *Lightning Rod*. Wing 17 and most of Wing 10 went at the *Buckingham Palace* with all they had, but they couldn't make a dent in her enormous sides.

English read the battle in a second. "Break off, Wing 17! Charlie, bring your people over to the *Restless!*"

"What? No!" Racer exclaimed. "You said target the *Buckingham Palace!*"

"Change of plans. Gather your force and join up with the *Battle Hardened* squadron. Concentrate on one ship and you'll be able to destroy her."

"Will that work?" Ogden asked.

"Take a look," English replied. "Our squadron is focused on the *Buckingham Palace*. The *Battle Hardened* is focusing on the *Restless*. We need to combine our firepower on one ship. We can do it!"

Ogden switched back to the communications system. "Did you hear that, Matt? Draw your fire to the *Restless*. Forget the *Buckingham Palace!*"

The *Lightning Rod* and her squadron reacted instantly. The *Lightning Rod* ignored the *Buckingham Palace* and turned every cannon on the *Restless*. The two destroyers converged on their target and the *Lightning Rod* squadron plunged in for the attack.

"Let's go, Thorpe!" Ogden ordered. "Gunny English, bring your wing about and let's get this done."

"Pull it around, Auggie!" English ordered. "Racer—Duran—target the plasma core. Auggie and Thorpe will cover you."

"With pleasure, Sir," Ezra replied.

"Hey, Duran," Racer called. "You want to play a little game of ping-pong?"

"You're on." Ezra gunned his engines to the breaking point and both fighters swooped low toward the *Restless's* hull.

"What are they talking about?" Ogden asked.

"Just a little game we used to play on the *Siskiyou*. It spread through the Force and then......On your port side, Thorpe! Watch it, boy!"

"You bastard!" Thorpe bellowed and yanked hard to port to smash three enemy fighters who were targeting Racer and Ezra.

The two pilots didn't notice anything but their wild dive to destroy the *Restless*. They rocketed wingtip to wingtip. Their birds hugged the *Restless* so closely that none of the enemy fighters could touch them without hitting the ship.

Racer came within range of the hull section over the plasma core. She fired and Ezra copied her. They traded shots one after the other and the hull section buckled.

"One more time, you big badass!" Ezra called. "Bring it in nice and tight and we'll have her through!"

"Wing 10 is clearing off!" English added. "Get in there, Auggie! Let's see you do some damage."

"Oh, hell yeah!" Racer cheered. "Make way for strong, silent Stoval, Duran! He's gonna show us how it's done."

"Stand aside, you amateurs," Stoval told them. "Watch and learn."

Racer and Ezra hooted and then gunned it as never before. They whistled past the *Restless* shooting back and forth at the hull section. They plunged away into the battle again with Stoval hot on their heels.

"It's through!" Ezra yelled. "Finish it, Auggie!"

Stoval hunched low over his controls and pounded the hull section with dozens of shots before he zoomed off into the squadron.

"*Lightning Rod* and *Battle Hardened* squadrons—get away from the *Restless*!" English yelled. "Fall back to the *Lightning Rod*! All squadrons—fall back!"

Dozens of fighters catapulted out of the battle as the *Restless* staggered. Explosions rippled down her sides and the hull started to cave.

English lost sight of the ship as the *Lightning Rod* squadron returned to the destroyer. "*Lightning Rod*—break off!" Ogden ordered. "Alter course for Earth on the double!"

"Yes, Ma'am," Radcliffe replied. "*Battle Hardened* breaking off as well."

The *Lightning Rod* shrank away from the *Buckingham Palace*. The larger destroyer didn't advance. She was too busy trying to get clear of the *Restless* in time to avoid going up in flames herself.

The *Foresight* and the *Starlet* had the same problem and the *Battle Hardened* pulled away. The *Battle Hardened* and the *Lightning Rod* picked up speed as the other four destroyers scrambled to clear the area in time.

"Punch it, *Lightning Rod*!" Ogden ordered. "We got a date with the Arsuk base."

The *Lightning Rod* sprang forward to full speed and *Battle Hardened* launched a second later. Their squadrons raced at their sides on a dead course for Earth.

"Take us back to the *Lightning Rod*, Thorpe," Ogden told him. "We need Gunny English in the air with Wing 17 where he belongs and I need to get to the bridge."

"Yes, Ma'am." Thorpe hustled up to the *Lightning Rod* and eased onto the flight deck. It really was a superb piece of flying to coordinate both ships in full flight, but English would save his praise for later.

Thorpe and Racer dropped off Ogden and Avila before they took off and vanished outside. English sprang down from Stoval's cockpit and headed for his own bird when Ogden stopped him. "Thank you, English. You did it. You destroyed the *Restless*."

"I would have done more, Ma'am. I'm sorry we lost so many people."

"Never mind. There's still time to finish this." She waved toward his bird. "Your fighter wing needs you, Gunny."

"Yes, Ma'am. I'm going."

He jumped in and launched without a second thought. This whole ruse accomplished so little. He only hoped he could do some more serious damage at the Arsuk Base if the rest of the Mars group wasn't already there.

Chapter 27

Radcliffe stood up from the captain's chair when Captain Ogden entered the bridge. "Captain on the bridge!"

"At ease, Matt. Great work."

"Thank you, Ma'am. The Mars group is over Arsuk now."

"Any resistance?"

"Not yet. It looks like our trick worked. None of the ships on the ground are even powering up."

"Let's get after it, then."

Radcliffe stepped over to his own station and took the helm. The *Lightning Rod* and *Battle Hardened* were already well on course for Arsuk.

They crossed the asteroid field and passed the Mars repair shop. It was totally deserted of the other ten destroyers the *Lightning Rod* left there.

"*Marigold* and *Lone Ranger* are hammering the base!" Radcliffe reported. "*Outrigger* and *Flint* standing guard."

"Where are the others?"

Radcliffe checked his readouts. "They're on their way to Paris with the *Catherine the Great*. The enemy is going after the Command Center again!"

"How can they be? There's nothing left but the hospital."

Radcliffe shook his head. "The bombardment has already started, Ma'am. There's a whole contingent of loyal destroyers defending what's left of the Command Center."

"Get over there!" Ogden ordered. "*Battle Hardened*, break off to the Command Center! All squadrons—defend the hospital!"

"Yes, Ma'am!" English replied through the system.

Radcliffe pushed the engines to the breaking point and crossed the North Atlantic in a heartbeat.

The battle raging over the Command Center had grown to a massive cloud of destroyers pounding each other. Dozens of squadrons swirled in a confused tornado of combusting plasma and exploding ships.

Wing 17 put on speed and vanished into the cloud. The *Lightning Rod* and the *Battle Hardened* got there a second later. The whole scene descended into such a jumble of destruction and chaos that Radcliffe hesitated to engage.

He checked his controls for any ship he could engage with. Captain Ogden didn't say anything for a minute while she checked, too.

"The *Foresight* and the *Starlet* are coming in from Io," Radcliffe announced. "Holy crap, they're heading for the Refugee Center!"

"Intercept!" Ogden ordered. "Any sign of the *Buckingham Palace*?"

"Nothing yet. I'll...." He broke off as the first cannon blasts stuck the Refugee Center.

"*Lightning Rod* squadron—divert to the Refugee Center!" Ogden ordered.

"Who the hell do these bastards think they are?" Frasier snarled. "Aren't they the ones who signed a civilian defense pact?"

"These are the same people who attacked their own Command Center," English replied.

"Pull the same maneuver, Gunny," Ogden ordered. "All fighter wings—take out the *Starlet*."

"You heard the lady, boys," English called. "Destroy that ship!"

A cheer went up from the *Lightning Rod* squadron. Wing 17 wheeled hard to the rear and sprinted across Paris. They got to the Refugee Center first and vaulted straight upward into the atmosphere to meet the incoming enemy.

Radcliffe coordinated with the *Battle Hardened* and both destroyers took up a position over the building.

Lightning Rod and *Battle Hardened* squadrons surrounded the *Starlet*. The *Starlet* and the *Foresight* opened fire and their squadrons did their best to defend the *Starlet*.

The *Foresight* squadron charged the *Lightning Rod*. *Foresight* fighter craft split formation to attack both the *Lightning Rod* and the *Battle Hardened*.

The maneuver played right into the *Lightning Rod's* hands. With one squadron taking on both destroyers, the *Foresight* squadron couldn't do much against either.

The *Starlet* joined the *Foresight* trying to target both the *Lightning Rod* and the *Battle Hardened*, but with each destroyer fighting one other destroyer, none of them could make much headway.

The two loyalist squadrons overran the *Starlet's* fighter wings in seconds. Both squadrons ran rings around the *Starlet* while Racer and Ezra plunged in for another devastating game of ping-pong.

"She's going down fast, boys!" Ezra called. "Roll it back and let's go pay the *Foresight* a visit."

The *Starlet* started to flounder and the fighter pilots retreated back to the *Lightning Rod*. The *Foresight* didn't see the *Starlet* in trouble until it was too late.

"Pull back, *Battle Hardened!*" Ogden yelled. "We'll cover your retreat."

"The squadrons are attacking the *Foresight*, Ma'am!" Radcliffe reported. "Should we pull them back, too?"

"Too late!" Avila called. "It's Duran—he's hit the *Foresight* plasma core! God damn, what a shot!"

"Withdraw, Matt!" Ogden ordered.

"I'm...." Radcliffe didn't get the words out before the *Starlet* imploded and then a devastating shockwave hit the *Foresight*.

"We can't get out of the way in time!" Radcliffe shouted.

"All hands—brace for impact!" Ogden called, but even that was too late.

The shockwave struck the *Foresight* and the ship started to go down right on top of the Refugee Center. "Full assault!" Ogden roared. "Get in there, Matt! Destroy the *Foresight* before she crashes into the building!"

Radcliffe unloaded all batteries on the *Foresight*. He gunned the *Lightning Rod* as close as he dared to the plummeting destroyer and smashed all cannons into the plasma core.

She woofed in a catastrophic ka-boom and severed the *Lightning Rod's* starboard engine panel.

"The *Lightning Rod* is hit!" English called. "*Battle Hardened*, the *Lightning Rod* is foundering! All fighter wings—close to defend the *Lightning Rod*!"

"Copy that, Wing Leader 17," someone replied from the *Battle Hardened*. "Fall back to the Mars repair shop, *Lightning Rod*. We'll defend your retreat."

Radcliffe struggled to bring the *Lightning Rod* under control. "How bad is it, Matt?" Ogden asked.

Radcliffe gritted his teeth. "Pretty bad. She doesn't want to cooperate."

"She did great." Ogden scanned the battle raging all over Paris. "The loyalists are driving the enemy away from the hospital."

"Ma'am...." Avila began and then he transmitted readings to every station on the bridge.

Massive battles burst on the map over Antigua Guatemala and the Pyrenees base, but the loyalists were quickly falling under rebel reinforcements coming in from all over. The rebels had mounted a much bigger force than anyone anticipated.

"Jesus!" Radcliffe whispered. "We can't let them get away with this."

"We're stricken, Matt," Ogden countered. "We can't do anything but get out alive."

"Let us go, Ma'am," English offered. "Let us help out."

"Negative, Wing Leader 17. Fall in and retreat to the repair shop. We'll be back to fight another day."

English's tone changed, but he said, "Yes, Ma'am," anyway.

Radcliffe could only watch the offensive falling apart all over the planet. The loyalists did their best, but it wasn't enough to quash the insurgency. Whatever the United Space Force was going to do to bring this rebellion under control, it wouldn't happen today.

Chapter 28

E nglish stepped onto the flight deck and Lieutenant Eismann rushed him. "Holy shit, man! That was something else!"

English laughed. He couldn't believe he actually made it back alive. He could even accept that Andy escaped. English would get him another time.

A second later, Wing 17 came in to land. Ezra, Racer, Thorpe, Babbitt, Ritchie, and Janacek charged each other, collided, and exploded in laughter, shouts, and rapid talk. "Did you see that goddamn ping-pong?" Janacek crowed. "You plastered 'em, son!"

"Did you see the shockwave when the *Starlet* hit the *Foresight*?" Babbitt croaked. "I thought we were all dead."

"We did it!" Thorpe screamed. "We actually did it! We saved the Refugee Center."

Racer grabbed English. "You made it back, Sir! You're a hero! We destroyed the *Restless*! I didn't think we could do it, but we did."

English laughed again. He didn't seem to be able to stop. "Yeah. We did it."

The next minute, the rest of Wing 17 turned up followed by the other *Lightning Rod* fighter wings. All the pilots mobbed Wing 17 and everybody talked and congratulated each other at once. The pilots hugged, clapped each other on the back, and relived the most heart-stopping moments from all their battles.

Charlie Frasier waded into the mix. "Hey, you damn pilots! We're going over to the carnival to celebrate! Come on! Get off this damn ship and let the mechanics do their work."

Laughter answered him and the whole crew streamed off the flight deck. Lieutenant Eismann joined them. They went downstairs to the cargo hold to enter the Olympus Station. More *Lightning Rod* crewmen got swept up in the procession.

Frasier flanked English, but English could hardly hear a word anyone said. His pilots and a few from Wing 10 kept elbowing over to him, laughing, and talking to him. Their eyes shone and their faces glowed with pride in what they'd accomplished today.

They jostled down the concourse, and when they met the *Battle Hardened* squadron coming on shore, the atmosphere disintegrated into a real celebration.

The whole crowd flooded to the Quad and upstairs to an enormous carnival set up on the Olympus Station's 75th floor. Things really started getting out of hand once they got there with drinks flowing and someone started playing dance music.

The loyalists might not have won the battle today, but English couldn't ask for a better result. The *Lightning Rod* squadron took out three destroyers exactly the way they planned.

Then they singlehandedly saved the Refugee Center. That was pretty damn good for a bunch of punks most people didn't think were good enough to stay in the service at all.

Racer came over to English and shoved a beer bottle into his hand. He took a drink and relief spread through him. He made it back alive when he didn't think he would. His plan worked. He supposed he should be proud of himself for that.

Thorpe, Babbitt, Janacek, Ezra, and Ritchie surrounded him. They all laughed, blushed, and talked to each other in excited snatches. English braced himself for whatever they were planning to do to him, but at that moment, a hush went through the group.

It started over by the terrace and spread through the throng. A bunch of people parted as the silence took hold. The whole crowd pulled back and the laughter died as Captain Ogden, Commander Radcliffe, and Lieutenant Avila walked into the carnival.

All three officers looked way too serious considering the circumstances. They didn't smile or even look at anyone as they advanced into the crowd. All three of them fixed their gazes right on English.

The pilots shrank from them—all except Wing 17. They closed tighter around English and he sensed them tensing for another confrontation.

Ogden halted in front of English, but he didn't really feel like coming to attention or looking at a spot behind her head. He'd come too far not to look her in the eye.

"Gunny...." she began.

The beer bottle in his hand felt suddenly ice cold. "Ma'am?"

Captain Ogden glanced around at the Wing 17 pilots surrounding English in a ring of protection. They all stared back at her without flinching or shrinking.

Then she straightened up and faced him. "I'm very sorry to have to tell you this, Sailor. The rebels attacked the Ufa Long-Range Alert Station in the offensive. The rebels targeted the station in retaliation for our strike on the Pyrenees Base and Antigua Guatemala. Ufa Station was destroyed....and Captain Daniel Caleb English was killed. I'm so sorry, Gunny."

Chapter 29

R adcliffe signed out of his workstation and left the bridge. He finished filing his reports on the operations at the Io Center, at Arsuk, and finally, at the Refugee Center.

He hadn't seen Captain Ogden since they came back from the carnival. The *Lightning Rod* and *Battle Hardened* crews were still down there celebrating and now Radcliffe was off duty. He was free to do whatever he wanted, but he didn't go back to the Quad.

He checked the ship's onboard logs and went down to the flight deck. It was deserted except for one person.

Sailor English sat on a tool chest at the very far end of the Wing 17 line. He had opened the launch bay doors and activated the EM field. He dangled his legs off the edge of the chest and stared out at the stars.

Radcliffe strode up to him and placed his hand on English's shoulder. English glanced over at him looking sadder than Radcliffe could ever remember him.

English raised his beer bottle in a silent toast and took a drink before he went back to staring out at the night sky.

Radcliffe eased the rest of the way over to the chest, but he didn't sit down on it. He didn't have any right to share English's pain.

Radcliffe leaned against the corner and noticed a bunch of photographs clutched in English's other hand, but English wasn't looking at them. He just kept staring straight ahead into space.

"He was a great officer.... very loyal," Radcliffe began. "He took a massive risk by sending you that letter. He did it for all of us—for the Force. He was a brave and selfless officer. He'll be remembered well. You did a great job bringing up officers who are a credit to the Force."

"Yeah, well...." English murmured. "I also brought up Andy, so I guess I'm quits."

"You're more than quits. Do you see the way your pilots look at you? Do you see the way they stand up for you? You're like a father to all of us. You have to know that."

English shrugged. "I hate to tell you this, but I don't want the rest of you. I only want him."

He sniffed and ran his wrist across his nose. Tears streaked down his cheeks. He didn't try to hide them from Radcliffe.

Radcliffe crushed English's shoulder again. Radcliffe's eyes stung at those words. As much as Radcliffe worshiped this man, Radcliffe would gladly sacrifice himself to give English back the son he loved.

What father wouldn't be thrilled to have Captain Dan English as a son? The whole force admired Dan English. He was a chip off the old block. His career shaped up to be as decorated and heroic as his father's.

Now it was over long before its time. Dan English would never earn another decoration. He would never receive the decoration he earned with his last most noble act. He gave his life for the Force and the rebels killed him for it.

"We've restored communications with the Command Center," Radcliffe began again. "We got a report from the Command Center Hospital. Your daughter's all right."

English nodded. "Thanks."

"We can give you bereavement leave if you want to go back to Earth. One family member gone is bad enough.... or two, if you want to look at it that way. If you want to go back to the Command Center and be there for your daughter, I'm sure Captain Ogden would let you go."

"I got nothing left to go back to, pal." English took another swig of his beer, but he didn't seem in much hurry to finish it. "Melanie has a job to do. She doesn't want me hanging around playing nursemaid. I belong here. I can't leave now. This is all I got."

"What happened to you? You were retired. You could have stayed that way. You didn't have to come out here."

English shrugged again and heaved a shaky sigh. "No one knows why I retired."

"Why did you? You weren't old. You could have stayed in command of the *Siskiyou* for years, but you just vanished. You evaporated. No one could understand it."

English made a slight movement with his photographs. He set his beer on the tool chest, shuffled the pictures between his fingers, and handed one to Radcliffe.

Radcliffe looked down at what looked like a young woman, but on second glance, he realized she wasn't young at all. Her face showed the clear lines of age, but she still radiated the youthful, energetic happiness of a much younger woman.

She looked strikingly like Dr. Melanie English, but this woman had much lighter hair and eyes. Other than that, they could have been sisters.

"She got a terminal diagnosis when the *Siskiyou* was out on that security run to the Europa Environmental Zone. Do you remember? I got word while you and the recon detail were still on the moon. I tendered my resignation as soon as I got word. I went back to Earth and went home. The Command Staff kept bombarding me with requests and even threats to come back, but I refused them all."

Radcliffe frowned. "I never heard anything about this. Was the real reason on your service record?"

"We kept it in medical confidence. I never told anyone why I quit. I just walked away and dedicated everything to taking care of her."

"So what happened? That was seven years ago. Why did you decide to come back now?"

"She lived a lot longer than anyone expected. She only died six months ago and.... well, I just couldn't hang around the house anymore. The kids were all gone. I was completely alone with no one. I had to get out of there. I had to get off the whole damn planet. I couldn't think of any better way than to get myself back on a ship, but it ended up being a lot harder than I thought."

Radcliffe gazed out at the stars. The truth turned out to be a thousand times more heartrending than the wild rumors surrounding English's retirement and then his mysterious return.

"The Command staff was delighted at first when I said I wanted to go back on active duty. Then they flipped when they realized I was serious about getting back on a ship. They tried to blackmail me. They said I could only go back on active duty if I took a reduction in rank. They thought they could humiliate me into staying on Earth and joining the Command Staff. They didn't think I would go through with it—I guess because they didn't know why I wanted to leave."

Now it was Radcliffe's turn to sigh. Of course. Those chumps on the Command Staff should have realized who they were dealing with. If Sailor English said he wanted to serve on a ship, he would. Bumping him down to gunnery sergeant meant nothing to him.

In a way, they gave him exactly what he needed. They put him on the flight deck with a bunch of kids who needed him most. The Command Staff posted him to the very crew who would most appreciate his unique leadership style. The *Lightning Rod* squadron was the perfect place for him.

Radcliffe handed back the photograph and English added it to his stack. He picked up his beer bottle and Radcliffe took the hint.

He climbed onto the tool chest and wedged himself onto it next to English. English moved over to make room for him.

Radcliffe had to sit sealed right up against English's side, but he didn't back away or try to add more space between them. His hip, side, and shoulder pressed against English's—the way it should be.

They both looked out at the stars and said nothing. There was nothing to say.

Chapter 30

E nglish rang the doorbell and heard the now-familiar call from Captain Ogden. "Come in!"

He walked into the same conference room, except that now there were only ten captains standing around the table instead of eleven. Captain Kimmel was gone.

"Come on in, Sailor," Captain Detrick called. "We're all thrilled to have you back."

"Thank you, Sir."

"We want to congratulate you on the successful completion of your mission," Captain O'Shea told him. "You did it. The rebels are down three destroyers."

"Yes, Sir," English replied. "I'm glad it worked out."

"The *Battle Hardened* has lost her captain, her XO, and two of her bridge staff," Captain Colby went on. "Captain Ogden has put your name forward to take command of the *Battle Hardened*. We'd all love to have you back, Sailor. We need a good man on the bridge there."

English stiffened. He wasn't expecting this. He might have fantasized about being promoted back to captain, but things worked out so differently since he came on board the *Lightning Rod*.

He was starting to become attached to his pilots and to flying. He wasn't prepared to give that up.

"Thank you for the offer, Sir," he replied, "but I'll stay where I am. I'm grateful, but I think I can do the Force more good on the flight deck."

"We're very glad to have you there, Gunny," Ogden replied. "The squadron wouldn't be the same without you."

He glanced over at her and she smiled at him. He was starting to feel something like attachment for her, too.

Captain Detrick held up both hands. "Well, if we can't tempt you, Sailor, Commander Novak from the *Boer* will have to take over on the *Battle Hardened*."

English glanced toward Matt Radcliffe. For a split second, English wondered if Radcliffe would be promoted to command the *Battle Hardened*. How would English feel about one of his closest allies leaving the *Lightning Rod*?

Radcliffe would be staying—for now. Promotions happened fast in wartime. English might have to step in to command a ship if things went wrong. Was he prepared to do that?

Of course he was, but not today.

"We're in communication with the Command Staff now," Captain Detrick went on. "We're strategizing about how to get back some of the installations the rebels stole from us in the last offensive. We'd like to include you, Sailor, but I understand if you don't want to."

"Thank you, Sir, but my fighter wing needs me. I'm sure there are plenty of people better qualified to run this war than I am."

"I doubt that," Captain Colby chimed in.

"If you really feel that way, you're dismissed, Sailor," Captain Detrick told him. "You'll be the first person we call if we need help making decisions."

English laughed. He couldn't help it. "You don't need me, Sir. You don't want a has-been like me running this war."

"You're exactly who we want, but if you feel more comfortable on the flight deck, you better go back there."

"Thank you, Sir."

English left the conference room in relief. He didn't want to get involved in planning the war or carrying out any more operations like the last one.

He still felt the sting of Dan's loss. He didn't talk to anyone about it after his conversation with Radcliffe, but English didn't go back into his cocoon the way he did before his meeting with Andy.

Dan's loss didn't hit him the same way. Dan would want English to carry on. Dan would want English to keep doing the best thing for the Force and for Earth. Dan would want him to keep fighting the good fight, the fight Dan gave his life for.

English strolled back out to the Quad. He'd been keeping a much closer eye on his pilots this time, but he made sure to do it from a distance so they didn't see him hanging around.

They never misbehaved again. They enjoyed themselves, but in much healthier ways than before and no one got in any more fights. No one accused the *Dannevirk* pilots of being traitors. All of that was in the past.

These kids were growing up fast. War had a way of doing that to a person. None of the old prejudices or timewasters seemed to matter anymore.

When his pilots did see him, they always smiled and greeted him. None of them worried about him finding out what they were doing because they never did anything he would disapprove of.

He leaned over the Quad railing and noticed Stoval, Ezra, and Ritchie on the tier below him. They stood in line for the movie theater and talked while they waited their turn to buy tickets.

Stoval noticed English first. Stoval's watchful eyes shot English a questioning glance, but Stoval didn't tell the others English was there. That was Stoval's way.

Then Ezra and Ritchie saw English, too. They leaned over the railing and frowned up at English, too. Then Ritchie waved. English waved back and walked away. He didn't want to interfere with their fun.

He headed downstairs, but he had nowhere to go but back to the ship. He didn't want to be on shore leave. He wanted to get back to fighting the war.

That was the legacy Dan left him. Nothing else really mattered. English didn't want to relax until the war was over. Then he could enjoy himself with a clear conscience.

He spotted Charlie Frasier dressing down one of his pilots outside a gambling den. English cut them a wide berth and made himself scarce.

He was just about to throw in the towel and go back to the *Lightning Rod*. He could always work on one of the Wing 17 birds if he had nothing better to do.

He passed a dance hall on his way to the stairs, but when he stepped into the stairwell on his way down to the concourse, a group of five men burst into the stairwell behind him.

He moved aside to let them go first, but to his surprise, they didn't go ahead. They surrounded him and crowded him into a corner before he realized who it was.

"You're Sailor English, aren't you?" one big bruiser told him.

English nodded and his gaze skipped around the group. The five men who cornered him were the colonists from the Acheron Colony—the men English rescued from the fire. They had been in Sick Bay all this time—or so he thought.

The big guy stuck out his hand. "I'm Zuronus Muliv. This is my deputy, Igarvis Oria." Muliv nodded to the hulk next to him.

"Are you boys okay?" English made a quick survey of their burns. Most of the party looked like they had completely healed from their ordeal.

Muliv leaned in close and lowered his voice to a husky whisper. "We've been talking about the Acheron explosion. My boy Azmar Dirutera here says he saw some people hanging around the Tecrium reactor before the fire. He thinks he can identify at least two of the saboteurs."

"Are you sure?" English asked. "Did you tell Commander Radcliffe about this when he took your statements?"

"He didn't ask about that. He was more concerned with getting the details of you bringing us on board the ship."

"Besides," Igarvis added, "Azmar was unconscious back then. He only got out of intensive care a few days ago."

English looked more closely and confirmed that Azmar's face was more severely burned than the other four.

"We don't want to talk to that commander about this," Igarvis went on. "We probably wouldn't have told him even if he asked. Azmar says the guys that did it were USF officers."

"What makes you think they were officers?" English asked Azmar. "Were they in uniform?"

"They weren't in uniform, but I recognized them." Azmar spoke in a gravelly voice as though his throat had been damaged in the fire, too. "They were off one of the destroyers delivering to the colony at the time."

"Which ship was it?"

"I don't know that. Six destroyers landed at the colony that whole month. The guys could have been from any one of them, but I remember seeing them out and about on the colony before that."

"Not just that," Muliv added. "Anyone would have to have a security clearance to get inside the reactor. Whoever they were, they didn't just walk in off the street. Someone let them in—someone high up the chain of command."

English thought fast. Why didn't he think of this before? No one without at least the rank of colonel would be able to authorize strangers to go inside the reactor.

"We had to tell someone," Igarvis went on. "We couldn't think of anyone else to tell besides you."

"Well?" Muliv asked. "What are you gonna do about this?"

English motioned them down the stairs. "Come with me."

"You aren't taking us to that commander, are you? He's just a kid. He might sell us to the same people who did this."

English didn't waste time telling them he trusted Radcliffe a lot more than he trusted these colonists. "I'm not taking you to him. I'm taking you to my quarters."

They followed him after that. He didn't try to talk to them until he got them behind closed doors. He had to be careful with this.

He waved them toward the couches in the middle of his quarters. "Take a seat. There's some food in the fridge over there. You can help yourself."

"You're being awfully casual about this," Muliv pointed out.

"I'm just trying to decide what to do. If you don't want me to contact Commander Radcliffe, then we have to go about this another way."

"How?" Igarvis asked.

"Just give me a minute." English sat down at his computer and set to work. He brought up the USF roster for the Acheron Colony on the day of the fire.

The colonists were right. Six destroyers registered at Acheron that week: *Continental Drift, Seagull, Jetstream, Afrikaans, Gryphon,* and *Lightning Rod.*

English tensed when he saw the *Afrikaans* among them. The destroyer came out against the *Lightning Rod* and the *Solar Flare* in that first battle, so the *Afrikaans* was a rebel ship.

He pulled up the duty roster and swiveled the screen toward the colonists. "I want you to run through this list and tell me if you recognize anyone."

Azmar came over and started scrolling through the pictures attached to each personnel file. Of course he passed by everyone on the bridge staff. They wouldn't get involved in sabotaging a Tecrium reactor on a well-known USF colony. That would be too obvious.

Azmar kept running down the roster and stopped. He pointed. "That's one of them right there. I'd know him anywhere."

He pointed to Lieutenant Scott Hornsby, and a few minutes later, he singled out Lieutenant Derrick Metcalf.

"You didn't recognize anyone else?"

Azmar shook his head. "I only saw the two of them. I didn't get a good look at the other three."

"So there were five of them?"

"Yep—at least, that's all I saw."

"Did they see you watching them?" English asked.

"Who knows? There were workers all over the place."

"Why didn't anyone else notice them around, then?" English asked.

"Maybe they did. How do I know? We were the only ones who made it out alive."

English frowned at his computer screen. So a bunch of officers from the *Afrikaans* went poking around the Tecrium reactor right before it exploded.

He made another check and confirmed his fears. The *Afrikaans* disembarked from the Acheron Colony right before the reactor blew up. The saboteurs probably thought no one would make it out of the reactor alive and they were almost right.

"The thing is," Muliv remarked, "someone with at least a colonel's rank had to authorize them to get inside the reactor."

"Yeah, I got that...."

"And it had to be someone off the moon," Igarvis added. "Our Colonel Konov wouldn't have done it. He wouldn't let a bunch of strangers inside the reactor."

English scowled again. These colonists weren't telling him anything he didn't already know.

In fact, the situation was even worse than they made out. Someone a lot higher than a colonel would have to override Konov's authority to let a bunch of lieutenants into a Tecrium reactor where they didn't belong.

A breach like that would have to come from much higher up the chain of command. Who did English know with that kind of authority?

He paced around his quarters for a second. "Well?" Muliv demanded again. "What are you gonna do about this?"

"I need to think about this. You boys are staying on the *Lightning Rod*, aren't you?"

"We don't have anywhere else to go," Igarvis replied. "We can't go back to Earth and the colony is finished."

English froze in his tracks staring at the men in front of him. Shit! Why didn't he think of this? How could he be so stupid? He never should have let everything else distract him from this.

"You boys go back to your quarters."

"What are you going to do?" Azmar asked. "Don't say anything to that commander, whatever you do."

"Okay," English agreed. "I won't."

Muliv fixed him with a hard glare. "You give us your word you won't tell him. We've seen you hanging around with him. *You* might trust him, but we don't."

English made an instant decision. "I give you my word I won't tell him, but I will have to tell someone."

"Who?" Igarvis asked. "Not the captain."

"I won't tell Captain Ogden, either, if you don't want me to, but I will tell someone."

"Who?" Igarvis asked again.

"You leave that to me. You trusted me with this information. I give you my word of honor as an officer and a man that I won't tell anyone I don't trust with my life. The person I tell will be absolutely trustworthy and absolutely loyal. No one will sell you boys out. I promise you that."

The colonists glared at him and then Muliv shrugged. "All right. We trust you."

"Thank you for telling me," English replied. "This information is going to be the best thing that ever happened to us. We'll be able to use this against the rebels and hopefully win the war."

Chapter 31

E nglish left his quarters thinking fast. He had to talk to someone—someone he really trusted. He trusted Radcliffe, but Radcliffe wasn't high enough in rank. English needed someone else. He needed another captain and he didn't plan on trusting Ogden again.

He set off through the *Lightning Rod*. He needed to get off the ship. The destroyer didn't seem big enough to hold all the information exploding out of his head.

The Tecrium fire at the Acheron Colony might have shut down the colony, but it didn't shut down everything. Of course! Everything came together in his mind. He kicked himself a few more times for not figuring this out long ago.

He left the ship and made his way back to the Quad. He searched everywhere and finally found the person he was looking for.

He went into a bar and approached the bartender. "I'm looking for Captain Detrick."

The bartender jerked his thumb over his shoulder. "In there. He's been in there practically around the damn clock."

"Thanks." English followed the gesture and stepped into a back room. He shut the door behind him and found Captain Detrick lounging on a couch.

He had set up an old-fashioned wooden desk on his lap. He scribbled with an old-fashioned fountain pen on countless sheets of paper. "How's the book coming along, Fletcher?"

"Pretty good. Pull up a chair."

English sat down next to him and watched his friend writing long hand. Detrick wrote out long sentences. He came to the end of one line and started on the next. He wrote in beautiful, perfect copperplate and focused on his work with unbroken attention to every stroke.

Detrick finally came to the end of another page and made a pointed dot at the end of the sentence. He started rifling his papers and re-reading what he'd written. "How did you find me? I come here to disappear, you know."

"I know. I wouldn't bother you if it wasn't important and I promise I won't tell anyone where you are—especially not your wife."

Detrick snorted. "Is that supposed to be some kind of threat?"

"How can it be when your other five novels have been so successful?"

Detrick organized his papers, set them aside, and started writing on another clean sheet. "What do you want?"

"I need a favor."

"You already interrupted me...and you already almost got yourself killed. Isn't that enough?"

"Someone sabotaged the Tecrium reactor to destroy the Acheron colony. A few of the colonist engineers at the reactor saw five officers off the *Afrikaans* inside the reactor right before it blew up.... which means the flow of Straisium is still intact. It's just sitting there on Ganymede waiting for someone to come and collect it....and we also encountered fighter craft hanging around Titan when they weren't attached to any destroyer."

Detrick's pen froze above the paper for a second and then he started writing again. "You still have these colonist witnesses you mentioned?"

"They're on the *Lightning Rod*. They barely made it out of the fire in time to save their own lives."

Detrick kept writing. "What do you want me to do about it?"

"Don't you get it? If Straisium is still available at the colony and rebel elements are hanging around the Jovian system, it means the rebels are trying to secure the supply. It explains why they're going to such trouble to control the system even though there's only a skeleton crew of loyal ships out here."

"That still doesn't help us."

"But it does!" English insisted. "We can secure the Straisium supply and cut the rebels off. They won't be able to fight anybody without Straisium. They'll be dead in the water if we cut their supply line. They would grind to a halt and the whole insurgency would collapse."

"How do you propose to secure the Straisium supply—and for the love of Christ don't say anything about volunteering to go down there and fight the rebels for it."

"Oh, come on, Fletcher!" English exclaimed. "Someone who was at least an admiral or a high-ranking colonel must have authorized these lieutenants to get inside the reactor which means the rebels already had people on the moon before the explosion. They could have moved their people to a safe location to take over the colony as soon as they got the colonists out of the way. Now they just have to get rid of us to set up a supply line to bring Straisium to Earth. I shouldn't even have to explain this to you."

Detrick looked up and set his fountain pen aside. "Will you listen to yourself? You had the option to take over as captain of the *Battle Hardened* and you turned it down. We offered to bring you into our conference and help us strategize how to win this war and you turned that down, too. You said you weren't qualified to organize the resistance and you belonged on the flight deck with the gasheads. Jesus, Sailor! I don't know what's wrong with you."

"What's your problem? You're a ship's captain."

"So are you! When are you gonna wake up and smell the coffee? Christ, Sailor! There is no one in the whole damn Force better qualified to run this war than you."

"Now, don't start blowing sunshine up my ass...."

"Do you honestly not hear the words coming out of your own mouth?" Detrick crammed the cap on his fountain pen, set his desk aside, and started gathering his papers. "Where is your head, Sailor? Now you come in here spinning me a tale about the Acheron colony and supply lines to Earth."

"Well, who the hell else was I supposed to tell?"

Detrick rounded on him. "Yourself, asshole! Tell yourself! If you were captain of the *Battle Hardened* right now, you could do it all yourself. You could fly off to Ganymede and destroy the rebel supply line and save the whole damn world just like you always do. Holy shit, what is wrong with you?"

English hunched lower in his seat. "I'm not in charge of the *Battle Hardened*."

"That's your fault, isn't it? Now Novak is being promoted to captain in your place. Do you honestly think she'll be able to pull off something like this?"

English looked away.

Detrick got to his feet, put his papers inside his desk, put his pen in his pocket, and positioned his desk under his arm. "We're having another conference tomorrow morning at ten, and for pity's sake, don't come around telling us that shit about you not being qualified to run the war. Do you not see how much we need you—how much the whole damn system needs you? How can you even think of letting Dan down like this?"

Detrick stood there just long enough to make sure English gaped at him in stupid shock. Then Detrick stalked out of the room and left English sitting there by himself.

Chapter 32

E nglish raised his hand, but he hesitated to press the doorbell. He didn't want to do it, but Fletcher Detrick's words kept stabbing him in the heart.

He *was* letting Dan down by doing this. This whole hair-shirted penance on the *Lightning Rod's* fighter wing was just some kind of self-sabotage that was letting down the whole Force.

Even knowing that, he still struggled to press the doorbell. He didn't want to do this. He wanted to disappear into his engines and his fighter craft and leave the big decisions to someone else.

Fate had other ideas, though, and if Dan expected more from him, then English had no choice.

He thrust out his hand, and instead of hitting the doorbell, he touched the release. The door swept open and he marched into the conference room without waiting for permission.

Captain Ogden moved out of the way to make space for him at the table.

"How you doing, Sailor?" Captain Colby asked.

"Pretty good, Gus. Thanks for asking."

Colby waved to a young woman standing next to Commander Radcliffe. "This is Commander Dayna Novak. She was XO of the *Boer* until yesterday."

English held out his hand to her. "Good to meet you, Commander."

She saluted and then shook his hand. "It's an honor to serve under you, Sir. I hope I can give you the best XO possible."

"I'm sure you will, Commander."

"We're all so grateful to you for taking command of the *Battle Hardened*, Sailor," Captain O'Shea added. "We'd love your input on our next move."

English's gaze darted to Detrick, but Detrick didn't meet that glance. Detrick must not have told anyone about English's revelation, which meant English would be telling everyone for the first time.

He straightened up and tugged down the jacket of his new captain's uniform. He still hadn't gotten used to it.

Then he stepped forward and laid his computer device down in front of the other captains. "Here's the deal. Ten days before the civil conflict broke out, the Tecrium reactor on the Acheron Colony exploded. The surviving engineers from the plant claimed it was sabotage and one of the witnesses claims that USF officers were inside the reactor right before it blew up."

"What?!" Radcliffe gasped. "They never told me that!"

"The man who saw these officers was in intensive care when you interviewed the survivors about the fire," English replied. "He was unconscious until a few days ago....and since it was USF officers who sabotaged the reactor, they didn't trust you to tell you anyway."

"So they told you instead?" Radcliffe demanded.

"That's right. This has nothing to do with you, Matt. They didn't know you. They didn't trust that you wouldn't sell them down the river to the same people who tried to kill them. It's that simple."

"What does this have to do with the civil war?" Captain O'Shea asked.

English switched on his device. It showed schematics of the Acheron Colony from before the explosion.

He pointed to the reactor. "The explosion epicenter was here—inside the reactor. This overlay shows the blast radius and the damage caused by the fire. You can see that the explosion killed all the remaining colonists and torched the whole colony, but it left the Straisium refinery intact."

A noticeable chill went around the table as his words sank in.

"The surviving engineers identified two of the five saboteurs as officers on the *Afrikaans*, which we know is in rebel hands. The *Afrikaans* left the colony right before the explosion. Her duty roster also lists forty-five active-duty crewmen who were inside the colony when it blew up—which means they are now listed as dead."

"Are you actually saying," Captain Ogden murmured, "that the *Afrikaans* planted people on Ganymede to secure the Straisium refinery after the explosion subsided?"

"I've run long-range scans of the blast site. There are exactly forty-five human life signs on Ganymede and they're all concentrated inside the refinery. They've brought the refinery back online. They just don't have any ships in residence to transport the Straisium to Earth."

"Holy shit!" Captain Colby breathed. "No wonder they're working so hard to eliminate us! They want to get rid of any resistance so they can establish a supply line to Earth!"

English glanced over at Detrick again, but Detrick didn't move or speak. He left everything on English's shoulders.

English should have expected this. He should have realized he couldn't just disappear. Fletcher Detrick was right. English owed the Force more than just a grunt on the flight deck. He owed his fellow crewmen the best officer he could give them. He owed Dan that, too.

"So what do you propose we do about this?" Captain Ogden asked.

English pulled himself up even straighter. "I'm taking the *Battle Hardened* to Ganymede to secure the Straisium supply. I'll do what I can to drive the rebels out of the refinery, but if that fails, I'll destroy the refinery. The rebels can't function without Straisium."

"The loyalists can't function without Straisium, either," Commander Novak pointed out. "If we destroy the refinery, the loyalist resistance will go down with the rebels."

"Not so fast, Commander. We still have the Lunar refinery, which means we need at least half of you captains to defend the moon against rebel incursion. We have to make sure the rebels don't get a toehold on the moon. As soon as we either recapture or destroy the Acheron refinery and secure the Lunar refinery, we'll have the rebels by the balls."

Captain Ogden puffed out her cheeks. "Phew! That is one hell of a plan."

"What do you need from us?" It was the first time Captain Detrick had spoken since English stepped into the room. He startled English so much that English jumped. "Just tell us what you want us to do, Sailor."

"I just told you. I want you to hold the moon no matter what. The *Battle Hardened* will take care of the Acheron refinery."

"That won't work," Captain Ogden countered. "One ship isn't enough on a mission like this. The *Lightning Rod* will go with you."

"I don't think...."

She cracked a rare grin at him. "Do you honestly think Wing 17 will stay behind while you go off and carry out this mission alone? We're going with you. In fact...." She glanced around the table at the other captains. "Most of us lost fighter wings and, in some cases, whole squadrons in the offensive. We'll need to do a full shakeup of all our squadrons." She turned back to English. "The *Battle Hardened* is short on pilots anyway. We can reassign Wing 17 to the *Battle Hardened* and run two condensed wings on the *Lightning Rod*. That will give both our ships two full wings each."

English couldn't speak. He never expected this. He hesitated to take command of the *Battle Hardened* because he didn't want to leave Wing 17.

She must have anticipated this. She must have read so much more into his feelings and his pilots' feelings than he ever gave her credit for.

"That's settled, then," Captain Colby replied. "The *Marigold* will stay on the moon. How about you, Leonard? You bring the *Outrigger*, too."

Captain O'Shea nodded. "You bet. No one is getting past us, Sailor. You don't worry about the moon."

"The *Lone Ranger* is going to Ganymede, too," Captain Detrick growled. "You'll need backup, Sailor."

English swallowed hard. His next words took all his resolve to choke out. "Thank you. Thank you all."

"We're the ones who should be thanking you, Sailor," Captain Colby replied. "We'll reassign half our ships to the Lunar refinery and the others to your detail. We'll be under your command until we get this done."

He should have said, *Thank you*, to them again, but he couldn't speak. He never expected this.

He expected when he left Earth that he would do his time on the flight deck. He had been prepared to spend years there. He wasn't expecting his own peers, his fellow captains, especially Captain Ogden, to thrust him back into command—especially command over them.

They all gazed back at him with open, accepting, grateful expressions. He couldn't let them down.

The meeting broke up and he left the conference room. He had something he needed to do. He couldn't go on with this until he faced his pilots.

Commander Novak caught up with him in the corridor outside. "Captain! Captain English!"

He didn't realize she was talking to him until she actually touched his elbow. He had gotten too used to being called, "Gunny".

She pulled up breathless and blushing in front of him. "Sir! I just want to say.... thank you. I'm so grateful to you for taking over the *Battle Hardened*, Sir. I just...."

"I'm sure you would have done an exceptional job, Commander. If you don't want to serve under me, I understand. I know you were probably looking forward to your first command."

"It isn't that, Sir. I was looking forward to it, but now...." She blushed again. "This is going to be so much better, Sir! This is the honor of my life, Sir. I never expected I'd ever be able to serve under a captain as decorated as you. It's...." Her hand flew to her heart. "I don't know what to say."

"You don't have to say anything, Commander. I'm relieved that you don't feel I bumped you off a post you deserved."

"Not at all, Sir! I was so thrilled when Captain Dahl told me you were taking over."

English found himself beaming at her. "Thank you, Dayna. I'm looking forward to working with you, too. With a little bit of luck, we'll be able to knock this mission out of the park and then we'll both be riding home high on the hog."

She exploded into a huge grin. "Yes, Sir! Let's do it."

"Great. You head over to the *Battle Hardened* and get her all ship-shape. I'll meet you over there in a little while."

"Yes, Sir!" She took off through the Olympus Station and English got serious. He couldn't shirk this another minute.

He went back to the *Lightning Rod*, but when he got to the flight deck, he hesitated again. He cast a long, heartfelt glance around the place that had become his new home. Now he was leaving it again.

Lieutenant Eismann left his desk, came over to English, and saluted. "It's such an honor to be able to call you 'Sir' again, Sir. You never really belonged down here."

"Don't say that, Brock," English choked. "I really don't want to be anywhere else."

Eismann's eyes moistened. "I know a few people who are going to be devastated when they find out you're leaving."

"I hate to tell you this, but I'm taking Wing 17 with me."

Eismann's jaw dropped. "No, you aren't!"

English nodded. "The captains just decided upstairs. Captain Ogden was the one who suggested it."

Eismann's hand flew to his head. "Holy shit! Now what am I supposed to do?"

"Most of the destroyers are running on two fighter wings, so we'll all be even. The *Battle Hardened* will have two also."

"Crap! I was getting used to having three. Wing 17 has gotten so damn good! They really shaped up. They're one of the best wings on board."

English smiled at him and his chest swelled with pride. "They're good kids."

"Charlie is going to be crushed."

"I better go talk to him." English turned away. He had some good-byes to say.

English strode off toward Wing 10 and spotted Charlie Frasier giving orders to some of the mechanics.

English walked up to him and Frasier turned around. He took one look at English's jacket and Frasier's face twisted in a pained grimace.

He checked himself, compressed his lips, and then stormed over to English. Frasier threw his arms around English and crushed him in a huge hug.

English's heart lurched. This was turning out to be a lot harder than he expected. How did the *Lightning Rod* come to mean so much to him so quickly?

Frasier pushed him back, held him at arm's length, and Frasier's face spasmed holding back emotion. "It was only a matter of time," he croaked. "I knew it would happen someday. It's for the best. You're too good for the flight deck."

"Don't say that, Charlie." English's voice cracked and he felt his eyes stinging.

Frasier nodded fast. "We're all better off with you up there. You go on where you belong. You know we're all behind you."

"I couldn't have done it without you." English gripped the back of Frasier's neck. He wasn't sure he could part from this man without losing his composure completely. They had only known each other for a few weeks and English already didn't see how he was going to function with Frasier by his side. "I have you to thank for this."

"Naw! You were this long before you came here. You were born for this."

Now it was English's turn to pull Frasier into a hug. He couldn't tear himself away from this man. He counted Charlie Frasier as one of the best friends of his life.

When he pulled back, English noticed Sean Duran and a bunch of the Wing 10 pilots hanging around.

As soon as English separated from Frasier, Sean snapped to attention and saluted him. The other pilots did the same, and last of all, Frasier saluted.

English saluted them back and then did his best to grin at them. "As you were, gentlemen. Don't let me interrupt your work."

"Yes, Sir," Frasier replied and English walked away.

English headed over to Wing 17. He really had no idea how he was going to face his pilots or what he was going to say to them.

Racer spotted him long before he got near their wing. She burst into a grin and then her face drained of all color when she saw his new uniform. She gaped at him with her eyeballs hanging out of their sockets. "What.... the.... hell....is.... that?"

The other pilots noticed what she was looking at and turned around to watch English cross the flight deck toward them.

Ezra, Thorpe, Stoval, and Babbitt all gathered around followed by Janacek, Ritchie, and Manheim.

"Oh, my holy blinkin' God!" Ezra whispered. "It can't be!"

"Are those......?" Thorpe's eyes dipped to the captain's bars on English's shoulders.

Babbitt gasped. "They made you a captain?"

Ezra smacked his knuckles into Babbitt's arm. "He already was a captain, fool! He's been a captain for decades. Slumming it with us was always going to be temporary."

"It isn't like that," English replied. "I'm just taking over the *Battle Hardened* because Captain Kimmel got killed on the *Buckingham Palace*."

"So.... you're leaving?" Racer gulped. "What are we supposed to do without you?"

"You're all coming over to the *Battle Hardened* with me," English replied. "Wing 17 is being transferred to the new ship."

"The whole wing?" Thorpe asked. "Birds and all?"

English nodded. "Birds and all."

"So...." Racer began again. "We'll have a new gunny?"

"I'm afraid so. It's like I said. We all have to do our best to win the war. None of us gets off easy. Trust me. I'd much rather stay down here with you."

English fidgeted in front of them. He felt more out of place in this uniform facing his pilots than he did at any other time so far.

He felt like an imposter. He felt like he was betraying them by becoming something other than their gunny. He never wanted to be anything else. He felt himself starting to get emotional when he thought he might never be their gunny again.

Manheim burst into tears and the others looked up at him with such obviously devastated expressions that English couldn't take it anymore.

"Now listen here, all of you. We're all going over to the *Battle Hardened*, but we're going on one more mission together—me and you—all of you. We're going out on a run and I'm coming with you."

"What happens if one of us accidentally calls you 'Gunny' again?" Ritchie asked. "Will we get busted for that?"

English couldn't help but smile at him. If that was their biggest worry, he could live with that.

"You won't get busted for calling me 'Gunny'. It would be an honor for me to still be your gunny. That will just be something special between me and all of you. Now listen. I need you all with me. We've got some work to do and we're going down on the ground to fight the enemy face to face. Understand? No swooping around and shooting them from the air."

"How the hell are we supposed to do that?" Janacek asked. "We're pilots. Don't you have security details for that?"

"Yes, I do, but I need you with me, too. There's no one on the *Battle Hardened* that I trust as much as you."

They started to brighten up and Ezra squared his shoulders. "We're with you, Sir. Whatever you need, you just let us know."

"Yeah, Sir," Thorpe added. "Wherever you need us, we're there."

"Good man." English clapped him on the shoulder. "Don't worry. You people are some of the finest crewmen I've ever had the pleasure to serve with. I actually turned down command of the *Battle Hardened* because I didn't want to leave you. I wouldn't go over there without you."

Chapter 33

E nglish headed down the concourse toward the *Battle Hardened*. He'd been on board several times since accepting command of the destroyer. Now it was time for the rubber to meet the road and actually take her out against the enemy.

He passed the terminal to the *Lightning Rod's* docking station. He'd already taken his leave from Captain Ogden and the rest of the *Lightning Rod* crew. His last stop waited for him at the turnoff to the *Lightning Rod*.

Matt Radcliffe smiled at English, but Radcliffe didn't even try to make it a happy smile. "I sure wish I was going to be your new XO."

"You have a place here, Matt." English hugged him. "You keep doing your duty and keep the *Lightning Rod* safe."

"Yes, Sir." Radcliffe laughed. "Now I can call you that again without feeling guilty."

"Thank you, son. Thank you for sticking up for me. I'll always be in your debt for that."

"You deserve this. The whole Force is better off with you in command."

English winced. "I think I'll be hearing a lot of that for a while."

"That's because it's true." Radcliffe hugged him again. "Go on, Sir. Show us all how it's done."

"Okay, son. You hang back and eat my dust."

Radcliffe laughed much louder this time. He was still chuckling when English walked away to the *Battle Hardened*.

He made his way to the bridge and Commander Novak snapped to attention. "Captain on the bridge!"

"At ease, Dayna." English sat down in the big chair. It felt strange and he got another wave of vertigo. He was taking someone else's place. Any second now, the real captain would come in and dress English down for sitting in his chair.

He checked the controls on his chair arm. Wing 17's birds were all registered on their new launch pads.

The ship's roster showed Henry Janacek, August Stoval, Ben Ritchie, Harlow Babbitt, Ezra Duran, Emory Thorpe, Ada Manheim, and Natalie Franz all on board and working on the flight deck.

Their new gunnery sergeant, Gunny Mark Ryner, was down there with them. Interviewing Ryner had been one of English's first tasks as captain of this ship.

He had been relieved to discover that Ryner was a salty old codger cut from the same cloth as Charlie Frasier.

English informed Ryner that Wing 17 was accustomed to a healthy dose of latitude when it came to protocol. English also gave Ryner license to be as hard on Wing 17 as he needed to be to maintain order and keep the pilots in line.

Ryner had the balls to grin during this conversation and English knew Wing 17 was in good hands.

"Sir!" Novak began. "The *Lightning Rod* is hailing you."

"Put her through, Commander."

The display on English's chair arm switched on and Captain Ogden smiled at him from the *Lightning Rod's* bridge. "Standing by the launch on your mark, Captain."

"The *Lone Ranger* is signaling readiness to launch, too, Sir," Novak reported.

"Take us out, Commander. *Lightning Rod* and *Lone Ranger*, you are clear to launch."

The *Battle Hardened* shuddered when Novak released the docking clamps and the destroyer started drifting out of the docking station. She reversed out of the hold and the *Lighting Rod* and the *Lone Ranger* released, too.

"Fall in formation, *Lightning Rod*," English ordered.

"Yes, Sir," Radcliffe replied.

The *Lone Ranger* pivoted into place and then the *Lightning Rod* took her position. The three destroyers formed a triangle with the *Battle Hardened* at its point.

English checked all three ships. They were all ready to fly with every squadron standing by to fight the moment he gave the word.

He checked the scans of the Acheron Straisium refinery for the thousandth time. Everything was the same there. Nothing had changed.

The same cluster of fighter craft still lurked behind Titan, but there weren't enough of them to threaten one destroyer, let alone three.

English had no more reason to wait around. "Acheron formation—full throttle!"

Novak and Radcliffe both gunned it at the same instant. The *Lone Ranger* hung close by the *Lightning Rod's* wing and all three destroyers sprinted to full speed in a split second.

English's heart leapt into his throat. He was doing it again. He was commanding a destroyer and his blood lit on fire. They were right about him. He was born for this. To hell with piloting a fighter craft. This was the real deal.

The three destroyers plowed across the asteroid field in no time and Novak veered toward Jupiter. "Launch all fighter wings!" English ordered.

Wings 6 and 17 launched from the *Battle Hardened* followed by Wings 10 and 12 from the *Lightning Rod* and the *Lone Ranger* squadron.

The fighter wings rocketed together to overtake the destroyers and all three squadrons joined into one seamless force.

English heard Ryner, Frasier, Lloyd, and other gunnery sergeants barking orders to their crews, but English didn't stick around to listen. He got to his feet and rode the elevator down to the flight deck.

At least a hundred security personnel waited for him there along with twelve large transport craft.

Their sergeants came to attention when English showed up. "Sir!" one of them barked. "The security detail is ready to deploy on your orders."

"Deploy, Sergeant. Get your people down on the ground ASAP."

"Yes, Sir." The sergeant turned to his men. "Deploy!"

The security personnel jogged onto their transports and English loaded up with his personal security detail. They surrounded him and the *Battle Hardened's* Master Chief Newlon handed English two sidearms and two rifles.

English buckled himself in and checked his weapons on the way down to the colony. He already knew what he would find there. The rebels had forty-five men at the refinery.

This security detail should be able to secure the refinery with no trouble.... or it looked that way on the surface. English knew better than to trust the way anything looked on the surface.

The transports and most of the fighters landed back on the flight zone where the *Lightning Rod* had originally been parked when the reactor exploded.

The colony looked very different now. The whole superstructure had been scorched black and most of the turrets and scaffolds had melted in the searing Tecrium heat.

The terrain around the colony was even drier and harsher than it had been before. The stinging wind carried an acrid smell of burned chemicals and melted metal to English's nose.

He strode outside and the security forces streamed into the colony on their way to the refinery. English set off after them. The *Lone Ranger* squadron and Wing 12 from the *Lightning Rod* rotated overhead to cover the colony from the air.

The three destroyers hovered directly overhead to patrol the atmosphere. No ships could come or go from the Straisium refinery. The rebels were trapped down here.

The ground troops vanished into the superstructure. Wing 17 came over and English's security detail let them in to surround English. "What's the plan, Sir?" Ritchie asked. "When do we engage the enemy?"

"Hopefully never. If the ground troops secure the refinery, we could be taking possession of this moon without a shot fired."

"That's asking a lot, isn't it, Sir?" Racer asked. "We can't expect the rebels to just hand us this refinery without a fight."

"You're right, Airman." English cast a flinty gaze across the colony. He didn't believe the rebels would lie down without a fight, either. "Let's go find out what's going on at the refinery."

He started forward when, without warning, a gigantic plasma jet erupted out of the superstructure.

It sizzled into the atmosphere and struck a catastrophic blow to the *Battle Hardened's* underside. "NO!" English roared, but it was too late.

Four more blasts rocketed out of the colony. Two of them plastered the *Battle Hardened* and the other two each hit the *Lightning Rod* and the *Lone Ranger*.

The *Battle Hardened* staggered in midair and a deafening explosion went off somewhere inside the ship. She listed hard to port and then started a slow, inevitable nosedive for the moon's surface.

She picked up speed by the second and smashed nose first into the ground beyond the colony.

More shots struck the *Lighting Rod's* starboard wing and the ship spiraled out of control. The plasma shots spouted from deep inside the colony.

The *Lightning Rod* fired her engines and dodged most of them, but enough hit their mark that the ship had to beat a hasty retreat. In a second, both the *Lightning Rod* and the *Lone Ranger* pulled away and headed off to get away from the colony.

"Shit!" Racer husked.

"Get under cover!" English ordered. "Get off the flight zone!"

He herded his people toward the superstructure, but as soon as they all started moving, gunfire broke out inside the colony.

Another plasma jet smashed into the transport that carried English to this moon. The large craft detonated in an unholy ball of fire and incinerated twelve security guards posted around the ship.

The shockwave flattened another twenty men. English ran from one person to the next. "Get inside the colony!"

"We can't!" Thorpe yelled back. "They'll gun us down!"

"They'll gun us down if we stay out here! The colony is our only chance to find some cover! Come on!"

English took off at a run heading for the blackened scaffolds in front of him. He ran straight into the gunshots, but staying out here would be suicide.

He made sure the rest of Wing 17 came with him and the security force followed. He charged thirty feet before he noticed Manheim standing frozen in shock again. She blinked at the colony in terror.

English ran back and yanked her forward by the arm. "Keep moving! Don't stop for anything! Head for that conduit over there!"

He steered Wing 17 in that direction. The security forces caught up and everyone packed in a tight ball.

Gunfire kept spitting from the colony, but English had judged its origin correctly. It came from a high catwalk between two Tecrium silos. As soon as the party got near the colony, the gunshots went over their heads. The rebels couldn't hit anyone down here.

English shoved Manheim and the other pilots against the nearest silo. Plasma shots pinged off its upper column and it rang all the way down to the ground. The silo was completely hollow and empty.

"Tell me you didn't plan it this way, Gunny," Ritchie began and then blanched. "Sorry, Captain."

"We don't have time for that." English stole a peek up toward the shooters. "They've got a lot more than forty-five."

"Where are the big guns coming from?" Duran asked.

"I don't know, but they must have stashed those here before the explosion, too."

"Why didn't they shoot the destroyers down when we first showed up?" Babbitt asked. "Why did they let us land at all?"

"Maybe the rebels wanted to see what we were doing," English suggested. "Maybe they saw us landing fighter craft and didn't think we were any threat to the refinery. Who knows."

"How do we get out of here?" Thorpe asked. "The *Battle Hardened* is down."

"We still have our birds," Ritchie added.

"Our birds won't evacuate the whole ground crew and the big guns would only hit us if we tried," English pointed out. "I didn't come all the way out here to run away. We came to neutralize these rebels and take the refinery and that's what we're going to do. We need to keep moving deeper into the colony. Let's go."

They headed past the silos into a narrow defile flanked by towers, scaffolds, and more high catwalks. "Too bad we don't have a map of this place," Babbitt pointed out.

"We do." English pulled a portable device out of his jacket pocket.

"You think of everything, don't you, Gunny?" Thorpe asked.

"I didn't think the rebels would land those big guns, but we're here now, so we might as well make the best of it." English switched on his device. "The good news is that this will show us where the enemy is hiding."

He tracked to the crew's location and found seven other dots moving fast through the warren of pipes and tunnels. "They're trying to cut around in front of us," Janacek pointed out.

"So we need to pull a trick on them." English pointed to some of the ground troops. "You boys loop around behind them and drive them into us.... here. If the enemy tries to retreat, cut 'em off."

Manheim went pale. "What do you mean by 'drive them into us'?"

"You have a weapon, Manheim. It's just like shooting drones in the arena. Just imagine you're scoring points on these targets, too."

"Except these targets are people," she pointed out.

"They're your enemies. Don't think about anything else.... unless you want to think about them going after your families. Let's go."

English made sure the ground troops were going in the right direction and then he led Wing 17 to a different location farther west.

He clambered up a ladder and positioned the pilots along another catwalk high off the ground. He checked his device. "Here they come."

Gunshots rang out in the maze ahead. "It's coming closer!" Manheim squeaked.

"Get ready...." English raised his rifle.

The group trained their weapons on the banging and cracking getting nearer by the second. All at once, a group of uniformed officers burst into view on a catwalk fifteen feet below Wing 17's position.

The security detail hounded the rebels from behind. The rebels took up covered positions to return fire before they retreated and ran to their next hiding place. They ran right into Wing 17's range.

English opened fire on them and all the pilots joined in. They hit five rebels, but as soon as the shooting started, another group hammered Wing 17 from even higher up the stack.

Thorpe went down screaming. Manheim screamed, too, but she was just scared. She dodged deeper into the maze to get out of the line of fire.

English fired upward into the stack, but he couldn't see the enemy on either side anymore. He raced over to Thorpe. The boy lay writhing and groaning on the catwalk.

"Easy, son." English checked him over and found two bullet holes, one in Thorpe's side and one through his upper thigh.

English scrambled to stop the bleeding and looked around in desperation. All the other pilots had found sheltered positions for themselves. Babbitt, Janacek, and Ritchie were shooting up into the tangle of pipes above their heads while bullets pinged and zinged everywhere.

Ezra and Stoval shot downward at the rebels on the ground. The rebel officers down there returned fire and English heard more weapons belching in the distance. He didn't see Racer or Manheim anywhere.

"Auggie! Help me!" English called. "The rest of you keep moving! Head for the refinery!"

"Where is it?" Ezra yelled over.

English shoved his device into Ezra's hands. "You guide us. The rest of you fall in behind Duran and be ready to shoot at a moment's notice."

"What about Racer and Manheim?" Janacek squinted upward toward the enemy position. "They aren't shooting anymore."

"They're moving off which means they plan to ambush us somewhere else."

Ezra checked the map. "There are two signals coming from over there. Maybe it's Racer and Manheim."

English glanced at the signal and then pulled Ritchie over to Thorpe. "You boys keep moving toward the refinery. I'll check on the girls and catch up with you."

"Are you sure, Gunny?" Babbitt asked. "Shouldn't we stick together?"

"You will be. Keep moving. There's an infirmary at the refinery. You can take Thorpe there and I'll catch up with you. We should be able to contact the *Lightning Rod* to come and pick us up. Go!"

Chapter 34

E nglish darted away into a maze of tanks and compressors. The path became so tight he had to wedge himself through.

Footsteps rang on the catwalk outside as the pilots headed off toward the refinery. The gunshots came from down on the ground and much deeper inside the colony. They were nowhere close enough to threaten Wing 17.

English pulled away and took off at a sprint for Racer and Manheim's position, but they weren't where Ezra pointed out.

English found a puddle of blood covering the walkway. It smeared the metal plate pulling into a dim alley behind another silo.

English darted inside and fell on his knees next to Racer. "Jesus, girl!"

"I had to move her, Gunny!" Manheim squeaked. "She followed me and ran right into the rebels' fire."

"Don't blame yourself. Shit!" English bent over Racer who slumped half-propped against the silo. She still had her eyes open, but she wasn't focusing on anything and her face had gone even whiter than usual.

The whole front of her uniform glistened with blood. English ripped it open and yanked up her t-shirt to find three bullet wounds, one in her chest, one in her stomach, and one in her neck.

"Son of a bitch!" English whispered and started stripping off his own jacket.

"I tried to stop the bleeding!" Manheim whimpered. "The rebels kept shooting at us. I had to shoot back to keep them away from her and she crawled here.... before she stopped."

"Give me your flight jacket, Ada."

English spotted a sharp edge of broken-off metal and hooked his brand-new captain's jacket on it. He sliced into the fabric and tore it to pieces.

He crammed the strips against Racer's wounds, but he already saw that it wouldn't be enough. Her eyelids started to droop. He couldn't fix what was wrong with her. He wasn't even sure if he could contact anyone with the medical expertise to fix what was wrong with her.

"We have to get her out of here!" he whispered. "You're too small to carry her, Ada, so you'll have to defend me."

"Defend.... *you*?" Manheim peeped. "How, Gunny?"

"With your weapon, Ada. You want to save Racer, don't you?" She nodded with her eyes as big as saucers. "You're a soldier, Ada. You shot and killed other pilots on the battlefield. You can do this."

She shut her mouth and gulped. Then she nodded.

"You go in front of me and shoot anything that moves—as long as it isn't Wing 17. Understand?"

She nodded again, and this time, she narrowed her eyes in determination.

English looped his rifle strap over his shoulder, made sure he had done everything possible to stop Racer's bleeding, and picked her up. He hooked her arm over his shoulder and strapped his other hand around her waist.

She groaned and then whined. "NO!"

"Easy, girl," he grunted. "We're gonna get you to safety."

"Gunny......." Her voice trailed off.

"I'm here," he panted. "Let's go, Ada."

"Where do I go, Gunny?"

"Go back to the catwalk where those rebels attacked us."

She turned her back on him and some indescribable change came over her like the one she went through at the arena.

Fear and tension drained out of her and she became something compact and dangerous. She shouldered her rifle, stepped to the edge of the silo, and jerked the weapon back and forth to scan the area.

She didn't turn around before she advanced. She snuck back along the trail of Racer's blood to the puddle where Racer had been shot.

Manheim kept checking and rechecking every possible angle, but there was no one around anymore.

"There," English panted. "You see that blood trail? Follow that."

It was Thorpe's blood. It left a clear path on the route Wing 17 had followed toward the refinery.

English and Manheim advanced for a few more minutes without seeing anyone. English thought he heard voices up ahead. He would give anything for an electronic map of the colony right now.

He just had to trust Ezra to lead him. Manheim got bolder with every passing minute. She checked quicker and walked faster. She satisfied herself that an area was clear and then nodded for English to come forward and follow her.

Racer's weight drooped heavier and heavier the farther they went. She hung limp and unmoving in English's arms. He didn't take the time to check how she was. He didn't want to know.

Manheim halted at a ladder descending to the ground. The blood trail ended here. "Now what do we do?"

English glanced around, and at that moment, gunshots erupted from off to his right. He ducked, but Manheim didn't hesitate an instant. She wheeled in that direction and opened fire.

English staggered for the nearest cover which was another tight corner between two more empty tanks. He lowered Racer to the ground and fumbled to bring up his weapon.

Manheim stood right out there in the open laying down a carpet of shots. English charged her and towed her out of danger by her shirt. "Get down!"

"They're behind that barricade!" she yelled back. "I think I saw five of them!"

"Are you sure? That isn't very many."

"I think I hit one of them. We can take them!"

English glanced over at her. Her wild blue eyes darted back and forth across the barricade she mentioned. The rebels took the opportunity to shoot over it, now that Manheim wasn't there anymore.

Two of them poked their heads up and then another two. If she was right, that left four rebels.

English raised his rifle, sighted down it, and took careful aim. He waited until one of the enemy came out for another look and English fired.

A scream echoed through the colony and Manheim laughed. "You got him, Sir!"

English didn't answer. He was already taking aim at another one. Manheim copied him, and the next time English's target appeared, she fired first. She hit her target square in the eye socket and the guy dropped without making a sound.

English stared at her in shock, but she didn't even notice. She was already squaring up to take another shot. She dropped the second one the same way.

"Manheim," English whispered, "you've been holding out on me!"

"Sir? What do you mean?"

"You're a born sniper. No wonder you had so much trouble in the fighter wing at first."

She frowned. "What do you mean? I'm no sniper."

"Forget it. Let's get out of here."

He waited until she finished off the last rebel and they started again. English slung Racer's body over his shoulder in a fireman carry, instructed Manheim to climb down the ladder, and then to cover him while he carried Racer down.

They picked up the blood trail, and in another fifteen minutes, they caught up with the boys. Thorpe was still conscious, so that was a mercy. "Any resistance?" English asked.

Ezra pointed to his device. "Look, Sir. They're all gathered around the refinery. You can hear the battle going on right now."

English listened. "You're right. Auggie, put Thorpe over here."

English laid Racer on the ground in a protected location and pushed a rifle into Thorpe's hands. "You guard her, Thorpe. We'll take the refinery and then come back for you."

Thorpe nodded. "Yes, Sir. You can count on me."

"Good man." English squeezed his shoulder. "The rest of you come with me."

They advanced much quicker without their wounded. The wing drew closer to the refinery, but Ezra didn't have to check the map anymore. The crew followed the noise.

It built to a deafening concussion as the friends crept up on the Straisium refinery. Gunfire erupted from all sides, and when Wing 17 got into position where English could see what was going on, his heart sank.

The *Battle Hardened's* security force had dwindled by half. The rebels had stationed gunmen at strategic points around the refinery's superstructure to pick off anyone who came near the building.

Random shots ricocheted out of the refinery and finished off the security personnel one man at a time. They dropped like flies with no way to hit back against their enemies.

The worst part was that English had no way to communicate with them to order them to withdraw. He couldn't even be certain withdrawing would make them any safer. The rebels had all the advantage of position.

"What do we do, Sir?" Janacek asked.

"It's simple, isn't it?" Babbitt countered. "We call in the *Lightning Rod* to bomb the refinery to rubble. That will stop the rebels from using it to supply their ships on Earth."

"The *Lightning Rod* can't get anywhere near enough to bomb this refinery, jackass," Ritchie countered. "Didn't you see the big guns outside? The rebels already destroyed the *Battle Hardened*. Do you want the *Lightning Rod* to go the same way?"

"Good thinking, Ben," English replied. "You're a genius."

Ritchie blinked at him. "I am?"

"For God's sake, don't tell him that, Sir," Babbitt groaned. "We'll never be able to shut him up."

"How many guns did you see over there?" English asked.

Janacek scratched his head. "Seven?"

"Ten," Stoval corrected.

English grinned at him. "You really should be an admiral, Auggie."

"Well, Sir, when you take over the Force, you can make me one."

English burst out laughing. He felt much better all of a sudden. "Come on, all of you. This way."

He took Ezra's device and crawled off into the colony. "Where are we going?" Ezra asked.

"We're going to do some damage on our own." He led the way to another protected hiding spot a mile from the refinery and peeked outside. "Now do you understand?"

The others squinted toward the giant cannons positioned along an artificial hill. The big guns aimed their barrels toward the sky, but the *Lightning Rod* and the *Lone Ranger* weren't there anymore.

Ritchie was right. The two destroyers wouldn't be able to get near the colony with the cannons around.

"How do we get up there?" Babbitt asked.

"We don't." English grabbed Manheim. "It's time for your moment of glory, Ada. Show these slouches what a real sniper can do."

"I told you, Gunny. I'm not a sniper."

"Sniper—her?" Babbitt exclaimed. "Now I've heard everything."

"You hear that, Ada? Now you absolutely have to prove them wrong."

She cracked a grin, wedged herself between Babbitt and Stoval, propped her rifle on the wall in front of her, and squinted down the barrel.

The whole wing crouched in breathless silence. "Who should I hit?" Manheim asked.

"All of them."

"You can't be serious!" Janacek muttered.

Manheim fired and one of the gunners seated on the cannon's firing cradle keeled over.

"Holy Christ!" Ezra whispered.

"Oh, no, she didn't!" Babbitt began, but Manheim was already shooting again.

She squeezed off four shots in rapid succession and dropped four more gunners before the rest realized what was happening.

A few gunners stood up in their cradles trying to see where the shots were coming from. They only made themselves bigger, more obvious targets. Manheim dropped three more. Only two remained.

"I don't believe it!" Babbitt exclaimed.

Janacek grabbed Manheim's arm and shook her while he cackled with glee. "Knock it off, Janacek!" she squealed. "I'm trying to aim here."

The last two gunners grabbed rifles from behind their seats, got off their cradles, and aimed down the hill toward Wing 17's hiding place.

"That's our cue," English announced. "Great work, Manheim. Let's go, people. Overrun that placement."

"Now you're talking!" Ritchie sprang to his feet and the whole wing took off running.

Ritchie, Babbitt, and Janacek got there first. The gunners fired a few times, but they couldn't hit so many attackers. In seconds, the three pilots gunned down the enemy and stormed the cannon placements.

"Now pay attention!" English ordered. "Get on board and start bombarding the refinery."

"No way, Sir!" Janacek argued. "We'd destroy the whole thing."

"No, you won't. Most of the rebels are on the front wall defending the place against our security detail. Start blasting and don't spare the plasma."

"Where are you going, Gunny?" Manheim asked.

"You don't worry about me. Just hit the refinery with everything you got....and cover the *Lightning Rod* and the *Lone Ranger* if they come inside the EM field. Go on!"

English turned away and charged down the hill on his way back to the colony. The pilots all scrambled into their firing cradles, and a second later, plasma spouted from their cannons.

It seared through the colony and smashed the refinery's front wall. English checked the device in his hand and skimmed sideways to enter the refinery through the back.

Wing 17's bombardment mounted until dozens of strikes pounded the refinery. English couldn't hear anything over the noise, but that only meant the rebels couldn't hear him, either.

Deafening crashes and booms shook the ground. Wing 17 was really going to town. Now it was English's turn.

He pulled his rifle forward and tiptoed to another entrance many blocks behind the building. The deserted loading dock led into empty corridors, storage rooms, and equipment warehouses standing still and quiet.

The rebels hadn't restarted the refinery equipment. They just defended the Straisium supply the engineers had already refined.

English crept from one doorway to the next. All those rebels out front wouldn't be running this operation. They wouldn't be shooting at security forces and getting shot by Wing 17 if the rebels had been running this operation. The officers in charge of this must be in here somewhere.

English followed his device down a few ramps and stairwells to the lowest level. The concussions shaking the refinery got louder until he couldn't hear himself think. Were any rebels still alive out there?

He finally found what he was looking for and peeked into a conference room buried a dozen stories beneath the surface.

Ten uniformed USF officers stood around the table talking, but English couldn't hear what they were saying. They pointed at their computers and their mouths moved, but the noise rose to such an ear-splitting din that no one could hear anything.

English hefted his rifle to his shoulder. He knew some of these men—the traitors! They deserved no mercy.

He didn't give himself a second to think twice. He pivoted into the room, opened fire, and spat plasma all over the room. Two of the rebel officers managed to pull their sidearms in time, but he dropped them before they could get a shot off.

English secured the room, but his blood ran cold when he saw their computers. More enemy ships were leaving Earth on their way to both the Lunar refinery and Ganymede. The rebels were coming out to take the Straisium supply and to keep it out of loyalist hands.

English pulled his device out of his pocket. He navigated to another screen to signal the *Lightning Rod* that the refinery was secure, but before he could send the signal, a jolt of searing pain electrified his insides.

He looked down and saw a ragged, bloody hole torn in his stomach. Blood bubbled from the wound. He couldn't understand how it got there except for the gut-wrenching pain tearing him apart.

He tried again to press the button to send the signal, but he couldn't move. The device fell out of his hand. Movement caught the corner of his eye and he tried to turn around.

A young airman in a USF uniform swiveled around the table aiming a rifle at English. English kept telling himself to shoot—to do something to stop this kid from killing him.

The kid leveled his rifle at English and fired again. Another stomach-turning jet of fire plastered him in the chest and he crashed down on the floor. He tried to force himself to think, but nothing was working.

His mind started to fade out. His eyes blurred and he rolled onto his side. He dragged his eyes into focus just enough to see the young airman aim his gun at English's head.

Then he saw it. The device rested on the floor right behind the kid's foot. English willed himself to flop onto his stomach. Blood pooled under him and he slipped in it when he tried to crawl toward the device.

His fingers closed on it with the last of his strength. Then a crushing weight slammed him in the back and he lay still.

Chapter 35

English snapped awake and tried to sit up, but an older woman pushed him back down on his pillow. "Easy, Captain. Take it easy."

He struggled to look around and spotted Racer lying on a bed next to him. English collapsed with a shaky sigh. "Thank God!"

"She's fine," Dr. Eva Cassidy told him. "You saved her life."

English snorted. "What am I doing here, then?"

"You secured the refinery."

He looked to his right and only relaxed slightly when he saw Thorpe sitting up on a third bed. "How many?"

"What do you mean?" she asked. "How many what?"

"How many ships are coming out from Earth?"

Dr. Cassidy made a face. "I don't know about that."

"You're lying. Tell me the truth. What's the position?"

Dr. Cassidy threw her own electronic device onto her desk. "You're as surly as ever. Fine. If you really must know, there are fifteen coming."

"So that's seven or eight for the Lunar refinery and seven or eight for us."

Dr. Cassidy sighed again and squared her shoulders. "No. I mean there are fifteen coming for us. There are another twenty going for the Lunar refinery."

English stared at her and then shut his eyes with a groan. "Wonderful."

"No rest for the wicked—except that you don't have a ship anymore."

"So.... the *Battle Hardened* is finished?"

"She exploded shortly after she crashed. The *Lone Ranger* is the only other ship around to help us hold the Acheron Colony."

English tried to sit up again. "I have to...."

"You have to lie down and keep quiet or you can forget all about going back on active duty. Is that what you want?"

English glared at her. "Doctors are the bane of my existence."

"Maybe you could change that if you stopped getting injured all the time."

"I don't get injured ALL the time."

She laughed at him. "Just every day or two, right?"

He turned away and wound up looking at Thorpe. Thorpe smiled at him and went back to reading something on his own device.

"How's Racer?" English asked.

"She's had several blood transfusions, but she's fine," Dr. Cassidy replied. "She'll probably be back on active duty before you."

English growled under his breath again, but he felt too crappy to think about getting up. He didn't want to know how long he'd been in Sick Bay. At least he was back on the *Lightning Rod* instead of stuck on Ganymede.

Dr. Cassidy went off to do something else and left English to his thoughts. He really hated Sick Bay, especially as a patient. He hated sitting or lying around while everyone else did the work, especially with fifteen enemy ships on the way to attack the *Lightning Rod*.

A moment later, the door opened and Captain Ogden came in with Commander Radcliffe. She stopped at English's bedside. "Well, you did it. You took the refinery."

"At the cost of one of our ships. I don't call that a victory."

"You wouldn't call it a victory even if we still had the *Battle Hardened*. You would go on about how many security personnel we lost or you would find something else wrong with the mission."

"Well?" he demanded. "How many security personnel *did* we lose?"

"I'm not going to tell you. You would only blame yourself. Our objective was to retake the refinery and we did it. You said you would blow it up rather than let it fall into enemy hands. That would have been a much bigger sacrifice than losing security personnel and achieving what we came to Ganymede to achieve."

He ignored this. He didn't want reassurance. "What's the defensive position? How are we going to hold the refinery against the rebel ships?"

She glanced down at her fingernails. "You know, English, you're on the *Lightning Rod* and she already has a captain. We don't need a second one, but we are short a gunnery sergeant on Wing 17....as long as you don't mind taking a massive reduction in rank."

He blinked at her for a second before he realized what she was saying. Then he laughed and even felt his throat tighten with emotion. "Yes, Ma'am. I can definitely do that."

She beamed at him. "Good. As soon as Dr. Cassidy clears you for active duty, I'm sure your fighter wing will be delighted to see you back downstairs."

She walked away. Commander Radcliffe grinned at English behind her back and English had to smile back. He was going where he really belonged.

Captain Ogden paused at the threshold and looked back. She cast an appraising glance first at Racer and then at Thorpe. "I'm glad you're on this ship, Gunny. You know, I need to promote someone to be my Master Chief now that Santiago Terranova is gone. I can always use an experienced officer on the bridge."

"Thank you, Ma'am, but I'd rather stay on the flight deck."

"I thought you would say that." She smiled again and walked out.

English sank back on his pillow and gazed up at the ceiling. He could finally accept lying here while he healed from his injuries. He was going back to the flight deck after this. He could live with that.

Dr. Cassidy cleared Thorpe first. Thorpe shot English a knowing glance before he left. No doubt Thorpe would go down and tell the rest of Wing 17 that English was back on deck.

English bit back a grin when he thought about the reception he would get when he got there.

He fell asleep thinking about it, and when he woke up, Racer was awake. In fact, Racer's voice woke him up. "How many times do I have to tell you? I feel fine."

English tried again to sit up, and this time, he succeeded. "What's going on, Airman?"

"Will you tell this damn doctor to clear me for active duty? I can't sit around here with the enemy coming in to attack us. I have to get downstairs. We have a battle to fight and Wing 17 needs me."

Dr. Cassidy turned around and addressed English. "Will you please tell this girl to lie down and be quiet so I can clear her for active duty? I can't do that until I run a few more tests."

"To hell with your tests!" Racer roared. "I told you I feel fine."

"I don't care if you just ran a marathon," Dr. Cassidy told her. "You aren't going anywhere until I run my tests. You might as well lie down and enjoy it while you can."

"Aw, come on, Sir! I can't do this."

"You have to, Airman." English leaned back on his elbow. "If you lie down and put up with it, she'll clear you for active duty before me. Then you can go downstairs and tell the others I'm still flat on my ass."

Dr. Cassidy laughed and Racer scowled at her.

"Just do it, Airman," English told Racer. "We need you on the flight deck and you'll only get there if you get cleared. Lie down and that's an order."

Racer huffed and finally flopped down, but she kept shooting hateful glances at Dr. Cassidy.

"These pilots!" Dr. Cassidy muttered. "They're the worst."

"Right after officers, right?" English asked.

"Doctors!" Racer snarled. "They should all be rounded up and shot."

"Keep a civil tone, Airman," English countered. "You can thank Dr. Cassidy for saving your worthless hide and mine after we got our asses handed to us on Ganymede."

Racer didn't reply and Dr. Cassidy shot English a suppressed grin, but he didn't return it. He wasn't too fond of doctors himself. He only tolerated them because he absolutely had to.

Dr. Cassidy finally stood back. "You're clear for duty, Airman. You can go. Just don't do it again, okay?"

"I'll do it again the very first time Gunny English tells me to," Racer fired back. She sat up and started putting on her uniform.

"You do that." Dr. Cassidy turned to English. "Your turn, Gunny."

"Do you want me to dance a jig or something?" English teased. "Or I could juggle."

She laughed. "Just lie there and pretend to be a corpse."

"Don't tempt me."

She started working on him. Racer smirked and crossed to the door. "See you downstairs, Gunny."

"Uh-huh," he muttered. That was two pilots with firsthand knowledge of where he was and what he was doing.

He shut his eyes and waited for the procedure to be over. Dr. Cassidy had just said, "You're all clear, Gunny. You can get up," when a pling came over the computer on her desk. She checked it. "It's for you, Gunny. Captain Ogden is requesting you to attend her in her ready room."

English's eyes snapped open. "Now?"

"Whenever you're clear for duty.... which is now."

"What does she want?"

"She doesn't say. She just calls you to the ready room as soon as medically possible."

"I wonder why." English sat up and looked around. "Where's my uniform?"

Cassidy pulled out a carton from under his bed. "Here."

He looked down into it. It contained a new gunnery sergeant's flight uniform, not a Master Chief's uniform or any other kind. He gazed wistfully down at it. Of course Ogden knew what choice he would make.

He got dressed and went upstairs to find Ogden and Radcliffe alone in the ready room. English saluted. "Ma'am—Sir."

"At ease, Gunny. What I have to say is personal, not professional."

"Ma'am?"

Ogden stood up and faced him. "I have a personal request—captain to captain."

"I'm not a...."

Ogden held up her hand. "I have a personal request and I understand if you don't want to do it. I want to ask you, as a personal favor to me, if you would put me in touch with your daughter Melanie at the Command Center Hospital."

"Why do you want to talk to Melanie? I mean, why do you want *me* to talk to Melanie? Communications are restored with the Command Center. You can contact her yourself."

"I know I could contact her myself. I'm asking you to do it for me.... or to introduce me to her through you. I want to make it look like you're contacting her. I don't know if the rebels are monitoring loyalist communications. They'll be less likely to think anything about it if you contact your daughter."

English looked away. "I don't know about that, Ma'am. After what happened with Dan, I wouldn't be sure the rebels aren't monitoring my communications specifically."

"Not necessarily," Radcliffe interjected. "Intelligence is trickling through the Command Center that Ufa was a rebel target long before Captain English ever sent you that letter. We have no evidence at this point that they were monitoring communications with Ufa at all. We don't believe they targeted Ufa because of you or your son."

English shifted his weight. "Even so, I wouldn't like to take the chance."

Captain Ogden sat back down. "Like I said, the decision is yours. If you don't feel comfortable with it or you think it would put your daughter in danger, I accept your decision. Just be aware that we're in communication with the Command Center anyway, so one more communication between us and the hospital shouldn't flag anybody's particular interest."

"Why do you want to communicate with Melanie, then?" English asked.

Radcliffe and Ogden exchanged a glance. English couldn't read anything into that glance.

Ogden held up both hands. "I can see you have some reservations about it. I'm asking you to think about it. We can discuss the reasons why when we...."

A boom interrupted her and all three officers glanced up at the ceiling. Then the siren started blaring

"Battle stations! All hands—battle stations! All fighter wings—stand by the launch! Battle stations! All hands—battle stations!"

"They're attacking!" Captain Ogden murmured.

All three broke for the door at the same instant. English got there first and bolted for the stairwell while Radcliffe and Ogden raced to the bridge.

English sprang down the stairs three at a time and joined the stampede of *Lightning Rod* crewmen all running the same way.

English exploded onto the flight deck and charged over to Wing 17. Half his pilots were already loaded up with the others climbing aboard.

English dropped into his seat. "Here we go!" Thorpe chirped. "Ready to kick some ass, Wing 17?"

"Show me the ass to be kicked and I'm your man," Ritchie replied.

"Who is it this time?" Babbitt asked.

"Fifteen destroyers coming out from Earth," English replied. "They want to take the refinery away from us."

"Good luck," Ezra muttered.

English's communications system crackled. "Squadron Command to Wing Leader 17. Stand by for an incoming message from the bridge."

English cocked his head. "There is? What is it?"

"I have a job for you, Gunny," Captain Ogden chimed in. "Take your wing down to the refinery and man those cannons. We'll lead the enemy into your range."

English looked around to find the rest of Wing 17 gaping at him through their cockpit covers. "Seriously?" Racer murmured.

"Yes, seriously," Captain Ogden replied. "Two destroyers against fifteen don't stand a chance, but with the ground guns helping out, Wing 17 might be able to make a dent in their numbers. You all showed yourselves willing and able to get the job done. What do you say, Wing 17? The *Lightning Rod* needs you."

"Yes, Ma'am," Thorpe replied. "We'll get her done."

"Thank you, Wing 17. Hit it."

"You heard the lady," English ordered. "Punch it, boys!"

Wing 17 punched it with Thorpe and Ezra in the lead. Ritchie, Babbitt, Racer, and Janacek dropped out right behind them with English, Manheim, and Stoval in formation.

The wing peeled around the *Lightning Rod* heading back to Ganymede, but the enemy saw them coming a mile away. Squadrons launched from the incoming destroyers, and in seconds, the enemy swarmed Wing 17 to block the pilots from getting near the moon.

Plasma hammered English's hull and he pulled out of a steep dive. "We can't get near the moon like this! There are too many of them."

"Pull it back, Wing 17!" Eismann ordered. "Cycle back to the *Lightning Rod* and stand ready to defend the ship."

"We'll all go down in flames if we do that," English pointed out. "We have to get to the ground guns. None of us stands a chance without that."

The enemy squadrons saw Wing 17 in retreat and piled in to surround the *Lightning Rod* and the *Lone Ranger*. The *Lone Ranger* got into trouble right away as four destroyers cut her away from the *Lightning Rod*.

Another six went after the *Lightning Rod*. Plasma explosions peppered the hull. English heard Eismann yelling orders through the communications system, but English couldn't make them out over the noise.

"Now, Wing 17!" English called. "Break for the colony—Beta formation!"

Chapter 36

Wing 17 plunged through the cloud of fighter squadrons flocking to the *Lightning Rod* and the *Lone Ranger*. The enemy must have received orders to focus on the two destroyers because no one pursued Wing 17 in its headlong dive for Ganymede.

The murky atmosphere parted and English took a turn around the cannon positions. "They look intact, Sir," Ezra observed.

"No one has been here since the *Lightning Rod* lifted you three to Sick Bay," Babbitt replied. "What's the plan, Gunny?"

"Get down on the ground and arm your cannon. The sooner we lay into these bastards, the sooner we can all go home for lunch." English descended. "Follow me."

The fighters lowered onto a dusty patch of ground near the guns, and in a second, the pilots hopped out and raced to their cradles.

Babbitt rotated his weapon toward the skies. Explosions rocked the battlefield up there. The steady shriek of engine noise and pounding booms echoed down to the Acheron Colony.

"Fire at will!" English ordered and all the pilots opened up at once.

The enemy offered plenty of targets. English sighted for the *USS Ironside*. The *Nostradamus* was back, so Stoval and Ritchie ganged up to attack the destroyer.

The others took turns blasting the squadrons to smithereens. Laughter, cheers, and taunts flew up and down the battery.

"Take that, you sons of bitches!" Thorpe bellowed.

"That's right," Ezra growled. "Come back around the other side where I can see you."

"This is fun!" Manheim squealed and unloaded rapidly. She hit five fighters in quick succession and giggled to herself.

Racer jerked her cannon back and forth pounding away with a rhythmic, driving beat. "Just how many of them are there?"

"Fifteen ships times three wings each with up to ten fighters per wing......" Janacek began.

"You're giving me a headache, Janacek," Babbitt countered. "Just shoot them. Who cares how many there are?"

"There are a lot fewer now," Thorpe observed.

English barely heard their conversation. He pelted the *Ironside* along her starboard flank. Stoval and Ritchie hit the *Nostradamus's* port engine and the combusting plasma got in English's way.

The next instant, Stoval and Ritchie hit the port hull just above the plasma reservoir. A rippling belch of flame cascaded down the *Nostradamus's* sides. She staggered and then the whole aft end detonated.

The explosion boomed forward chewing up the ship one section at a time and then, in a catastrophic woof of exploding plasma, the whole ship ruptured.

"Hell yeah!" Ritchie stood up in his cradle, raised his arm, and high-fived Stoval across the gap between their guns. "Eat it, you cocksuckers!"

"Outstanding, boys," English told them. "Now help me out with the *Ironside*."

Ritchie sat down and both gunners turned their cannons on the *Ironside*. The rest of the pilots were still enjoying themselves too much with the fighters.

"Target the destroyers!" English called down the line. "Forget the mosquitos! Manheim—stop playing with your food! Target the *Copernicus*—you, too, Racer!"

Grumbling answered him, but eventually, they all rotated their guns around and started in on the destroyers.

English, Stoval, and Ritchie made short work of the *Ironside*, and a second later, the *Copernicus* lost her starboard tailfin.

The destroyer groaned to one side and started spiraling out of control. "She's going down on Europa!" Janacek cheered.

"Bring it around to the *Golden Hind*," English ordered. "We're doing it, boys! Keep taking 'em out to give the *Lightning Rod* some breathing space."

He picked out his next target. It was the *Henrietta* and that ship exploded, too, with four gunners all joining in to tear her apart.

Another explosion shimmered across the sky and English looked around for his next target. His heart dropped when he noticed four enemy destroyers making an end run on the *Lightning Rod*.

More enemy ships had further isolated the *Lone Ranger*, but she still held her own, now that the ground gunners had cleared so many of the squadrons.

The *Lightning Rod*, on the other hand, was running out of options. The four enemy ships withdrew behind the curtain of combusting plasma where the ground gunners couldn't hit them.

English and his pilots had been so occupied with the destroyers in front of them that English didn't see these four until now.

The *Edmonton* veered around the *Lightning Rod's* other side where English's gunners couldn't hit the enemy at all. The *Edmonton* unleashed a hellish barrage against the *Lightning Rod*. She couldn't defend herself with all four attacking from every side.

The *Argonaut* and the *Kilbirnie* smashed the bridge in while the *Southern Cross* wheeled to the port side.

"Concentrate your fire on the *Southern Cross*!" English ordered. "Manheim, you and Racer take the *Kilbirnie*!"

The gunners wheeled their weapons toward the battle, but before they could do any damage, the *Octopus* skidded into their path again.

She took a vicious pounding on her starboard flank and the tail swiveled hard away, but the destroyer didn't leave.

English cringed when he saw explosions going off along the *Lightning Rod's* hull. No way could she stand an attack like this. English couldn't even see the *Edmonton* plastering the *Lightning Rod* from out of sight.

The noise escalated to an ear-splitting din. The *Octopus* stumbled under continuous bombardment from Ganymede, but she would not get out of the way no matter what Wing 17 did.

"Manheim......!" English called, but it was too late. The *Kilbirnie* broke out of line, lunged forward, and smashed the *Lightning Rod* square in the nose.

The *Lightning Rod* skidded in reverse. Her squadrons converged to hammer the *Kilbirnie*, but the enemy overpowered the *Lightning Rod* in seconds.

The four destroyers closed their dragnet and drove the *Lightning Rod* even farther away from Ganymede. In a matter of seconds, they propelled her deeper into space and out of the ground gunners' range.

"Load up!" English bellowed. "Get in the air pronto!"

Manheim and Janacek squeezed off a few more shots and then the whole wing broke for their fighter craft. English scrambled into his cockpit. The split second the controls took to turn on seemed way too long.

He yanked his bird into the air and gunned the engines for the *Lightning Rod*, but the *Octopus* still blocked his path.

The destroyer veered into Wing 17's way and unloaded all her batteries on the incoming fighter craft. The first shot deflected off of English's bird and punched Racer's starboard wing.

"I'm hit!" she shrieked. "I'm losing navigation!"

"Get back to the *Lightning Rod*!" English ordered. "We'll cover you!"

The other pilots closed in a protective huddle around Racer, but they could barely save themselves. The *Octopus* spat plasma into their formation and then the destroyer's squadron came out to finish the job.

Enemy fighters smashed through Wing 17's formation and one of the enemy collided with Ritchie's bird.

"My port engine is gone!" he roared. "I'm going down!"

"Hang on, boy!" English called. "I'm coming to get you."

He ripped his fighter out of the battle and skated back around the confusion. Ritchie's starboard engine was still working, but his efforts to steer only made his bird flounder even worse. He spun off into open, empty space.

English aimed his fighter at Ritchie's, hit the throttle, swooped in, and struck a glancing blow across Ritchie's cockpit. "Hey!" Ritchie yelled. "What are you doing?!"

"You're heading for the Acheron Colony now. Get down on the ground and go back to the refinery. The rebels had food supplies there. You can hold out until the *Lightning Rod* or one of the other destroyers comes to get you."

Ritchie looked down at Ganymede coming closer. His expression hardened in determination.

English turned back to the battle. The *Octopus* squadron was still giving Wing 17 holy hell. The other four enemy destroyers blocked him from seeing the *Lightning Rod*.

"We can't get through!" Janacek called.

"I have an idea!" English replied. "Duran and Thorpe—with me! The rest of you occupy these fools so they don't come after us."

"You got it," Manheim squeaked and she powered forward to engage four enemy fighter craft.

English pulled out of the battle with the other three on his ass. He rotated sideways and came at the *Octopus* from starboard. "Duran, work your magic!"

"We won't be able to get near her with so many of these pests around," Ezra remarked.

"You don't have to get near her or even do any damage. Just draw her away from Wing 17. Thorpe, you and me are gonna give these jackasses a run for their money."

The four pilots reacted in an instant. Ezra and Thorpe pulled sideways and started playing ping-pong on the *Octopus's* outer hull. English veered into a corresponding dive on the port side.

Their attack worked much better than English expected. The *Octopus* squadron stopped fighting Wing 17 and surrounded their mother ship to drive the attackers off.

"Break for the *Lightning Rod*!" English ordered.

Janacek, Racer, Stoval, and Manheim sprinted under the *Octopus's* enormous belly and English lost sight of them. He vaulted over the *Octopus* spraying plasma anywhere and everywhere.

He almost collided with a bunch of enemy fighters rushing him from the other side. "They're giving us all kinds of grief!" Ezra called. "We can't get a decent target. There are too many of them!"

"Fall back with the others!" English ordered.

"What about you, Sir?" Thorpe asked.

"Go!" English bellowed. "I'll deal with these assholes."

Chapter 37

"What the hell is going on out there, Matt?" Captain Ogden demanded.

"Wing 17 is on Ganymede, Ma'am!" Radcliffe reported. "They're firing on the destroyers.... or some of them are. The rest are going after the enemy squadrons."

"Get our birds back here on the double! We have to...."

Another brutal smash stuck the *Lightning Rod* from starboard.

"The *Edmonton* is flanking us, Ma'am!" Radcliffe told her. "We can't...."

More cannon fire bombarded the ship from in front as the *Argonaut* and the *Kilbirnie* advanced to pound the bridge.

"Counterassault—all batteries!" Ogden ordered.

"We're already running all batteries at capacity!" Avila replied. "The *Southern Cross* is moving to port."

"Withdraw!" Ogden roared.

"We have nowhere left to withdraw to! We're completely cut off!"

Ogden checked the readouts on her controls. "Pull back to Europa."

"The *Southern Cross* is pivoting to block our retreat! We're trapped!"

"*Southern Cross* squadron is blocking Wings 10 and 12 from getting through," Avila reported. "We're on our own out here!"

"Wing 17 coming in fast!" Radcliffe interrupted. "Four birds coming from Ganymede!"

"Only four?"

"Another two breaking away!" Radcliffe told her. "Gunny English is stranded on the *Octopus*. He's peeling back. He can't get through."

"Ma'am!" Avila shrieked. "The *Kilbirnie*......!"

The *Kilbirnie* took a running charge and plowed nose first into the *Lightning Rod's* bridge. Avila pitched out of his chair and Radcliffe staggered onto his knees. The impact flung Ogden to the floor.

She scrambled back into place. "Cannon batteries—report!"

"No answer, Ma'am!" Radcliffe forced himself upright behind his station. "Four batteries down. The others aren't responding."

"So.... we're defenseless?"

"Wing 17 wheeling to starboard! The pilots are heading back to engage with the *Southern Cross* squadron. They're through! All three fighter wings coming in."

"Tell them to concentrate on the *Southern Cross*."

"What about the *Edmonton*?" Avila asked. "She's the weakest. We could break through."

"The other three would only come after us again. Lay into the *Southern Cross*. We might be able to help Gunny English."

Another cascade of plasma shivered the *Lightning Rod's* hull. Continuous concussions blasted the ship's rear end as the *Southern Cross* wheeled back and forth across the *Lightning Rod's* tail.

The *Lightning Rod* squadron buzzed around the *Southern Cross* trying to draw her away, but with the other three destroyers laying down a steady barrage of shots on the *Lightning Rod's* front end and sides, the squadron couldn't do anything to help the destroyer.

Radcliffe cast one backward glance toward the *Octopus*. He didn't see English anymore. The *Octopus* squadron surrounded their mother ship. The destroyer had taken considerable damage, but one fighter craft couldn't make a dent in so many fighters.

Radcliffe gulped down a pang of grief. English must be gone, but the *Lightning Rod* had much bigger problems right now.

The *Argonaut* carpeted the *Lightning Rod* with withering blasts. The four enemy squadrons overran the *Lightning Rod's* fighter wings. The enemy squadrons ran constant strafing runs down the *Lightning Rod's* sides targeting the engines, the plasma core—any vulnerability they could hit.

The *Argonaut*, the *Edmonton*, and the *Southern Cross* held the *Lightning Rod* in an unbreakable fist. They blocked off every avenue of escape while the squadrons picked the destroyer to pieces.

All at once, the *Kilbirnie* gave one more vicious punch, smashed the *Lightning Rod* with ramming speed, and sent the destroyer spinning off to nowhere. At the same instant, the *Southern Cross* squadron landed a punishing strike against the starboard engine panel.

Four engines detonated and the *Lightning Rod* skidded sideways.

Radcliffe scrambled between the helm and the throttle trying to right the ship. "She's crippled, Ma'am! We're losing helm control."

"Bring the backup...."

The *Kilbirnie* rammed the *Lightning Rod* hard in the side. "Starboard engine panel is completely gone!" Radcliffe bellowed. "We're going down on Europa!"

<u>End of Book 1.</u>

If you enjoyed this book, please consider leaving a review. You can also support me on Patreon at <u>www.patreon.com/InvisiblePublishing</u>.

Keep Reading

Battlefleet Series: Book 2

The insurrection to take control of the United Space Force is heating up and spreading all over the solar system. The *USS Lightning Rod* gets caught in the middle of a dangerous game of cat-and-mouse between traitors hidden in the ranks, mutinous crews trying to take control of ships in favor of one side or the other, and both sides want to use Gunnery Sergeant Sailor English as a pawn for their own ends.

The forces trying to tear the Force apart infiltrate English's own family. They will pit him against his own son who is acting as a captain for the rebel cause and actively coming out in battle against the *Lightning Rod*. The situation comes to an explosive head when English gets the crazy idea to leverage his relationships with his own children in favor of the loyalist cause. The aftermath will leave him, his family, and what's left of his life in ruins.

You can find it at your favorite book retailer.

Sign Up Once--Get all Theo Mann's free books including brand new releases

Humanity on the brink of annihilation.

A mysterious package, a corrupt officer, and a conspiracy that goes all the way to the top? What could possibly go wrong?

When a routine mission goes horribly wrong, Warrant Officer Ewing Archer and a handful of faithful friends get trapped in a battle to save the last survivors of Earth.

The human race has abandoned the ecological disaster of Earth. Now all that remains is a network of interconnected ships, stations, and satellites surrounding the planet.

But when war breaks out, Archer becomes a firebrand that could destroy it all....or save it.

Sign up at www.theomann.com to read it for free

About Theo Mann

I write 70 books per year—and yes, before you ask, all these books are my original creative work. Nothing written under my name is AI-generated or ghostwritten because I write better than AI and any ghostwriter out there.

People don't read fiction for entertainment or to escape from reality. People read fiction to see their humanity reflected in another person's character and story.

This is my promise to you. When you read my books, you'll see your own humanity reflected in the characters and stories. I take this commitment to my readers very seriously. My books are an intimate form of communication between us. I would never disrespect my readers by turning that over to a machine or another writer. This is my bond between me and you as my reader.

I write 20,000 words per day as my daily work output. If anyone with a public platform would like to challenge me to prove this in a controlled environment, feel free to contact me on this website's contact page. How do I do write so much? Find out more on my blog, *Crimes Against Fiction* at www.theomann.com.

I worked as a professional ghostwriter for fifteen years. Now I'm on a mission to set a Guinness World Record by writing 700 books over the next ten years and 1400 books over the next twenty years, all originally written by me.

See my website for the full book list. I'm also the author of *Proof for the Existence of God* and the *Crimes Against Fiction* blog.

If you have a story idea, or if you would like me to explore a series in more depth, or if you'd like me to explore a character by writing a spinoff series about that character or world, leave me a message on my website's contact page. I answer all reader emails, so ask me anything, tell me what you liked and didn't like, and let me know where you'd like your favorite series to go. I would love to hear your ideas and find out what you'd like to read next.

Find out more at www.theomann.com.

Also by Theo Mann (so far)